THE HEART OF A RAKE

The Silver Vixens
Book 1

Abigail Bridges

© Copyright 2026 by Abigail Bridges
Text by Abigail Bridges
Cover by Dar Albert

Dragonblade Publishing, Inc. is an imprint of Kathryn Le Veque Novels, Inc.
P.O. Box 23
Moreno Valley, CA 92556
ceo@dragonbladepublishing.com

Produced in the United States of America

First Edition March 2026
Trade Paperback Edition

Reproduction of any kind except where it pertains to short quotes in relation to advertising or promotion is strictly prohibited.

All Rights Reserved.

The characters and events portrayed in this book are fictitious. Any similarity to real persons, living or dead, is purely coincidental and not intended by the author.

AI Statement: No AI or ghostwriting was used in the creation of this story, or any story, published by Dragonblade Publishing. All text, structure, content, ideas, and concept are 100% human generated solely by the author whose name appears on the cover. It is prohibited to use this material, or any copyrighted material, for AI engine training.

ARE YOU SIGNED UP FOR DRAGONBLADE'S BLOG?

You'll get the latest news and information on exclusive giveaways, exclusive excerpts, coming releases, sales, free books, cover reveals and more.

Check out our complete list of authors, too!

No spam, no junk. That's a promise!

Sign Up Here

www.dragonbladepublishing.com

Dearest Reader;

Thank you for your support of a small press. At Dragonblade Publishing, we strive to bring you the highest quality Historical Romance from some of the best authors in the business. Without your support, there is no 'us', so we sincerely hope you adore these stories and find some new favorite authors along the way.

Happy Reading!

CEO, Dragonblade Publishing

Additional Dragonblade books by Author Abigail Bridges

The Silver Vixens Series
The Heart of a Rake (Book 1)

The Ashton Park Series
To Stop a Scoundrel (Book 1)
A Rogue Like You (Book 2)
Nothing But a Rake (Book 3)
The Duke I Came For (Book 4)
By the Rosemary Tree (Novella)

The Lyon's Den Series
Into the Lyon of Fire
A Lyon in Waiting
To Uncage a Lyon

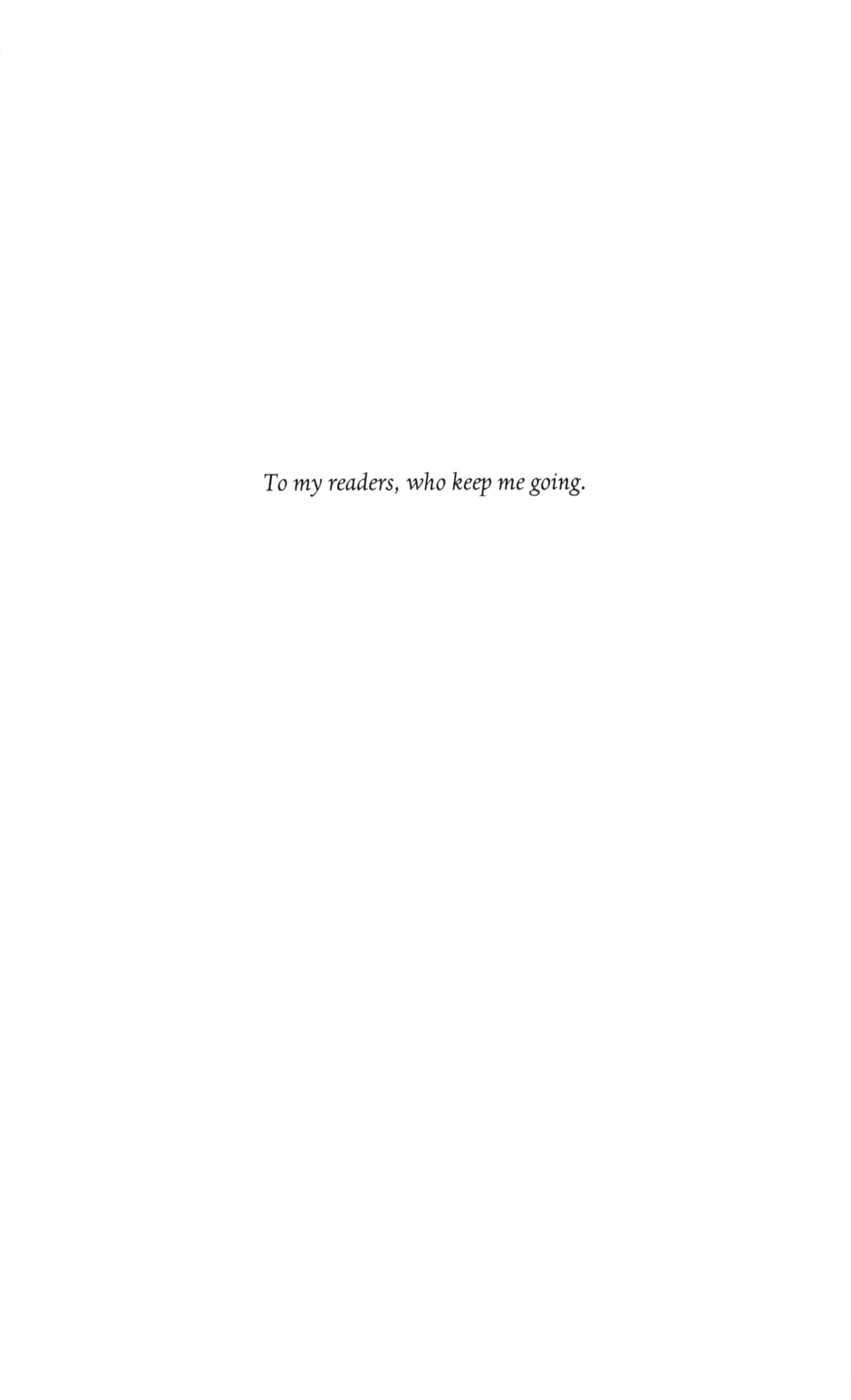

To my readers, who keep me going.

CHAPTER ONE

Saturday, 16 July 1814
Stella Ashley's residence, Bloomsbury, London
Quarter after two in the morning

L ORD MARK RYDELL adjusted his somewhat dingy white cravat, bending to check its appearance in the mirror of Stella's dressing table, his notoriety much on his mind. Established well before his time on the Peninsula fighting alongside his brothers, his nefarious reputation had been studiously curated since his return. Being absolutely appalling to well-bred ladies had become a beneficial hobby. And keeping Stella, an actress with her own spurious reputation, comfortable and well-funded in this Bloomsbury town home, helped feed all the rumors about his dubious character.

This pleased Mark to no end. A useful thing this reputation of his, which kept marriage-minded waifs and their mamas at bay and gave him the freedom to pursue far-less-noble pursuits.

His mother, however, would be disgusted by his current location. His oldest brother, Matthew, the current Duke of Embleton, would merely scold, a touch of humor in the words.

Still . . . Mark did try to keep up his physical appearance, his preference for elegant and well-made black-and-white kits as much a part of that reputation as his mistress. His valet would be annoyed by the state of the silk. Wrinkled, of course, as it had most recently been wound around the voluptuous actress's wrists.

Mark truly did not care what his family—or his valet—

thought, however, as they knew him well, and how much of his reputation was merely a façade with a purpose.

To make people leave him alone.

Besides, his valet, Howe, existed in a state of apoplexy more often than not, ever since the war had made the fripperies of English dandies a bore and a bother to Mark—thus the black-and-white kits. But Mark did appreciate Howe's attention to detail; thus he straightened and smoothed the cravat as much as he could.

Behind him came a sound—half-moan, half-purr—from the bed. Appropriate, he thought, as Stella was a bit of a cat. Her voice slurred as she pushed thick blonde tresses out of her face, the words husky and elongated. "Why are you dressed? You could stay the night, you know." She pouted. "You never do anymore. Not since you got back from that bloody war."

Mark tugged on the cravat again, then rolled his shoulders, fatigue dragging them down. "I need to return home. My family breakfasts at eight. I have no interest in dealing with my mother's complaints about any overnight absences."

Stella rolled and stretched, her lovely, plump form and luring gaze a distinct invitation to return to her bed. "Who eats that early? I thought the nobility never emerged before noon."

"A myth, except during the season. And you have never met my mother. Or my brother. One thinks he is still in military service to the Crown. The other might as well have been. The household routine does not vary even if we have not returned home until dawn, and Mother is rather traditional in her household scheduling. Breakfast is on the sideboard precisely at eight and removed by half-past nine. Luncheon at one. Dinner at half-past five, unless there are guests or an event. Tea at eight, unless my mother decides otherwise or if guests have arrived. Supper precisely at ten. Or never."

"How annoying. Sounds far too tedious and routine for you." She stretched and lolled again, her smile turning as mischievous as the gleam in her brown eyes. "You should introduce us. I could entice them to change their ways."

The thought amused him. If such an event occurred, however, he would have to stand well away from either his brother the duke or his mother, the formidable duchess Phyllida. Their response would be . . . explosive. "I am fairly certain my mother would prefer to see you on the stage than in her son's arms."

"How delightfully dull of her."

Mark chuckled. Despite her teasing, Stella well knew her limited role in Mark's life. And of his in hers. A role that had gradually become even more limited over the last few weeks, his mind elsewhere. "Do you need anything?"

She sat up, letting the covers fall away as she left the bed and reached for a dressing gown. "My bill at the modiste's is overdue."

He nodded, appreciating her body but not tempted to linger any longer. "The one here in Bloomsbury?"

"Yes. She is quite patient, but—"

"I will take care of it. Anything else?"

"Will you be at tonight's opening?"

Mark hesitated, tilting his head to one side as he considered the possibility. Stella Ashley, one of London's most-favored actresses, sold out any theater at which she appeared. Her performances were pure delights, and tickets were always in demand. But his mother's plans for him took precedence, including tonight. The duchess had become rather determined to see him marry this season, despite his repeated insistence that he would not. His mother believed all men should marry by thirty, and at six and thirty, he was well past her deadline. Mark acquiesced to her invitations in part to keep the peace—and in part because he did enjoy meeting new women. He liked women. All of them. A great many of them in the past.

Long in the past.

"Not tonight," he murmured. "I am escorting my mother to the Huntingdale ball. She is unfortunately determined to find me a bride."

"I suppose it would be selfish of me to hope she fails." Stella tied the sash of her dressing gown, even as she still undulated toward him, her hands rubbing across his shoulders. "You really should wear something more colorful. You are too handsome to spend your life in black and white."

This had been a constant campaign of hers, almost as persistent as his mother's for marriage. "I had more than adequate experience with bright colors in the army, thank you. Black and white suits me."

"It does not suit you. It makes you appear much duller than you are." Stella pressed her breasts against his chest. "So will you be there tomorrow?"

Mark gave her a quick kiss on the cheek and eased her away. "Tomorrow." He paused. "How is she?"

Stella stilled, her eyes studying him as she stepped back. "Why?"

"Stella . . ."

She turned away from him, tightening the knot on the sash. "She is fine."

"Still with your mother?"

"Why do you pretend to care?"

Mark took a deep breath to steady his temper. "Because I do, whether or not you believe me."

She turned back to him, eyes flashing. "Do you? Do you even remember her name? Then you plan to visit sometime soon?"

The question she always asked. And the answer he always gave. "It would only confuse her. Olivia. It would only confuse Olivia."

"Not if you start now. She is barely three years old. She is smart. And growing up quickly." The defiance in her eyes faded into something more wounded, more vulnerable, and Mark realized he faced the genuine Stella for the first time that morning. She had stopped acting. At last. She reached for his hand, her warm fingers curling around his. "I know you care, and I also know how hard that is, given who you are. If you wish to stay away, I understand. But that is hard for me as well. And eventually, it will be even harder for her. To know that she is a ba—a by-blow. A scandal waiting in the wings."

Mark winced, then kissed her cheek. "I will consider it."

"That is all I ask."

He suddenly felt the need to be out—in the air, in the fog. Out. Mark left Stella's bedchamber and trotted down the stairs, pausing in the narrow entry hall to pick his top hat off the hall table. As he settled it on his head, he noticed a crack in the wallpaper, barely visible in the light of the candle Stella's maid had left burning for him. He scowled, then picked up the candle, holding it high, as he looked about. Lots of cracks, and a deep yellowing he had never noticed before. Not that he had spent all that much time in the house since he had purchased it four years ago, just before she became pregnant, nor had he been in it during the daytime hours. Glancing up, he saw water stains on the ceiling and a distinct separation of the crown molding from the wall.

He set the candle down with a shake of his head. The house had been pristine when he had purchased it, but obviously Stella had not maintained it, nor had she brought issues with the house to his notice. Of course, she mostly used three of the eighteen rooms in the house—her bedchamber, the kitchen, and her maid's room. Stella did not entertain guests at the house and mostly took her meals out at restaurants and parties.

Mark snuffed out the candle, closed the door behind him, and descended the front steps with a syncopated trot, his mind still on the house. Stella was an accomplished and popular actress, but when they had met, she had occupied a rat hole of a bedsit in Convent Garden. Despite her income, she preferred to save the money, and a good portion of it went to pay for the doctors who cared for her mother, ill at the time with recurring bouts of pleurisy. Both qualities had attracted Mark to Stella, and their association had benefited them both. She now had a reliable protector, a secure roof over her head, and he had a regular—and safe—place to satisfy his physical needs, as well as his less than traditional desires.

Neither of them had expected a daughter. They had taken all the expected precautions to prevent such an occurrence, but it had happened, and neither had a doubt that he was the girl's father. Olivia's dark, wavy hair, her long, narrow nose, and her wide-set, deep-blue eyes matched his own features—not her mother's fair hair, brown eyes, and pale skin. Olivia also looked enough like his younger brothers that she might have been an offspring of his parents. She even toddled as they had, with a giggle that would have been recognizable at Embleton House.

He knew those last two qualities because—despite that he had kept it from Stella—Mark had often stood outside the house in Whitehall where Rose Ashley, now reportedly recovered, resided with the first-born grandchild of the Duchess of Embleton. Two extraordinary facts he hoped to keep forever hidden from the women in his life.

Secrets. Did not every man have his share?

Saturday, 16 July 1814
Sculthorpe Manor, Berkeley Square, London
Ten of seven in the morning

WHY WAS HE *still here?*

Judith Amelia Lovelace, Lady Sculthorpe, a widow of two years and a dowager countess for six months, had stirred and stretched, luxuriating in the soft downy covers of her bed. Then she had rolled onto her side and been startled by the presence of the blond curls and bare shoulders of Lord Peregrine Gower.

Damn it, Perry . . .

Thin streams of early morning sun streaked through gaps in the window curtains, illuminating her bedchamber and casting odd shadows and dancing streams of sunlight over the burgundy linens and cherry-wood furnishings. Not Judith's preferred taste in décor—far too dark—but she had become accustomed to them over the past two years. She had gladly surrendered her original suite of rooms with its rose, cream, and oak accouterments—also not to her initial liking—when her stepson became the earl.

In fact, little of the décor in Sculthorpe Manor had been chosen or arranged to Judith's desires, something she had acquiesced to more than two decades ago. That had been the provenance of her former mother-in-law, and as the second wife of a second son, Judith had no voice in the way the household functioned . . . at least until her husband had unexpectedly found himself the earl. Now her older stepson held the title as well as his father's bedchambers. And Judith had moved her life from the countess's rooms down the hall to this smaller but adequate suite of rooms. After all, the bedchamber of her previous suite adjoined the earl's and living adjacent to his stepmother had not been Edmund's preferred arrangement, even prior to his marriage.

Nor hers.

Judith still smiled at the memory of his broaching the subject to her. His father, the fifth Earl Sculthorpe—*her* Edmund—had been dead and buried less than a week, and her stepson's awkwardness about taking over his father's title and rooms had been charming and sweet. But Judith knew all too well how these things worked. While not his mother—Edmund's mother had died in childbirth with Daniel, her second child—Judith had been the only mother her stepsons had known. Her husband had wed the seventeen-year-old Judith for his second wife just before Edmund turned four. Now at a mere four and twenty, the newest earl headed a major aristocratic household consisting of his bride Margaret and his brother Daniel, as well as Judith and her three sons, his half-brothers. Although none of them had seen Daniel in months, he remained Edmund's responsibility.

Quite a handful. But Edmund had done well. So far. Although she had changed bedchambers, Judith had remained countess until Edmund's marriage to the lovely Margaret six months ago, and Judith tried not to interfere, offering advice only when asked. Judith herself had become the countess at twenty, and she had managed the Sculthorpe properties, including this house, for eighteen years. Passing those responsibilities on to Margaret and staying out of the way had not been easy but was the proper thing to do.

And a relief. Judith's widow's portion and dowager properties—insured by her husband's will—remained in the estate for the time being, as she saw no reason to separate them. All in all, a huge estate for the young couple to manage. But Judith had taken over the duties herself when barely more than a girl, and they would learn as they worked, just as she had.

Besides, she had other things on her mind.

One of those things now gave a sleep-laden snort. Perry shifted but did not awaken.

Judith's mouth pinched. Perry had been a frequent visitor to her bed over the last year or so—since she had shed her widow's black—and he knew the rules, one of which was that no one stayed past dawn. While the entire household knew Judith had nighttime visitors, she never wanted to spread the details in front of them or provide the gossips with too much information to bandy about. No matter what people thought they knew, Judith had been discreet and private.

Repressing the urge to poke her errant visitor, Judith propped up on an elbow and looked at the clock on her mantel. Almost seven. Too early for the nobility in the household, although the servants would be up and moving about with their morning chores. They would breakfast at half-past seven . . . the perfect time for Perry to make his exit.

Also a good time for a quick jaunt upstairs to the nursery. Judith pushed back the covers and stood, shivering in the chill of the room as she retrieved her night rail and dressing gown from the floor and slipped into them. She noted both had been victims of their bed play—the night rail had a tear and the sash of the dressing gown hopelessly knotted—and Judith reminded herself to mention the repairs to her maid. She grabbed a ribbon to tie back her mussed hair and left the bedchamber, pulling the door firmly closed behind her hard enough to waken Perry but not the rest of the house. With a sly grin, Judith turned toward the nearby servants' stairs and padded upward.

The stairwell held the scrumptious scents of fresh-baked bread, fried onions, and gammon drifting up from below stairs, and Judith's mouth watered as her hand slid along the rail, polished smooth by generations of servants. She had not eaten much at the lackluster supper at last night's ball, and her stomach rumbled as she pushed open the door to the fourth floor. The carpet here felt thinner than the ones on the floors below, but still a comfort to her chilled toes.

She stopped in front of the nursery door, listening. Sweet giggles sounded from behind it. Her baby boy, William, the last one in the nursery at almost four. Smart, rambunctious, and keenly observant, he had left his toddlerhood behind, making her heart ache every time she noticed something new in his growth—which seemed to be each and every day. She knocked lightly on the door, then entered.

In the far corner of the room, William and his nurse sat at a low table, sharing small bits of food. Nanny stood, eyes wide. "Your ladyship!"

"Mummy!" William dashed toward her, some kind of dark jam spread across both cheeks.

"My jammy boy!" Judith squatted, gathering the child into her arms. "You are so big these days!" William giggled, bouncing on his toes, and hugged her, sharing his jam with her shoulder. And he *was* tall, much more so than either of his brothers at four. She could no longer scoop him up the way she loved to do without risking her back.

"You are too early!" He gave a quick pout. "Nanny will be upset."

Judith swallowed a laugh. "I suspect she will be more upset with your waste of good jam."

Nanny trotted after him, a serviette flailing in one hand. "Oh, my goodness! I'm so sorry, my lady. We were not expecting you so early."

"See!" William grinned.

Judith held out one hand for the serviette and used it to clean her son's cheeks, then her dressing gown, as she smiled at the young woman. "No reason you should. So few of us rise this early. But I was awake and didn't want to wait for this morning's visit." She handed the cloth back, smoothed William's ruffled ebony curls, and kissed the top of his head. "I had to see my beautiful boy."

William again giggled and squirmed.

Nanny gave her a knowing smile. "You are missing your George."

Judith's chest tightened. She patted William's back and urged him to return to his food. As he skipped toward the table, she straightened and nodded at Nanny. "I still think he was too young to be sent off to Eton."

"He is twelve, my lady. Some go much younger."

"Which is a travesty. We send our boys away too soon." Judith pressed a finger to her trembling lips, her gaze lingering on William. "George was barely past his father's death."

"I know how hard that was for him. Master Robert seems to have fared better."

Judith straightened and composed herself. "He was eight. It affected him in a different way." She looked at the nurse again. "Do you speak to Mr. Thompson much about Robbie's studies?"

"Only in passing. But he seems to be doing well."

Judith nodded and gazed at William again as he munched on a crunchy piece of jam-coated toast, replacing the recently cleaned smears on his cheeks. As he chewed, he bounced a tiny wooden horse on the table, as if it were cantering through the park.

Judith sighed. Her precious boys. She and the fifth earl had waited until Edmund and Daniel had matriculated to Eton to have children, with George born less than a year later. Robbie had come along two years after that, and William another six years later, after two losses. Too long. William would never know his father, and Robbie would have scant remembrances, if any.

But no one, not even their family physician, had realized how ill the earl had been. He had hidden that—as with much of his life—from everyone, even his wife and his heir. A good man but remote with all things, even his heart, especially after his time overseas, fighting in the colonies. Judith had learned to deal with the memories and nightmares that had haunted her husband, but she remained determined that her sons would not be so distant from those who cared about them. And she prayed they would never have to go to war, never have to deal with the evil that warfare did to good men.

Thus her frequent visits to the fourth floor.

"Mum?"

Judith turned. Robbie stood in the door of the nursery, his dark eyes still bleary with sleep, his nightshirt loose and rumpled on his thin frame. Judith smiled and went to him, rubbing his shoulder. "How is my sleepy one?"

He gave her a half-smile. "Sleepy."

She hugged him. "Did I wake you?"

He gave a weak gesture toward his brother. "William, I think. Incessant giggles."

"'Incessant'? My, Mr. Thompson is indeed earning his salary."

Robbie stood a little straighter, pride shining in his eyes. "He tells me I am making excellent progress with my Latin and vocabulary. He tells me we will start reading botany soon."

"And mathematics?"

He sniffed, then wiped his nose on his sleeve.

She pushed his arm down. "Not so much on manners, I see."

His cheeks pinked. "I do not understand them. Manners make no sense."

She kissed the top of his head. "There are many things in life that do not make sense, Robbie. We must do them anyway. Manners will make life smoother. They make being with other people easier. You will find, for instance, that your mother is much happier when you do not smear your sleeve with snot."

He snickered. "Yes, Mum."

The longcase clock on the first-floor landing chimed the half-hour, its mellow bongs echoing through the house. Judith gave Robbie a quick hug. "Now. Go get ready for your breakfast and studies. I must return downstairs."

He returned the hug and tolerated one more kiss before shuffling out of the room. At a tug on her dressing gown, she looked down at William, whose sweet face and bright brown eyes gleamed up at her. All three of her boys had inherited their father's dark features and tawny skin—such a contrast to her own fair appearance—looking enough like their half-brother Edmund that no one would question their relation to him. And she knew they would grow up to be just as handsome, just as attractive for the ladies. That Edmund had married so young and apparently so wisely had been a blessing.

But this one, her William, with those dark twinkling eyes and mischievous manner, he would be trouble. He could benefit from firm male guidance—Judith hoped Edmund would be up to the task.

She bent and gave William a silly kiss on his relatively clean forehead, making him giggle again. "I must go, jammy boy. It will be a busy day for both of us, I'm sure."

He pouted.

"You will be nice to Nanny today?"

He nodded. "Always!"

Nanny gave a scoffed laugh, and Judith bit her lip. "We must work on your ability to tell the truth."

His eyes widened, then he brightened. "Can I ride? Mr. Robins likes me to ask questions about the horses."

For a moment, Judith wondered if their groom truly liked having her son around—or if it were Nanny's company he preferred. She had seen the two of them exchanging shy looks. "It's quite chilly outside—"

"Please!"

"I really do not know what happened to our summer—"

"I will wear a jumper!"

Judith looked at Nanny. "Ask Mr. Robins if he has time for a pony ride."

"Yes!"

Nanny grinned, her cheeks flushing pink. "Yes, my lady. I'm sure the exercise will do him some good."

"And give you a rest. Or perhaps a chance to chat with our handsome groom?"

Nanny's cheeks grew even rosier. "Perhaps, my lady."

Oh, she would miss this woman! In a few weeks, William would shift to Mr. Thompson's care and tutoring, and Nanny would be in need of a new position. But good nannies were in great demand, and Judith reminded herself to write an excellent reference for her.

She stroked William's curls again. "I will see you this afternoon." Sometimes Judith thought she had survived her husband's death solely because of the daily visits with her boys. Her marriage had been no love match—nor had she expected it to be when she had accepted Edmund's suit. Neither had had much to offer in the beginning, and she had not been his first choice. But in the long term, they had been good for and to each other, eventually becoming friends and constant if not exactly exciting lovers. His illness had gutted her, but her boys . . . they had restored her hope, and she craved their presence. She had added the morning visits when the afternoons were no longer enough.

William raised both arms. She gave him another quick hug, then headed back downstairs. She peered into her bedchamber and let out a sigh when she saw that Perry had taken the hint. Her bed was empty. Perfect.

She went inside and rang for her maid, Epworth, and worked again to get the knots out of her dressing gown's sash. Epworth knew a great deal about her mistress's activities. She had been Judith's one and only lady's maid as well as her confidante for the past twenty-two years, and she often guided young nobles up to Judith's bedchamber. Still, Judith had no desire to explain the knots had been the result of Judith's instructions to the young—and relatively inexperienced—Perry. Even after several months, the man still failed to grasp the concept that some knots were not supposed to be escapable. One twist of her wrists, and Judith had been free to turn the tables on him. Which delighted him far more than her.

She sighed, pulling the last jumble free, tossing both the dressing gown and sash onto the bed. Tonight the Huntingdale ball awaited, and she and Epworth had a lot to do. With a grin, she wondered which handsome treat she might entice to join her afterwards. While her boys had restored her hope, in the events of the *ton*, Judith had discovered a different kind of contentment in the ebullient life she had missed by marrying at seventeen. She would turn forty in two years, and she remained determined to make the most of what youth and beauty she had left.

CHAPTER TWO

Saturday, 16 July 1814
Huntingdale House, Mayfair, London
Half-past eleven in the evening

JUDITH PRESSED A gloved palm to her cheek, feeling the heat of her face through the pale-green silk. She gave a slight curtsy of thanks to her dance partner, who took his cue, murmured his own gratitude for the spirited reel, and backed away. Judith rested her other hand against her stomach, pausing to catch her breath, then lowered both as she headed for a beverage table near the far wall, mulling over two rather unkind thoughts.

The first was that the young gentleman should never again dance a reel, ever. His awkward prancing through the fast-paced dance reminded her of an ancient horse with a stone in its shoe. Steps that should have been light and rapid had been heavy and hobbled as he favored his left foot, as if it dragged a ball on a chain. He had trod on her toes twice, startling her. Judith suspected his bed play would have the same flaws in rhythm and immediately felt a stab of grief for his future wife. And while he seemed to be a kind soul—one could never really tell, since gentlemen tended to be on their best behavior at a ball—his conversational skills bore far too much resemblance to his dancing ability for her comfort, all one sided and stilted.

Judith paused and gave her dance card a quick glance to reassure herself that he had not claimed a second trip around the floor. Then she patted the side of her small, light-green cap to see if he had dislodged it in his overenthusiastic turns and gyrations.

No, it still retained its place on the crown of her head, and all the feathers still pointed in the right direction. The color perfectly accentuated the silver highlights in her chestnut hair, as did the metallic trim along the split sleeves and hem of her silk gown of the same pale green. A similar-colored ribbon circled the gown under her breasts, culminating in a bow at the back and ribbons trailing down along the train. Judith pushed one of the pins holding the cap more firmly into place, took another breath, then sauntered closer to the beverage table.

Her second unkind thought was that Dorothea, Countess Huntingdale, should never again host a ball, ever. The house's ballroom—too small by far for anything other than a limited gathering, such as a soiree or musicale—quickly overheated, especially in July, even in this exceptionally cool year. Being an adept hostess among the *ton* consisted of far more skills than what dishes to serve at supper and which musicians to hire for dancing.

Battlefield strategy, for instance, came to mind.

And the Earl Huntingdale, while notable in Parliament, did not appear to have the social stamina to deal with the offended members of the *ton* who had not received an invitation. Again, a weakness of the hostess, who did not seem to know whom best to invite and whom to ignore.

Unfortunately, at least for Judith's interest, this resulted in an appalling lack of suitable dance partners and potential lovers.

Judith did feel a pang of sympathy for the four daughters of the Huntingdale family, the first of whom would make her debut in three years. Poor child. With that inept a mother, she would surely be delivered into the cesspool of the *ton* woefully unprepared for the political and social manipulations of those around her.

Judith glanced around the ballroom as she strolled. The next slot on her card remained empty, a relief since she needed a break from the crush to regain her bearings and take another stock of the room. Although now crowded with dancers attempting a cotillion without running into the walls, the small room *was* elegant, with its pastoral frescos covering the ceiling and walls. Plaster medallions covered with gold leaf anchored the four primary chandeliers, also gold, each of which held at least 120 candles, adding to the growing heat. The parquet floor gleamed with polish—making it treacherous for satin slippers—but in the center, an elaborate chalk painting of the Acropolis, now smeared beyond recognition, had aided the dancers.

Judith glanced down at her own chalk-covered slippers and hem, hoping Epworth could clear the dust remnants settling amidst the silver embroidery. She could hear the scolding tongue clucks of her modiste as well as her maid in the back of her head. The intricate stitching that circled the base of her dress would take some gentle and determined brushing. Although most ladies did not wear a ball gown twice, Judith often did, especially since her husband's death. She had been frugal before with the household finances. Now she was downright stingy with her widow's portion. As a dowager countess and no longer a debutante seeking a mate, new gowns for every season made for an unnecessary luxury. Tonight's gown, in fact, dated from the 1811 season, refreshed by her modiste with new trim and frills, along with the feather-festooned cap.

Turning away from the dancers, Judith picked up a cup of lemonade from the beverage table, sipped, and winced. The lack of sugar in the swill made for a bitter and lasting aftertaste.

"I'm afraid it's either that or the ratafia. They will not bring out the champagne until midnight."

Judith looked over her shoulder to see a tall, dark-haired man standing beside her stepson. His mouth formed an arrogant smirk, but his deep-blue eyes gleamed with an unexpected humor. The elegant simplicity of his black-and-white evening kit stood apart from some of the gaudier attire of the other gentlemen—including her own stepson's burgundy, green, and gold—but the cut of his clothes and the quality of his silk waistcoat and cravat spoke of a casual wealth and status.

Judith set down the cup. "Probably the most judicious choice our hostess has made all night, given that this is worse than the sluice at Almack's. And I would rather drink poison than ratafia. Champagne too early and her guests would quickly gulp down her best offering, leaving none for the supper."

"The supper will not be much better either." The smirk did not relent, even as he spoke.

"Spoken like a true veteran of the Marriage Mart."

"Only of the edible fare. I have steered clear of all other offerings."

"A hard-won wisdom, my lord?"

Those eyes sparkled. "A spurious wisdom, I'm afraid, my lady."

Edmund cleared his throat. "Excuse me. Lord Mark, may I present my stepmother, our dowager countess, Lady Sculthorpe, Judith Lovelace. Mother, this is Lord Mark Ry—"

"The Duke of Embleton's son?"

Lord Mark gave a crisp bow. "The second one, yes, although it is my oldest brother who is now duke. It is a pleasure, Lady Sculthorpe."

"I did hear about the loss of your father. I am sorry."

His lips pressed together. "I thank you."

"And you are second of eleven, if I remember." Judith waited for the man's response and was not disappointed.

His eyebrows arched and the smirk vanished, as did the gleam. "Nine these days."

"All children are important to be counted." Judith's own losses were never far from her mind. "All are precious."

His eyes narrowed, studying her, tiny creases appearing at each side. He tilted his head to one side, and the candlelight over his head caused the faint silver streaks in his ebony hair to glimmer like a light dusting of snow. Yet "handsome" did not quite describe the clean lines of his jaw and aquiline nose, his sculpted cheekbones, or silken curls. To have such a man focus on her made Judith's stomach tighten with an unexpected glee, and she fought to keep her expression calm, not completely succeeding.

Edmund cleared his throat again.

Judith touched her stepson's arm. "Do you need some air, sir? It *is* rather stuffy in here."

That gleam returned.

Edmund's cheeks pinked. "No." His voice dropped to a whisper. "Mother, please." He straightened and took a deep breath. "I brought Lord Mark over because I know him to be a good dancer. I realize he is a little older than those you usually choose—"

Mark's eyes snapped toward Edmund. "I beg your pardon?"

"So few men my own age can maintain pace with me."

Those eyes turned back to hers. "Do I hear a challenge in that statement, Countess?"

"Lady Sculthorpe, please, as I am the dowager. Perhaps you did. If you think there is one to be heard. Are you my own age?" A rude inquiry, but that had never stopped Judith before.

"The next dance, I believe, is a quadrille." He held out his hand, ignoring her question.

She raised hers, the dance card and its attached pencil dangling from her wrist. "Probably wise to start simply."

Edmund rolled his eyes as Lord Mark signed the card. "Now you see why I prefer to attend Society events with my wife. She is far more docile."

Lord Mark paused, then added his name to a second dance. "Docility is not always an admirable quality."

Judith watched him sign. "Ah. I like a man who has lofty expectations."

Lord Mark released the card. "I merely enjoy adventures where I can find them. Large or small."

With another roll of his eyes, Edmund wandered off, and Lord Mark offered Judith his arm.

She took it, amused by some of the sly glances and fluttering fans that followed her escort to the dance floor. Lord Mark was exceptionally attractive—uncommon for such a staid and limited event. The more eligible bachelors of the *ton* often sought out a larger field of play, such as Almack's or a grander ball. *Perhaps he does not consider himself eligible, given his reputation.*

Their stroll around the edge of the dust-covered floor continued, smooth and measured, and Judith could feel the strength in his forearm. She glanced up at him. "I see by the unsubtle glances we are receiving that your renown is everything I have heard. Is it truly well earned?"

"I suppose that would depend on what you have heard."

"Ah. Notoriety is not always what it is made out to be. So here is a theoretical question for you."

He looked down at her. "Theoretical?"

"I prefer theoretical questions to coy small talk."

"A distinct change of pace for a lady of the *ton.*"

"How many women, would you say, must a man take to his bed before he is considered a rakehell, in contrast to how many men a woman can take to her bed before she is considered ruined, a wanton? Or a harlot?"

Lord Mark gave a low snort. "Am I to assume you are implying one number is significantly higher than the other?"

"Infinitely so."

The orchestra ended their melody, and the dancers shifted on the floor. Lord Mark and Judith took up a corner position near the violins, as the musicians paused to retune their instruments. As three other couples joined them, he leaned closer, his eyes sparkling again. "One for the wanton, if unmarried. Two or more for a harlot. Perhaps five or more if she would like to become a wanton harlot. More on both counts for a widow, I would think. Society tends to be kinder to women who have already had a turn at fidelity and the provision of an heir and spare."

She ignored the barb. "And the rakehell?"

"I suppose it would depend on the quality of the women."

"Intriguing distinction. Nobility."

"Five. At least it was for me. But they were married, so I had the aid of their husbands to spread the . . . um . . . details."

Behind them the orchestra settled and turned their attention to their conductor. "Am I to assume you did not stop at five?"

"Ah, Lady Sculthorpe, you see before you a man aiming for the status of a true scoundrel."

"Your mother must be so proud."

"Not a word I would have chosen, but she is here tonight. I am officially her escort. You may ask her if you like."

"Do not think I will not."

He released her hand and faced her. "Such hesitation on your part would not cross my mind. But first we must dance."

As the lively strains of the quadrille swirled around the ballroom, the dancers spread into four groups of four couples each. Judith smiled at her partner, reminding herself to thank Edmund later. Even if her acquaintance with Lord Mark Rydell advanced no further than this chat and a dance or two, Judith had been thoroughly entertained, unlike her previous dances with gentlemen who barely knew how to discuss anything beyond horses and whisky. Items she ordinarily knew a great deal more about than they did.

Plus, he was rather lovely to look at. *Was he really here only to escort his mother?*

Feeling a blush of desire rising in her belly, Judith turned her attention to the other three couples. She had a passing acquaintance with two of the women, but she knew none of them well. The ranking member of the group, and thus first gentleman of the dance, was a viscount from Kent and his wife. The second and third couples took their spots, with Judith and Lord Mark taking position as the fourth couple, which would give them a few moments to get their bearings. The music, a spritely tune led by the violins, lifted into the air, the partners bowed to each other, and the first lady stepped off, reaching for the hand of the second gentleman opposite her.

Ignoring the growing chalk dust cloud around her feet, Judith found herself moving through the fast paces of the dance with joy. The bouncy steps, in-and-out and circles, the star shape left her a bit breathless but exhilarated. Each "return to partner" meant a tight grip from Lord Mark's hand and the light in his eyes shone even more as he focused on her face. The turns that brought them closer together allowed a faint scent of soap, pine, and mint to reach her, a pleasant aroma that did not overwhelm as so many of the gentlemen's colognes did. He was indubitably the best dancer of the evening, his steps light and sure as he moved through the intricacy of the quadrille with a smooth and confident ease. His firm leadership through the steps differed pleasantly from the limp fish hands most men employed.

Perhaps skilled dancing was a requirement of an excellent rake. While that had not been her experience so far—and Judith had substantial experience with less-than-excellent young rakes— she decided that finding out the exact skills of this somewhat-older version might be well worth her time.

MARK BOWED AT the end of the dance, then escorted the dowager countess back to the beverage table before leaving her, as they had both lost track of Edmund. Mark had recognized the earl had ulterior motives when he wanted to introduce his stepmother but not precisely what those motives were. Now Mark had a couple of strong suspicions, and he could not decide whether to admire the man for a wily plan or call him out for being so devious. Mark decided to let the evening play out instead, wondering if the dowager had been included in her stepson's scheme.

He rather hoped not, given how much he had truly enjoyed their encounter.

Mark knew that aristocratic men often married much younger women, especially for the second or third marriage. Still . . . to hear the woman referred to as a dowager countess had led him expect someone in her dotage, white-haired and tottering. Lady Sculthorpe had instead been a pleasant surprise with her wit and beauty—a woman he would have pursued with enthusiasm before the war. He relished their banter and enjoyed her quick and precise steps in the quadrille, the rush of color in her face from the exertion making her even more alluring. A lovely face with emerald eyes that shone, surrounded by a well-styled mane of chestnut curls and complementing an enticing figure that held a womanly fullness that made him want to linger in her company. The faint hint of lilies had followed her on and off the dance floor, and the tinge of pink in her cheeks made him wonder how she would look, how she would smell in the fullness of her arousal.

Definitely not white-haired and tottering.

Although neither of those terms described his own mother, despite her being more than twenty years older. While Phyllida had reached her early sixties, she remained statuesque, with an almost military posture and blonde hair only now going to gray. While her tendency to continue wearing the black of mourning usually dragged down her otherwise youthful look, tonight she wore a lavender gown—a pleasant change made for the purpose of attending the ball—but she had refused all offers to dance.

Nor was Phyllida yet a dowager, a word that would not apply to his mother until his brother Matthew married.

Still . . . the contrast between the two women locked in his brain as he turned over the suspected reasons for the introduction, and he glanced back at Lady Schulthorpe, who had already been lured into another dance by a young lord.

An extremely *young* lord.

Mark paused, his brow furrowing as he watched the couple spin through the dance. *Why* was *she dancing with someone barely able to shave?*

A thump hit his chest, and he started, glaring down at his mother—and the fan that had just landed against his waistcoat.

"Stop staring at her." The words hissed through taut lips.

Mark stepped back and closed his hand around her fist—the one clutching the fan. "Do you even know who she is?"

"Of course, I know. I know everyone in this room. And she is not for you. Why were you dancing with her?"

"As a favor to her stepson. He asked me to dance with her. So I did."

"Why?"

"Because I am quite an accommodating gentleman." He tightened his grip on the fan hand as she tried to jerk it away.

"You are hardly ever that accommodating. But I meant why did he want *you* to dance with her?"

"I–I am not certain."

"But you suspect."

"Suspicions are not facts."

"Let go of my hand."

"Only if you promise not to whack me with it."

"Are you going to dance with her again?"

"Yes. A nice, quiet cotillion later in the evening. I promised, and I will not embarrass her by withdrawing. Are you going to hit me?"

His mother released a long sigh. "No."

He released her hand. Slowly. And on guard. He offered his arm, and she took it, letting her fan dangle from a cord around her wrist. He led her toward a row of chairs against a far wall. "Why do you say she is not for me?"

Phyllida peered up at him. "Lady Sculthorpe is almost forty with three sons of her own. And rumor has it she has exchanged virtue for pleasure."

"I would not fault her for something I vie for."

His mother's expression sharpened. "Do not be coy. You need your own family."

"I do not see why. I thought Matthew was in charge of providing the next heirs." A previously determined bachelor, his older brother had, in truth, relented to the idea of marriage only earlier that day.

They reached the chairs, and Phyllida settled gingerly onto one of the cushions. "I do not hold out much hope for Matthew. He is far too sour. You have the more pleasant personality, when you wish to."

Mark scowled, uncertain if that was a compliment or a complaint. "Mother—"

"Her." She gestured briefly at a young woman speaking with an older matron. Mother and daughter. "Lady Catherine. You danced with her earlier."

Mark clenched his teeth to hold back his immediate reaction to the suggestion. He sat in the chair next to Phyllida, then leaned closer to whisper, "Not if she were the last woman on earth. Her mother is a bear with beastly claws, and Lady Catherine's head is filled with tealeaves and ribbons. Having a conversation with her is slightly less enticing than watching clothes dry."

His mother pressed two fingers to her lips. When she had her humor under control, she whispered back, "Young ladies are not brought up to be scintillating conversationalists."

"The more's the shame."

"Are you not on anyone's dance card?"

Mark released a low growl. "Yes. I am promised to Lady Carys Morgan for the next one."

"She is kind, if somewhat too Welsh."

"A motherly description of someone who always appears to have just stubbed her toe."

"You really must stop."

"You wanted me here."

Phyllida looked at him, a serious aura of dismay clouding her eyes. "Not to insult the daughters of my friends."

Mark sighed and squeezed her hand. "I apologize, Mother. I just wish you would relent on this quest. I am too lost to be a husband to anyone."

"You say that, but I will never believe it."

Because you have not heard me screaming in the middle of the night or seen my bruises from hitting the headboard. Yet another thought he would never express to her. "You should."

She turned her hand, returning his squeeze. "Even Pandora's box held a flutter of hope in the end."

He stood. "I should find Lady Carys."

Stepping away, he skirted the edge of the ballroom as he searched for the lady in question. His eyes, however, kept drifting to either Edmund, Lord Sculthorpe, who Mark had finally spotted clustered with a group of his peers, or the dowager countess, who had been chosen for the upcoming dance by yet another *young* lord. This one he knew—Gower—who gazed down at Lady Sculthorpe like a besotted schoolboy.

Annoyance congealed in his gut, and Mark could not fathom why—whether it was the men's ages or that they seemed to look at her with the adoration of starving puppies salivating over a beefsteak.

A cleared throat got his attention, and he jerked, looking down at a young woman who could not have been more than seventeen—or five feet tall, making her more than a foot shorter than he was. Lady Carys. Mark dug deep, found his smile and his manners, and offered the lady his arm.

And the night suddenly felt even longer than it had before.

CHAPTER THREE

Sunday, 17 July 1814
Sculthorpe Manor, Berkeley Square, London
Half-past ten in the morning

THE LONGCASE CLOCK on the first-floor landing sounded half-past ten, and Judith's mouth twitched. She had been awake for more than an hour but had remained in bed, staring at the burgundy damask-lined canopy, her mind lost in the events of the night before. She had not even bothered to ring for Epworth, which she should do soon lest the entire household began to think she had taken ill. Only her monthly courses took Judith out of her daily activity, and Epworth would know those had finished a few days before. Otherwise, half-past nine was late for Judith, much less an hour after, even though she had only returned home at three that morning. Between her boys and her desire to be up and out of the house in all but the most beastly weather, Judith never slept late. Too much life awaited outside these walls to lie abed, and the bright rays of sun that pierced through the curtains told her it would be a lovely day to be out.

But not even in her own mind could Judith decipher why she so focused on the previous night that she had become immobile. Her thoughts tumbled over themselves as she stared at the pleated cloth over her head, her eyes following the lines of the fabric from the four corner posts to the center medallion again and again.

Even more surprising, Judith had spent the night alone. Perry had wanted to join her, making it so obvious that she had almost scolded him on the dance floor for his indiscretion. She had not done so, nor would she ever indulge in such a public display, and normally she would have felt flattered by his attention, preening under his compliments. But he had seemed far too much like a relentless child, whining for a treat and annoying her. Over the evening she had become increasingly unsettled, unwilling to choose any of her previous lovers or cultivate a new one among the interested parties.

Instead, she could not rid her mind of a twisted smirk and glistening blue eyes. A wit of uncanny sharpness. A firm grip. A keen, muscular dancer. Dark hair with a bare wink of silver.

Ridiculous.

Lord Mark Rydell had to be at least five and thirty. At least. More than a decade older than most of her lovers. Perry Gower was but three and twenty. Judith preferred the younger men, those not yet ready for a wife, eager for an enthusiastic tumble and little more. She also refused to take a married lover. And Rydell, a rake with a reputation for preferring married women, reportedly had a current mistress, an actress. Judith had circulated in the *ton* long enough to know most of the scoundrels, their relationships, and their family histories. And she knew Rydell's as well.

But much of the scuttlebutt about his sexual proclivities stemmed from a time before he had joined his brothers at the battlefront. Although the youngest of the children remained in the family home, the three oldest Embleton sons—including the heir at the time but now the duke, Matthew—had followed Wellington to the Peninsula. Lord Mark Rydell was a soldier who had been more than five years at war, venturing back to England only on rare occasions. They had, obviously, returned to England when their father had died, but the *on dit* about them told of men who had not returned unscathed. Matthew was said to be surly and unapproachable. The third son, Luke, had returned to France after healing from an almost crippling wound. And Mark, now the heir with all the responsibilities that go with that position, had supposedly lost the ability to sleep, with a tendency to wander at night in the most dangerous sections of the city, seeking fights in the roughest of boxing salons and gambling hells. Reports of numerous lovers had all but disappeared. Except for the actress. And only the actress, a relationship that had developed during one of his trips back to England. Rumor had that he had purchased the townhouse where she lived more than four years ago.

Convenient. Long term. Almost as if she were a wife.

How very curious for a man who seemed to revel in his reputation for bedding dozens of women.

Thus, between his desires and hers, no two people in London were *less* suited to each other.

So why did Edmund insist on introducing him to me?

Edmund knew she took lovers but had ignored it in his everyday dealings with her. Margaret had slyly mentioned "the young men of the *ton*, so adorable, like new toys" when she and Judith had been alone in the boudoir. Margaret had been tending to her needlework while Judith attempted to read. Docile or not, Judith knew her daughter-in-law craved the juiciest of details and had blithely ignored the comment, finally setting aside her novel and turning the conversation to the latest issue of *La Belle Assemblée*. Fashion always distracted Margaret.

Something was amiss. Had Edmund begun gambling? Did he owe Rydell money? Did he think he could pay it back with Judith's portion? That she would surrender it to Edmund if she married a duke's heir?

No, that made no sense. She knew exactly how deep the coffers of the Sculthorpe estate ran, and any but a stupendous debt could be paid by selling some of their holdings or artwork. And unless a marriage was in the plotting, no guarantee could be made that Judith's money could be circumvented into another's pockets. And Lord Mark would remain the heir only until the new duke had children of his own.

So did the motive arise from the other direction? Was Rydell looking to marry a rich widow? She would qualify, but her sources indicated that the Embleton sons wanted to avoid the state of marriage altogether. Lord Mark was a second son, but there were no indications that his family withheld funds from him, especially as long as he remained the heir. If the rumors about the actress were sound, then he had to be supporting her, which was *not* a frugal proposition. Judith knew of the woman, knew her reputation. Stella Ashley had expensive tastes and made no secret of it.

And even during the second dance, Rydell had given no indication that he was there for any purpose other than enjoying himself. The cotillion—not a dance for in-depth conversation—had been a slightly faster one than most, and his strength as a partner once again had shone during their moments together. Despite the rumors of battlefield injuries, he showed no signs of physical weakness. If anything, he seemed the opposite of wounded, with firm muscles, a trim waist, and obvious strength in his legs and arms. He had flirted with her, yes, but all men did.

And he had once again challenged her to meet his mother. Judith had accepted, but the duchess was not to be found, which had puzzled and concerned him. When his mother could not be seen in the small ballroom, he had escorted Judith to the next dance partner and excused himself. Neither of the Rydells had been seen again.

Judith scowled. He had remembered who her next partner was from seeing the name on her card. He had commented on others, humorously, cautioning her about which ones would be a danger to her slippers.

He had clearly taken note of the other men with whom she had danced.

Why would he do that? Were he and Edmund working together in this?

On what?

Judith scolded herself for her speculations, searching for something that most likely did not exist—an ulterior motive for

Edmund wanting to connect her with Lord Mark Rydell. *Perhaps he is just an intriguing friend.*

"Or you could just ask Edmund." Judith said it aloud, then smiled. She did have a tendency to put too much thought into such a situation, especially when it puzzled her, often seeing connections where none existed. "Do not be a dolt. It was one evening. Two dances."

She took a deep breath and pushed up in the bed, shifting the pillows and bracing her back against the headboard. "But," she whispered, "if Edmund has some nefarious reason in mind, he might not be honest about it. Do I want to push him into a lie?"

Her mouth twisted. "Or he could choose to be honest."

After a moment, Judith sighed. "Or you could stop dwelling on nonsense, get your arse out of the bloody bed, and start your day." Perhaps a stroll in the park would clear her head. It was Sunday, after all, and Rotten Row would be crushed with people enjoying the delightful weather—the summer had been unseasonably cool, which meant sunny, warmer days brought out the *ton* in thick droves, as if they were all glad to get out of their houses.

Throwing back the covers, Judith slid her legs over the side and stood, padding to the bell pull. Tea would help, along with a bit of toast. Perhaps some butter and jam. Judith no longer had the figure of a debutante wraith, but last night's gown had been a bit loose—she could allow herself some delicious jam. She sat on the dressing table stool and pulled her nighttime plait—the protective style she kept when sleeping alone—around to the front, slipping the ribbon off the end and running her fingers through the golden-brown strands to separate the braid, as her mind moved from the ball to the park. The sun would be blissful, and she made a mental list of the friends she might see. She would wear the blue today, a walking kit that came with matching kid day boots, a spencer, and a lovely buckskin bonnet, complete with an ostrich feather dyed to match the deep tourmaline blue of the gown.

Blue.

And those eyes were in her mind again, the crinkles in the corners reminding her again that Rydell was not one of the young pups of the *ton*. Older. And infinitely more experienced with both Society . . . and a woman's bed.

Her nipples tightened. So did her thighs as warmth spread between them.

She stood up. "Damn it!" The tap on the door did not calm her. "Enter!"

The door opened slowly, Epworth peering in, eyes wide. "My lady?"

Fool!

She waved Epworth in. "Yes, come in, Epworth. My apologies. I am afraid last night has left me a bit out of sorts." Her maid bore a tray of tea, fruit, cheese, and buttered toast, and Judith sighed as she spotted the pot of jam on the tray. "Thank you. Just what I need to turn the morning around."

Epworth set the tray on the bench at the end of Judith's bed. "Was it the Embleton gentleman?"

Judith froze, then her eyes narrowed. "Why would you ask that?" A question out of place for most servants, but Epworth had served her too long and too well. And Judith had long relied on her maid's knowledge of the downstairs world.

Epworth shrugged. "You know how the servants talk. The news from the ball about you and Lord Sculthorpe is that the Embleton gentleman was the most attentive to you both and the only one to dance with you twice. He is said to be most handsome."

"Lord Peregrine also—" Judith gave a dismissive wave, then eased down onto the dressing table stool. The gossip could be useful. "I danced with others, but Rydell was indeed attentive. What else are they saying?"

Epworth poured the tea, added milk, and brought Judith a cup on a saucer. "That each of you is a strong dancer, but that when the two of you danced, the whole ballroom watched."

Not something Judith had noticed. "Well, he is somewhat notorious." She accepted the tea, sipping thoughtfully.

"They also said that he—he and his mother—left before the supper."

Judith could not remember seeing either of them after that cotillion. She looked at the floor, trying to envision the tables at the late-night meal. Neither the food nor the guest list had been particularly enticing or memorable. "I do not—"

"That she was taken ill."

Judith's focus snapped back to Epworth. "Ill?"

Epworth smeared jam on a slice of toast and added it to a small plate that also held several slices of pears and a bit of cheese. She set it on the dressing table. "If you will turn around, my lady, I can brush out your hair as you eat."

Judith did, watching Epworth in the mirror. "You said the duchess was ill?"

"Apparently nothing serious. One of the footmen said she seemed to rally once her son agreed to leave with her."

Judith almost choked on her tea. She coughed, and Epworth gently removed the cup and saucer from her hand as Judith settled, the cough turning into a low laugh.

"My lady?"

Judith straightened on the stool and held out her hand for the tea, which Epworth returned to her. "Men, my dear Epworth. No matter how old or wise they become, they will never understand the ability of women to rule the world."

Epworth grinned and reached for a hairbrush. "And what are we wearing today, my lady?"

"The blue walking dress. The tourmaline one. With that feathered bonnet. If I can persuade Edmund to let me have the curricle, we will be quite the sight in the park this afternoon."

"You will indeed, my lady. But you always are."

Sunday, 17 July 1814
Embleton House, Mayfair, London
Half-past two in the afternoon

MARK GROWLED, A low dark sound in the back of his throat. "You cannot leave a ball on the pretense of being ill, then saunter through Hyde Park the next afternoon as if all is well with the world." He paced in front of the receiving room fireplace, his annoyance burrowing deeper into his gut.

On the settee, his mother flipped over her embroidery hoop to check a knot. "Do not be ridiculous. Of course I can. Any woman my age would have felt faint in the heat and nauseating crowd of that ball. I only needed fresh air to be right as rain." She turned the hoop over again and continued to stitch. "Where is your brother?"

"White's."

"Again? He is avoiding me."

"Of course he is. Your campaign to have both of us marry before the season finishes is enough to make any man madder than a hatter."

"Will you please sit? Your pacing is doing the same for me."

Mark dropped down on an armchair opposite her settee, tucking his legs in under the seat and leaning toward her. "You summoned me, Mother. What do you want?"

"As I said, I want to go to Rotten Row, and I want you to escort me. It is a beautiful day, and the whole *ton* will be out. I want to take the landau and see who is promenading."

"You mean you want to see which women might be out with a suitor and who might be with their chaperones. You want to make a list of eligible ladies."

"That is one reason to go to the park."

"I am not getting married."

"*Au contraire,* brother—"

Mark, started, jerked around, then glared at his brother. "Do not do that," he muttered.

Matthew winced. "Sorry."

"Matthew!" Phyllida set aside her hoop. "So surprising for you to join us. I thought you had taken rooms elsewhere."

Matthew sat down on the settee next to their mother, making Phyllida grab her hoop and gather her skirts a bit closer. "Do not tempt me." He gave Mark a sly glance but said nothing to indicate that the two of them had, indeed, discussed hiring rooms for Mark—not Matthew—but for reasons that had nothing to do with their mother or their marital state. Or lack thereof.

Phyllida placed her embroidery on the low table before the settee. "What did you mean with that *'au contraire'*?"

Matthew straightened as he glanced from Mark to his mother. His voice, slightly lower than Mark's own baritone, carried a bit of humor in its tone. "After last night's ball, the betting book at White's has a wager on when Lord Mark Rydell will bed 'a certain fair widow of renown,' which all the wags are saying means the estimable and feisty dowager countess, Lady Sculthorpe."

Phyllida's eyes flared. "That damnable hussy!"

The brothers stared at their mother, then Mark slowly tilted his head to peer more closely at her. "Do you want to explain that comment?"

"I saw it last night!" She glared at Mark, gesturing at him with one hand. "The two of you. Flirting as if no one else was in the room. As if no one could see how . . . how inappropriate the two of you were."

Matthew's eyebrows arched as he looked at Mark. "What exactly did the two of you do during that quadrille?"

"The last dance was a cotillion." Mark gave a long, weary sigh and leaned back in the chair. "Is *that* why you took ill? To get me away from her?"

Phyllida looked at the ceiling, as if appealing to heaven for help with her clueless sons.

Matthew cleared his throat and tried to smother a grin with one hand.

"Bloody hell, Mother, I have told you I have no interest in marrying, but that does not mean I do not enjoy the company of women. I always have and I suspect I always will. I am not a monk. And given how many men the lady danced with last night, I suspect she is of the same mind. Gower kept stroking her back as if she were his favorite horse, for pity's sake. Sculthorpe introduced us—"

"Sculthorpe? The earl?" Matthew's expression turned curious.

"Yes. Her stepson. We have done business together, and he thought I would enjoy dancing with her. And I did. I even *liked* her, which is more than I can say about my other partners for the evening." Mark waved his arms in front of him. "They felt completely skeletal in my arms and their heads are full of wisps. Lady Sculthorpe is a fine dancer and can converse about things other than new frocks and whether the sun will shine tomorrow. We had a pleasant evening. That is all."

"And if she had asked you to her bedroom?" His mother's clipped words were a clear challenge.

A challenge he gladly accepted. "I would have gone. As I said, she is an excellent dancer."

"I see."

He knew he should not continue, but—"With fine, strong legs and a superb round arse." He made a cupping motion with his hands.

"Mark!"

Matthew burst out laughing, and Phyllida swatted him.

Mark stood. "I suspect it is my turn to visit White's."

"Mark!"

"Matthew can take you the park."

His brother snorted. "When pigs fly."

Mark ignored them both, leaving the receiving room and heading for the entrance hall. Near the front door, their butler Stephens waited with a chapeau and a light cloak. Mark paused, then reached for them. "Expecting rain later, are we?"

Stephens nodded. "So they say. And it is still cool."

"You heard everything, or just expected us to head to the park?"

"The duchess does have a way about her."

Mark coughed. "So she does." He pulled the chapeau onto his head and draped the cloak over his arm before heading out the door. He paused briefly on the pavement, then turned toward White's, the brisk air and his long strides easing some of the tension from his back and neck, tension that had been there throughout the night, since Edmund had insisted he meet Lady Sculthorpe. Tension that had escalated when Mark had realized his mother's ploy to get him away from the ball had been due to his enjoyment of the short time with the dowager countess.

What was it about this woman? Edmund, whom he had met at a boxing salon years ago, before Mark had gone to war and Edmund had become an earl, seemed determined to put him in front of his stepmother, whereas Mark's own mother seemed driven to keep him away from her.

Edmund. Matthew's inquisitive look returned to his mind—his brother obviously thought the introduction as odd as he did. Mark again mulled over possible reasons for Edmund's insistence on introducing his stepmother, none of which made any sense. He did know one thing—when he checked the wager book at White's, that bet would be in Edmund's handwriting. Handwriting that Mark knew well from the vowels he had often carried for the man. Because Edmund, for all his placid nature and upstanding moral appearance, could not resist an odd bet, the odder the better. And he frequently lost. A lot.

Sometimes more than a lot.

Could it be that simple?

Possibly.

But in this moment, Mark would lay out the stack vowels he carried from men all over the city that there was more buried in the motive behind this introduction. And the only way to eliminate the mystery entirely would be to follow his mother's advice and stay away from Lady Sculthorpe.

Except . . .

Mark did not want to.

He had found Judith Lovelace, Lady Sculthorpe, fascinating. Her intelligence, her humor, and her beauty—they all called to him. The silver gleaming in her chestnut hair, her radiant emerald-green eyes, her strength and confidence on the dance floor—all of them reminding him that she bore little resemblance to the wan debutantes he had found far too young, too innocent, too provincial, and too thin for his tastes. Lady Sculthorpe had the hips of a woman who had given birth, and while still trim, she had a body that told him she did not shy from a hearty meal. Most of all, she acted comfortable with him, apparently unphased by the persistent rumors about his past. The way she had looked up at him, as if admiring who he was, matched no other woman on the floor. She did know his reputation—a reputation carefully cultivated to ensure the *ton's* younger ladies would avoid him— and did not seem to care.

"All children are important to be counted. All are precious."

Mark stopped cold, his boots scuffing on the pavement as the words appeared in his mind abruptly, unexpectedly. Lady Sculthorpe's words. An unusual sentiment among the *ton*, who usually viewed their own children as products of a lineage, mostly ignored until they came of age. A necessity but not a privilege or a blessing.

Would she feel the same about a child of scandal, a by-blow, a child of a mistress? Would she think that child as precious as her own?

Mark stared down at the pavement, his chest tightening with a sudden, unwanted ache. Could she?

The ache sharpened, and Mark took a quick breath, then changed the direction of his steps. White's could wait. The club and that bloody book were going nowhere.

He needed to see Olivia.

CHAPTER FOUR

Sunday, 17 July 1814
Whitehall, London
Half-past four in the afternoon

THE SQUEAL OF a young child, Mark decided, had to be the most joyous sound on the planet. A happy noise layered with the glee of living and the wonder of discovery. Rose Ashley, Stella's mother—now that she was well enough—had become a rather adept gardener, and the small back garden of the house where Olivia and her grandmother lived held a plethora of flowers, multicolored rocks, small bits of carved stone, and a dozen or so delightful mud puddles, perfect for splashing whenever Granny had looked away. Abandoned bits of iron and wood, rescued from neighborhood piles, had become trellises for vines and homes for birds. Also hundreds of insects, which did not bother the girl in the least. Instead she clearly found the many varied shapes and colors of the crawly things fascinating, eagerly scrambling after them, sometimes on all fours herself.

At three, Olivia had lost some of her baby plumpness and walked with more confidence. But she spent a great deal of time bending down, touching everything in front of her, exclaiming over each new bug or flower, asking endless questions of her grandmother, and listening patiently to the answers. She laughed as she bounced through puddles and snatched at a bird in a bush—both of which earned her a scolding from the old woman.

In his carefully chosen and shadowed alcove across the alley, Mark watched, as fascinated by his daughter as she was by an everyday flower. Observing her made his chest tighten, a craving that burrowed deep within, a longing he knew would never be satisfied. He had discussed with Matthew the possibility of acknowledging Olivia publicly—it was not unheard of for aristocratic men to do so—but his brother had urged him to wait until the lineage had been secured. They also doubted Phyllida would welcome the girl into their home, and Mark could not protect her otherwise. For her to be publicly known as his child would leave the girl vulnerable to predators and other schemers. Perhaps someday. But not yet.

And there would be no other children, at least not legitimate ones. Mark cast his gaze to the ground. While he could not share this with his mother, he knew to his core that no woman would want to spend an entire night with him, much less a lifetime. Better to keep them all at bay, playing the rogue. While he had become renowned as an adventurous, skilled, and tender lover, when sleep did come—a rare event—it far more resembled the horrors of battle than a gentle slumber in a lady's arms. Screams. Limbs flailing wildly. Terrors that sent him stalking the halls, sometimes even while still asleep. Mark occasionally awakened bruised and bloody from hitting solid objects unawares. More than once, he had come to consciousness in the mews behind their house, his brother at his side, both unaware of how he had gotten there.

Since they had returned to Embleton House from the war, Matthew had helped Mark mask some of the ills of the nighttime, but the two of them had now put into place a plan to find Matthew a wife, which would bring another innocent into the house. Mark needed his own home, with locking doors and servants sworn to secrecy, so that search had also begun.

Olivia screeched, a less than happy sound.

Mark stiffened, his head jerking up, heart clutching. He stepped from the alcove before halting abruptly.

The girl had taken a tumble, tripping over some unseen object. Her grandmother helped her up, brushed off her clothes, wiped Olivia's hands on her apron, and kissed a palm, murmuring to the child. Olivia nodded, brushed away a tear, and smiled. She gave her grandmother a quick hug about the neck, then pointed to a stand of lavender. Olivia wandered that way as Rose began to pinch dead blossoms from a nearby rosebush. The girl brushed fingers over the purple blossoms, then lifted her head—her eyes meeting Mark's.

Mark stilled.

Olivia tilted her head to one side, studying him, and raised her hand. Her smile seemed to brighten the day, and Mark returned the greeting. Olivia waved. Mark did as well, then pointed at her grandmother and pressed a finger to his lips. Olivia glanced at Rose, then nodded at him.

With a sigh, Mark slipped back into the shadows.

Olivia resumed her play, and Mark watched until the two returned to the house, most likely for a nap or early supper. The afternoon had turned ever cooler, and overhead the gathering clouds held the promise of the rain Stephens had mentioned. Mark slung his cloak about his shoulders and headed toward his original destination of White's.

Reaching the storied club, he passed between the two stone pillars at the edge of the pavement and trotted up the steps to enter the comfortable realm of men. Sanctuary. He handed the cloak and chapeau to one of White's butlers, ordered a brandy, gathered up an abandoned newspaper, and found a spot near the fireplace in one of the front rooms. He would wait to view the betting book until he knew who else lingered in the club.

He did not have to wait long. He had barely begun to read when he heard his name.

"What-ho, Rydell! I figured you would be in the park chasing the merry widow. I heard she traipsed along Rotten Row today, bold in her curricle, a bluebird on the hunt for a mate, taking a gander at every blade on the path like an urchin eying a row of sweets." A man dropped into the chair opposite, his emerald-green frock coat, purple waistcoat, and cream buckskin trousers contrasting with Mark's usual black-and-white kit.

Mark did not care for the peacock colors that some of the younger gents wore. He peered around the newspaper at the new arrival, smirking. "You are the one dressed for an outing with the ladies, Harding. Did your tailor mistake you for a parrot or has he gone blind?" The cut was his favorite remark about the preening dandies among them, and he used it often.

"Ha!" Harding leaned back in the chair and motioned for a footman to bring a brandy as two other gentlemen wandered closer. "The ladies appreciate a man who can afford the finer things in life. It satisfies them to know they could have a secure position with me."

Mark folded his paper and set it aside. "I supposed you would have to satisfy them with your wallet, Harding, since I hear you are unable to do so otherwise."

Men around them chuckled, murmuring, as Harding bristled, red spots blooming over his cheekbones, emphasizing the kohl lining his eyes—another habit of the young blades Mark disdained. "Apparently, sir, you suffer from the same lack of proficiency, since your current paramour has been sniffing around other sources for her . . . satisfaction."

A guffaw sounded behind Mark's shoulder, followed by a jovial, "Oh, touché, Harding."

Mark let out a long sigh of exasperation, intentionally masking the spike of concern that had tightened his gut. *Surely Stella would not . . .* "If you are referring to a particular lady of my acquaintance—"

"That wanton is hardly a lady—"

"Then you have no true understanding of our arrangement—"

"My understanding is that your pockets—or some other element of your bearing—simply do not reach deeply enough. The *on dit* is that she is currently attempting to pick the pockets of other nobles, and that she has tried on more than a few for size."

Mark shook his head and took a sip of brandy, letting his gaze linger on Harding a moment. He set the glass aside, twisting it to study the residual glaze of liquor on the side of the glass. "Do you know why the ladies of the *ton* refer to you as 'the Apprentice'?"

Harding's eyes narrowed. "I have not heard—"

"Because you have yet to become skilled with your tools."

A raucous round of laughter echoed through the room, as Mark stood, clapping Harding on the shoulder and leaning closer. "If you do not believe me, just ask at Almack's. Those women know all the best rumors." He straightened. "Gentlemen, if you will excuse me, I have a bet to place, then I am off to the theater with my shallow . . . pockets."

Mark checked the wager book. As suspected, the bet about "a certain fair widow of renown"—no one would dare mention a lady by name in the book lest they wanted to be called out—was in her stepson's handwriting. He then gave a jolly farewell to the butler. But as he strode the pavement outside, a deep dread built in his gut, and he prayed that his suspicions—and Harding's insinuations—about Stella had no foundation at all. The alternative held an unimaginable horror.

Sunday, 17 July 1814
Theater Royal, Haymarket, London
Nine in the evening

MIDWAY THROUGH THE second act, Judith's left foot began to tingle, and a cramp crept up her calf, tightening the muscle and escalating the ache. She shifted in her seat, trying to stretch her leg out without kicking either Edmund's or Margaret's chair and pressing down with her toes. The family box on the third tier of the Haymarket Theater had more than enough room for the three of them, but they had crowded close to the front in order to hear the actors over the murmuring of the crowds below as well as in the adjacent boxes.

Theater attendance—almost an essential requirement among

the *ton's* elite—drew people to the various performances in droves, although the quality of the plays had less appeal than the glittering gowns and kits of the Beau Monde. As with Rotten Row, the theater was as much about seeing and being seen than being entertained. Most people, even those in the rowdy crowd below, appeared more interested in the latest gossip and who in the aristocracy sat among them than in the actors on stage. Craned necks and twisted shoulders held more favor, and the appearance of a high-ranking noble meant whispers spreading among the audience like so many waves on the beach. Judith herself had finally abandoned her attempt to hear the words of Richard Sheridan, although her attention had not been drawn by one of her peers. Instead, she focused on the actions of one specific actress, a blonde who pranced across the boards, gleaming and in complete control of the stage. Stella Ashley. Her radiant smile and abundant physicality usually enraptured an audience—and apparently one lord in particular.

What had attracted Rydell to this woman? Judith's thoughts toyed with the edge of jealousy, which annoyed her to no end. She had never been jealous of Edmund, even when she had been one of many debutantes vying for the widower's attention. *Why should I be jealous of Rydell? He is hardly the only man in London to pay attention to me.*

Stella Ashley gave a shout of surprise and seemed to float—actually float!—away from another actor. A skilled movement given her ample figure and tight costume.

The cramp in Judith's left calf seized, shooting a spike of pain up into her thigh. "Oh bloody hell," she muttered, frustration overwhelming her. She pushed from her chair, pointing down at her leg when Margaret turned to look at her. "Cramp. I need to walk it off." Margaret nodded and Judith pushed through the dark, curtained alcove at the back of the box and into the corridor outside.

She took a deep breath, pressing down with the ball of her foot as she limped back and forth a few steps. Normally this time of year the corridor held as much sweltering heat and lingering odors as the theater's interior, but the cooler days had left it a pleasant break from the people and candelabra-heated boxes. Judith muttered to herself about blonde actresses, errant lords, and annoying cramps as she tried to work free of the agony.

Until she realized a man stared at her from four boxes away. A dark-haired man with an unrelenting smirk.

Judith froze. Dear God, he was too handsome for his own good.

He sauntered toward her, his head tilted to one side, his top hat canting precariously. "Are you ill, Lady Sculthorpe?"

"No. Blasted cramp will not let me sit still." She pressed down with her toes again and winced.

"Ah." Rydell glanced around, then took her arm and guided her back through the curtains and into the alcove.

As the darkness closed around them, Judith hissed, "What are you doing?"

In the dim light from the corridor, which pressed through a narrow space between the curtains, Judith could see the gleam in his eyes. He pressed a finger to his lips, then pushed her back against the wall. Before she could react, he knelt in front of her, placed his top hat on the floor beside them, and lifted the offending leg, bracing her foot on his thigh.

Her eyes widened. "Rydell!"

"Shh."

With a firm grip, he closed both hands on her calf and began to massage the muscle, his fingers methodically loosening the tension.

She glared at him, her words a whispered hiss. "Are you mad?"

His smirk became a wicked sort of grin. "Merely mischievous. Do you wish me to stop?"

Judith bit her lip, her breath catching in her chest. His actions—scandalous as they were—held no seductive intent. He could have been grooming a horse. But his ministrations had brought relief to the pain in her leg and foot, and the heat of his palms, the pure strength in his hands and arms sent a rush of desire up through Judith's body. Warmth bloomed in her belly and between her legs.

"I—" She stopped, her words faltering.

"How is the cramp?"

She nodded, trying to catch her breath. "Much better. I—thank—"

Rydell's expression changed then, the smile fading into something calmer, alluring. His eyes narrowed, his gazed focused on hers as his touch on her leg gentled into long, soft strokes, drifting higher.

Judith gasped. "You must not—"

"Shh."

His fingertips traced the edge of the ribbon holding her stocking in place. The heat between her thighs spread, and Judith found herself fighting to keep her breathing calm and regular. She clutched her fists into her skirts, fighting the urge to slip her fingers into his dark curls. "Rydell—"

"Shh."

One finger tugged at the ribbon's bow, and Judith realized with a start what he had in mind. "You cannot—"

The ribbon loosened. He freed the top of her silk stocking and eased it down her leg. "But I can."

Judith pressed her head against the wall, panting as he removed her slipper and pulled her stocking free, tucking it and the ribbon into his coat pocket. He replaced her shoe and eased her foot to the floor. He stood slowly, leaning into her, their bodies almost touching. "I wish," he whispered, "to own a part of you."

Judith's lips parted in a gasp, his words galvanizing her, an unexpected and stark craving spearing through her. Rydell took her upper lip between his own, tugging, worrying it, as he cupped her face in his hands.

I cannot do this! It is scandal! In everything she had done, every lover she had taken, she had never been this public, this outrageous, this—

He teased her mouth with his tongue, gliding it along her lower lip, as his last words resonated deep into her soul. *I wish to own a part of you.* Desire, a deep craving for this man, flooded over her, consuming her with a demanding need to be with him in every way possible. She had never desired any man this fiercely, this—

She released her skirts and pushed against his shoulders, breaking her mouth from his. "You must stop."

He did, pulling away slightly. "You did not enjoy—"

"I did." She shot a quick glance toward Margaret and Edmund, who still faced the theater, although Margaret's attention had drifted to the boxes opposite theirs. "But I cannot want you this much—need you—" She swallowed hard, trying to regain some composure, forcing her voice into a tight whisper. She had to break this hold on her. She shook her head, her thoughts wild. "Besides. I thought you had someone, someone who you—" She gestured vaguely toward the stage.

Something shifted in him. Rydell stiffened, his expression souring with his mouth becoming a thin line, his eyes narrow and downcast. "So did I."

"I am your second choice then?"

He looked back at her, his gaze piercing. "Hardly." But he stepped away. "I have to take care of something. It may take a while. But I will find you again." He scooped his hat off the floor, but paused, looking over his shoulder. "And you are no man's second choice. Unless he is a fool."

Then he left.

Judith took a deep breath and released it slowly, letting her arousal, her inflamed passion for Lord Mark Rydell leach from her.

It took several deep, slow breaths before her legs steadied enough for her to walk to her chair behind Margaret and Edmund. Neither gave her a scant glance, and she hoped they would not notice one bare foot and ankle as they left for home.

I wish to own a part of you.

The words spoke of a desire Judith had longed for her entire life. She had had few courtiers in her first and only season—the second daughter of an almost impoverished household had little to offer but wit and competence. She had been no one's first choice, not even Edmund's. But he had been a scarred and wounded veteran of the war with the American colonies, a widower with two sons, and not even an earl. A second son with few prospects beyond his own investments. Wealth and a title could have won his first choice for a second bride—or possibly his second, third, or fourth choices—but another year would pass before an accident would take both his father and older brother from the lineage. Despite his pursuit of some of the more desirable debutantes, he had been turned away at almost every door. So Edmund had to settle for Judith after the others rejected him, as he had often told her the first four years of their marriage, especially after he had become earl. "If only I had waited another year." A phrase he often used when their relationship turned unpleasant.

But Judith had persevered in the marriage, and she had proven to be an excellent and faithful wife as the years passed. Finally, in the years after George's birth, Edmund had grown to care for her deeply. They had gradually become suited partners in a quiet and decent marriage.

But Judith had longed for passion. For a man to desire her with a mindless longing. So as a widow she had sought it among the young blades of the *ton*. To no avail. The passion of a puppy is sweet but often without control or direction. Judith had frequently needed to comfort her lovers when their performance in her bed peaked almost before getting started. She had to fight laughter at their overwhelming disappointment, consoling them with kisses and promises of a brighter future.

But it had all begun to tire her, even as she continued to desire the presence of a man in her bed.

I wish to own a part of you.

Judith's chest tightened, the words of the actors below slipping over her unheard. *Did he realize what he was saying?*

Judith wiggled her toes inside her left slipper and bit her lower lip, her mind recalling the feel of his fingers on her thigh, his lips against hers. A smile slowly crossed her face as she suspected he knew quite well what he had said. He wanted to claim her.

First choice.

CHAPTER FIVE

Monday, 18 July 1814
Bloomsbury, London
Half-past one in the morning

MARK STARED AT Stella, barely curtailing the rage that threatened to swamp him like a rogue wave. "Are you mad? Have you completely lost all your senses? Shropshire? Why would you even consider him?"

"He's a duke!"

"He has the pox!"

The red flush that had colored Stella's face since he had barged into her bedchamber drained away like the first pint of a drunkard. Wide eyes and a gaping mouth stared back at him. "How was I to know?"

Mark jerked an arm toward the door. "You might have asked your maid, since everyone but you in this bloody town knows it! Or actually looked at the cock he fucked you with!" His fury made his arm shake and he dropped it to his side as he took two more steps toward her.

With a yelp, Stella backed away, stumbling over the stool at her dressing table and thudding to the floor, landing on her backside. "Don't hit me!"

Mark smeared both hands over his face, then through his hair, trying desperately to tamp down the fury that had consumed him since he had seen Shropshire—a duke in title only since the man had lost all his worldly goods at the tables—saunter into Stella's backstage dressing room and later out the front door of this house. His house. Mark steeled himself, forcing his voice calm. "I have never and would never hit you. But you . . . you have no idea what kind of damage you may have wreaked. Now get up off the floor and explain yourself. Start with how long you have been fucking the man."

Stella scrambled to her feet, clutching her dressing gown around her body. She sidled toward the bed, bracing herself against one of the posts of the headboard. "Two"—she swallowed hard—"two weeks." She blinked rapidly, then muttered, "Three. Maybe three." She held up a hand in protest before he could reply. "But he went to Mrs. Phillips's Warehouse. We used a sheath. French letters. Just like you and I do. I swear to you!" She curled her arm against her chest, her voice dropping to a whisper. "I swear!"

Mark squeezed his eyes shut. "You addle-pated ninny, those barely stop a baby, and sometimes, clearly, not always that." He glared at her again. "Is he the only one?"

She chewed her lower lip.

So. No.

I have been an absolute fool.

He rolled his shoulders as he looked around the room. Mark had spent so many delightful hours here, reveling in Stella's charms, basking in the idea that he had found a safe—"You had better pray you have not given me this. Better yet, you had better pray he did not give it to you. It is a truly awful way to die."

"How do you know—"

"I have been at war, woman!" He stopped, pulling in deep breaths, trying to rein in sudden, unexpected memories that flooded his mind, streaming out of his fury. He clenched his fists at his side, his voice low. "I have seen horrors not even people in the Rookeries have known. You cannot conceive of the destruction, the pain . . ."

He thought it impossible, but Stella paled even more. "What are you going to do?" she whispered.

He shook his head, still stunned by what had happened.

"Well, I will not be in your bed ever again. And you should prepare to not be in this house any longer."

She stiffened. "You are evicting me?"

"I have no choice. It is my house, and you have made it notorious. Your dallying with Shropshire is already on the books at White's."

"It can't be!"

"Oh, but it is, my dear. And we had an arrangement, which you have now forfeited. Go live with your mother or ask Shropshire for a set of rooms—oh, that's right, he has no money. You certainly chose wisely." Mark despised the cruelty in his voice, but he could not fight both his anger and the deep betrayal he felt. Or the loss of the misguided trust he had placed in this woman over the years.

The mother of his child.

His throat closed, and he coughed, fighting to regain his breath.

Stella stepped forward. "What do you mean, no money? He's a duke!"

Mark almost laughed at her naiveté, something he would not have thought of her. "He is also an inveterate gambler. He lost most of the title's wealth five years ago and has been selling the properties since. He has a bare set of rooms not far from here and a seat in Parliament due to his title. No heirs. The title will revert to the crown when he dies. Which will be not too long from now, if the rumors are true."

She sank down on the bed. "What have I done?"

Mark sighed. "You have been as big a fool as I have."

Stella looked up at him, eyes pleading. "Olivia . . ."

"I will take care of Olivia. And your mother, if she gets ill again. I meant it when I said you might go live with her, because at least then there will be some money, along with your wages. But our association is ended. I will give you until the end of the month to vacate this house."

"I do not think I can live with my mother. She does not know about"—she waved a hand around the room—"this."

"Then do what you can. But I can be no part of it."

Her normal color returned, and she looked down at her hands, apparently resigned. "What will you do with the house?"

"I am not sure. Clean it. Rent it. Sell it. I will decide later."

"The jewels?"

"They are yours to keep. They could help support you."

"But my maid—"

"I will keep her on until I make a decision about the house. If the new tenant or owner does not need her services, I will provide a reference, so she does not have to say she worked for you unless she wishes to."

Her voice turned bitter. "How thoughtful."

Mark held his tongue. Stella could be as acrimonious as she wished, but they both knew she had created this drama, and he could have easily chucked them both out on the street this very day. After a moment of silence, he gave a sharp nod. "Very well. I will ask Matthew's man of business to check in when you are gone. Goodbye, Stella."

He turned and headed down the stairs, snatching his top hat from the table near the door and jamming it onto his head.

"Lord Mark?" The soft voice came from the doorway of the small parlor at the front of the house. He turned to see Stella's maid, a wisp of a girl with brown curls peeking from beneath her cap. She clutched her hands over her stomach, fingers twisted in the cloth of her apron. "Thank you."

He nodded. "Clara, is it?"

She bobbed her head.

"Do not fret. This will not be visited on you."

She gave a long sigh, tears filling her eyes.

"Mark, please!" The wail echoed down the stairs and through the front hall. Clara winced.

Damn it, Stella.

"Take care of her," he muttered to the maid, then he left, striding out the door and onto the pavement. He made his steps as long and heavy as he could, his boots pounding the hard surface beneath them. His anger, no longer a blasting flame, simmered deep within, a burning that drove him on. His cloak swirled around him as he pushed through the fog moving in off the river, and his vision tunneled, his thoughts a chaotic miasma.

Even now he could be ill with the beginnings of the *ton's* most dreaded illness. Many of the elite men carried the scourge of syphilis, and his own brother had warned him when Mark's internal terrors from the war had turned him from the gentle-women who wanted him to spend the night to paid companions—and Stella. Matthew had even reminded him of the adage so truthful in this age: "One night with Venus; a lifetime with Mercury." But mercury, the supposed cure for the pox, often caused more damage than the disease. In France, in the rural areas that never knew medical aid, he had seen what the pox did to people over the years, the horrors it wreaked on mind, body, and spirit. The agonizing deaths.

Why could you not have left well enough alone?

Blindly, Mark turned his steps away from Embleton House and toward Covent Garden. He would never be able to sleep tonight, and this fury needed to be exorcised. An obvious solution awaited, deep in the bowels of one of the worst parts of the city. Gentility, nobility needed to give away tonight to the rawness of physicality. The boxing ring called, as did the wagers circling it.

It would be a rough night.

Monday, 18 July 1814
Sculthorpe Manor
Half-past eight in the morning

EPWORTH LOOKED AT the lone stocking a long time, glancing between it and Judith. "You *lost* it? At the theater?" The disbelief in her voice spoke volumes and tweaked Judith's lingering touch of guilt. Epworth knew she had not misplaced a stocking.

"I think I must have had too much ratafia."

Epworth's eyes narrowed, the sharp cockney coming out in her words. "You don' like ratafia. Never touch the stuff."

"Well, any port in a—oh, let us forget about the stocking." She snatched the remaining one from Epworth and rolled it around one hand. "It is gone and that is that. Let's get me dressed. I want to see my boys, then breakfast, and I need to be at the modiste's by eleven. I want to go to the park after luncheon. Is the countess awake?"

Epworth grinned, then motioned for Judith to sit at her dressing table. Judith tucked the stocking into one of the drawers as Epworth began to brush out her hair. "At half-past eight? Possibly but unlikely. Although his lordship did ask for breakfast to be on the sideboard by nine."

Judith examined her nails for splits or cracks, then picked up a wooden tool from the table and began pushing back her cuticles. "He probably has some sort of business to attend to. I heard our steward is coming in from the country house. Apparently, the crops are not faring well in this cooler weather."

Epworth changed the brush for a comb and began to style Judith's hair. "And all this rain. Like God's calling on Noah again." She paused to open a box of ribbons. "What will you be walking out in today?"

Peering into the box, Judith pointed at a yellow silken loop. "Let's chase a bit of the gloom away, shall we? And hope the rain gives a pause."

Epworth pulled the ribbon out, shook it free and draped it over her own shoulder as she continued to plait, pin, and twist Judith's long chestnut strands. "By the by, the servants were all a-chitter this morning about something that happened at the theater last night." She leaned closer, her tone sly. "About the Embleton gentleman."

Judith froze, staring at her maid in the dressing table mirror. She licked her lips, which had suddenly gone dry. "Um, what about him?"

Epworth's voice dropped to just above a whisper. "Apparently, that actress he's been, um, visiting got herself into a spot with another man. Before and after her show, right there in the theater. Word is, you could hear 'em rutting—oh, pardon me, my lady—talking, through the door of her dressing room. And the Embleton chap right outside, hearing it all, pacing and fussing like a mare in heat. He didn't break in or nothing, but they said he looked like a thunderstorm. Apparently followed 'em back to the place she lives. When her maid came out to buy milk this morning, she told some folks her mistress had to move. That the gentleman who owned the house had tossed her out on her heels."

Judith could not believe it. "He evicted her because she—she—"

Epworth had embraced the heart of it now. "Her maid—Clara, sweet girl if a bit dim—said it had to do with the man she—well, it were the Duke of Shropshire."

Judith's stomach clenched as she stared at Epworth in the mirror. "No! Why would she—"

Gesturing with a rat-tailed comb, Epworth nodded. "Clara said her mistress claimed to not know about his—well, what everyone else knows."

A veil of dread settled on Judith. "That he has the pox. But everyone does know that. Do you think she is lying?" Mark's face returned to her mind . . . and the look he had given her when she had said something about current mistress. Cold and dark.

"She must be. How could she not?"

"Perhaps she thought he had money."

"Well, my lady, he *is* a duke, pox or not."

"But an impoverished one. The man is a scoundrel who gambled away everything he owned . . . or gave it to one of his many doxies."

"I don't think everyone knows that part of it." Epworth began weaving the yellow ribbon into Judith's hair. "My lady, I don't understand that. I thought every title came with an income. And land? Stuff they cannot sell."

Judith shook her head. "You are speaking of what is called an entail—property, usually, although sometimes money—that is tied to a title and cannot be divested from it. The property and its management provide an income, although some titles have a yearly stipend from the crown. Shropshire's does not, and the only entail was his country house and a small acreage around it. The larger estate—family-owned land—earned an income through tenancies and farming. When he became duke, the estate had been stable and rather wealthy, even by Beau Monde standards."

Judith paused, thinking suddenly about other men who had followed the duke's same path. "But like a lot of profligate men in the aristocracy, Shropshire could not manage his way across the auction lot at Tattersall's. He virtually lived at gambling hells and brothels instead of learning to manage his heritage. Finally, he had to sell what he could and abandoned the rest. His beautiful house now sits empty and rotting. Unless one of the new merchants with all their growing wealth buys it, it will probably collapse in a few years."

"What a shame."

"Indeed. But even if the actress did not know about the money, it seems odd she would take such a chance with his reputation."

Epworth paused, her expression thoughtful. "When you've been desperate, my lady, and starving, that fear never really goes away. You would do anything not to go through it again."

Judith gazed over the absolute riches that littered her dressing table. Riches she took for granted every day. Silver-handled brushes. Combs with mother-of-pearl teeth and bejeweled edges. Gold inlay boxes holding ruby, emerald, and diamond earrings and bangles. She could live for several years by selling just the things that lay in front of her.

Shropshire was a fool. And, desperation aside, so was Stella

Ashley. "So what"—she swallowed—"what did Lord Mark do after he . . ."

Epworth gave a light shrug. "No one is sure. But one of the Embleton hall boys was out with their housekeeper at market this morning. He said the gentleman came home around dawn, stumbling in the back way, all bloody, bruised, and soaked to the skin by the late rains. Cast up his accounts in the kitchen yard, looking like he'd been keelhauled."

Or gone several rounds in the boxing ring.

Judith peered at Epworth in the mirror. "As my Lord Sculthorpe used to look sometimes?"

Epworth shrugged again, her eyes focused on Judith's hair. "Perhaps."

Judith closed her eyes. She had seen it, knew what it looked like when a man turned to that sport out of anger or pain. Edmund had done it when his nightmares grew too powerful or his frustration too great. Some of her lovers even participated in rough sport, thrilled at how bareknuckle fights exhausted and cleansed them.

She shuddered. She would never understand.

"Are you all right, my lady?"

Judith opened her eyes and forced a smile, sitting a little straighter, pushing the affairs of men to the back of her mind. "I will be, once I see my beautiful boys." She smiled at Epworth. "Let us get the day started, shall we?"

CHAPTER SIX

Monday, 18 July 1814
Embleton House
Half-past two in the afternoon

"YOU LOOK LIKE hell's own hound. What in God's name happened to you?"

Mark raised his newspaper to conceal a wince, turned a page, and stretched his feet out toward the low fire in Matthew's study. He ached with every movement—remarkable, given how numb his spirit felt.

His brother was not having it. Matthew closed the study door and turned the key, then stood in front of Mark's wingback. "Put down that blasted paper and talk to me. The servants are all chattering about your return this morning, looking like the cat's latest hairball. Many of them were already awake when you cast up your accounts in the kitchen yard, then broke two sconces trying to maneuver the back stairs. Your young valet is tight-lipped as always—"

Mark kept the paper up. "Nice to hear Howe is earning his money."

"But the rest all know the hall boys dragged a tub and buckets of hot water up to your room for a bath before breakfast. Which was also brought to your room. As was lunch. Neither of which you ate."

"Food remains particularly unappealing at the moment."

"No doubt, as it would have to compete with the brandy still in your gut. I can smell it from here, even after your bath."

"There were a few applications of said liquor after said bath."

"No doubt. Mother is fit to be tied and demanding answers, and it took a great deal of persuading to keep her out of here—"

"God, no."

"So tell me what the bloody hell happened before I have to quiz every servant. Because I know they will be full of tales far more gruesome than the truth."

"I would not promise that."

"Fine. So no Banbury tale about an honest boxing match. You've been in a row to end all rows."

Mark sniffed, although one side of his nose remained blocked. "Why"—he stopped, swallowing something heavy and thick the brandy had not been able to clear out—"why should I have to explain—"

"Because I'm the bloody duke, that's why!" Matthew's tone softened but only slightly. "You did not look this bad when you took a load of grapeshot in your back—"

"I was farther away."

"And you are my brother, you arse."

Indeed. Mark finally folded the paper and laid it on an accent table next to his chair, where a significant amount of brandy waited in a bowled goblet. He nodded at the wingback opposite his. "Sit."

"Mark—"

Mark took a sip of the brandy, which burned the cuts on his lip and inside his mouth. He grimaced. "Trust me. You will want to sit."

Matthew did. "Mark—"

"Stella bedded Shropshire."

The three words rocked Matthew back into his chair, a rough bark of startled disgust bursting from him. "She must be mad! Why would she?"

Mark shrugged one shoulder, then stilled as every muscle in his chest, and at least two ribs, protested. "I am not sure. Perhaps she thought I was tiring of her . . ." His words faded as he stared into the brandy.

"Were you?"

He took another sip, managing to avoid the wince this time. "Perhaps. But I thought I disguised it well. I would never have completely abandoned her."

"Because of the girl."

Mark nodded. "Yes. The girl. Olivia. Her name is Olivia."

"But now you have."

"Yes. Stella. But not Olivia." Another sip. This time with the wince. "Matthew"—he looked at his brother over the rim of the glass—"she bedded Shropshire."

Matthew stared at the fire, his eyes half-lidded. "How long?"

"The past two or three weeks. She could not be certain."

His brother faced him again. "No. I meant you."

"Ah. I was with her Monday last, which would have been the first time after she took Shropshire. Then Friday night. Saturday morning. So it will be at least another two to three weeks before the first sore would appear."

"If you have it."

"Yes. If I have it."

"Will you take the mercury?"

"Or a bullet."

Matthew paled. "Mark, you cannot—"

"Oh, yes, I can." Mark set the brandy aside. "What I cannot do is tolerate *all* of it. The night horrors, the constant pain, the madness the disease can bring on—"

"Not for a long—"

"It does not matter!" Mark pushed out of the chair, pain twisting every joint and fiber of his body, raging through him like a ravening fire. He groaned, then leaned against the mantel, staring into the flames, fighting for control.

Matthew joined him. "What happened last night? After."

Mark straightened a bit. "Boxing. Truthfully. But also a row in a pub. Another in the Rookeries."

"Did they rob you?"

Mark hesitated, then nodded. "I gave it to them, poor buggers. I was trying to find out—they told me—" No. He could not tell his brother that part of it. Not yet. "There were others—they had no idea what they had taken on."

"A drunken soldier with no will to live?"

"Something like that."

A knock on the door silenced them both. Then Matthew called out. "Please leave us!"

Stephens, their butler, called back. "Your Grace, a Bow Street Runner is here. He insists on speaking with Lord Mark."

Matthew cut his gaze toward Mark. "Are you sure it was just a row in a pub?"

Mark straightened and took a deep breath. "I believe so. At least I do not think I killed anyone."

Matthew shook his head. "Mother may be right about you."

Mark finally found his smirk. "Heaven forfend."

His brother crossed the study, then unlocked and opened the door. "Bring the man up."

As the butler's footsteps faded, Mark leaned against the back of his chair, squeezing his eyes tight, then reaching for his brandy.

"When he is gone, you should go to bed."

"I do not think—"

"I want Dr. Oakley to look at you. Make sure nothing is bruised or broken that you do not know about."

Mark took a long breath, wincing again. "Trust me. I know about them all. Mostly bruises, although a couple of ribs may be cracked."

"And will need wrapping."

"Howe can—"

Stephens appeared in the doorframe, holding the brim of a soiled bowler with two fingers. "Mr. Jeremy Smith." He stepped back and a tall man moved into the room. His blond hair, which needed a good washing, had been mauled by the bowler, but his rough woolen suit and waistcoat appeared clean and well-made, if plain and on the shabby side. He nodded at Matthew. "Lord Mark

Rydell."

Mark stepped from behind his brother before Matthew could take offense. "I am Lord Mark Rydell. This is my brother, Matthew, Sixth Duke of Embleton."

Smith executed a short bow toward Matthew, although his gaze remained on Mark. "Apologies, Your Grace." He straightened, his blue eyes narrowing a bit. "Rough night, my lord?"

Matthew gave a low growl. "That should be none of your concern. State your business."

Smith's focus remained on Mark, his face impassive. "I am afraid, Your Grace, Lord Mark's overnight activities may be a part of that business."

Mark remained silent, an uncomfortable twist growing in his gut. Some of the men he had battled had left the worst for wear, but surely they had not—

"How so?" Matthew's voice remained calm, but the gravel in it told Mark that he too had become worried.

Smith took a slip of paper and a rough pencil from his pocket. He unfolded the paper and glanced down at the writing. "Lord Mark, do you own a property in Bloomsbury? Near Russell Square?" He gave the house number as well.

That twist in his gut tightened as Mark fought the urge to look at Matthew. "I do."

"Is that your primary residence?"

Mark swallowed. "No. I live here."

Smith looked up at him, his eyes narrow. "Who occupies the property?"

"A woman, a friend, along with her maid."

That blue-eyed gaze did not waver. "Her name?"

"Stella Ashley."

"The actress?"

"Yes."

"And you were with her last night?"

Matthew bristled. "Now look here, Smith—"

Mark put a hand on Matthew's arm. "No. It's fine. Our arrangement was not exactly a secret."

"Was?" Smith's eyebrows arched.

He nodded at the runner. "Yes. I was there briefly, around midnight. I ended the arrangement. And I asked her to move elsewhere."

Smith hesitated, glancing down at the paper again, then back up to Mark. "*You* ended it?"

"Yes."

"Why?"

Mark tried to stand a bit straighter, although his ribs did not approve. "I—she—Miss Ashley has found another protector. I am not interested in sharing her affections."

"Was the parting amicable?"

Mark's gut began to ache. He did not like where this conversation was headed. "As reasonably as could be expected. She continued to shout at me as I departed. Her maid could attest to that. The girl and I spoke as I left."

The runner paused, his mouth tightening. "So Miss Ashley was still alive when you left?"

Oh, dear God. The numbness that had consumed Mark's mind now spread over his body with a chilled flush. He staggered backward. Matthew grabbed his arm to steady him as Mark whispered. "What do you mean . . . 'still alive'?"

Smith folded the paper and tucked it away. "Miss Ashley is deceased. Her maid found her body in the back garden this afternoon. She had been strangled."

Monday, 18 July 1814
Hyde Park, London
Half-past three in the afternoon

JUDITH PAUSED AND closed her eyes, relishing the warmth of the sun's unexpected glory. Clouds had hung low and heavy over the city earlier in the day, but now the sweet rays from above warmed her through the silk of her golden yellow gown and the soft linen of her chemise. She had donned tawny-colored boots of fine kid leather, which matched the straw of her bonnet with its yellow ribbons dangling strategically around her face and down her back. Another gown carefully refurbished by her modiste; the bright color of the silk had been augmented by delicate medallions of green embroidered on the puffed sleeves, around the hem, and on the backs of her matching gloves. She felt as golden as the day.

Judith had left the curricle to stroll along the Serpentine, soaking in the summer beauty of the park. In the height of the season, depending on the path chosen, a stroll could mean either the overwhelming fragrances of flowers or the scents of horses, trampled grass, and dust. Slow, soft breezes brought along the laughter of children or calls of friends. Judith smiled at the knots of children racing back and forth between their nannies and the water's edge, where ducks and geese gathered, begging to be fed.

"Do you think Nanny brings William and Robbie to see the birds?"

Epworth, stepping closer to stroll at her side, nodded. "I believe she brings William quite often. Robbie, less so now that Mr. Thompson is preparing him for Eton."

Judith sighed, whispering, "Too soon."

"Mr. Thompson does say that both Master Robert and Master George are exceptional in their studies. Scholarly even."

"I do hope so. I hope there is something out there for them that is not the church or military service."

"Both are honorable professions."

"True, but I wish we could—"

"Good afternoon, Lady Sculthorpe!"

Judith turned, and Epworth took four discreet steps behind her, gaze pointed to the ground. Epworth might take liberties with her—which Judith allowed and even relied on—when they were alone. Neither would ever reveal such a thing in public.

Judith's eyes widened as her fair-haired lover, Lord Peregrine Gower, approached with a frail slip of a girl at his side. A chaperone—not a maid, most likely a sister or cousin, given her garb—followed a few steps behind them, lips pursed so tightly she looked as if she were about to break into a whistling contest with the birds. The wan beauty next to Perry seemed familiar, however, and Judith greeted them with a smile and a nod. This was hardly the first time she had unexpectedly encountered Perry in public.

"Lord Peregrine. How pleasant to see you! You are looking well today." Indeed, with his height—well over six feet—and his silk indigo frock coat and top hat, rouged cheeks and kohl-lined eyes, he made quite the luminous sight in the afternoon sun. "I believe we last saw each other at the Huntingdale ball." *Ah, that was it. The girl had been at the ball. Had danced with Perry . . . and Mark.* Judith blinked, turning her attention to the sour-faced miss, whose light-blue frock, slight frame, and pale complexion rendered her almost invisible next to the preening Perry. Even her hair seemed . . . fragile. As if the wrong turn of her head would cause it to shatter. She clutched her reticule in front of her with both hands, as if terrified the thing would jerk from her grip and skitter away. Judith's eyebrows arched in anticipation.

Perry leapt into the gap. "Lady Sculthorpe, may I present Lady Carys Morgan."

Judith smiled at the girl, who could not have been more than seventeen. "Lady Carys. I believe I saw you at the Huntingdale ball as well."

Lady Carys gave a sharp nod and quick curtsy, then looked up at Perry as she nudged him.

Perry jumped as if the child's elbow were as sharp as the collarbones protruding from her neckline. "Ah, yes. That is, in fact, where I met Lady Carys. Lord Mark Rydell introduced us. She is a superb dancer."

Lord Mark's opinion to the contrary . . . Judith swallowed a laugh. "I see. And you are already . . . walking out? In the park?"

Do not say it. Do not say it.

A blush started at the top of his cravat, spreading rapidly, a clear recognition of her implication. A young man did not stroll with a young woman in Hyde Park, even with a chaperone, if he did not have serious intentions toward her. Intentions already known to her family. "I—um—I know this may seem very unexpected. Very . . . sudden."

Judith gave a dismissive wave. "Not at all. Happens all the time. You meet someone, and you know immediately you will be suited to marry and spend the rest of your life together, forsaking all others."

Epworth had a sudden coughing fit.

The blush turned blotchy, and Perry tugged at his cravat. "Yes, well, I—um—"

Judith turned a blazing smile on Lady Carys. "Congratulations, my dear, on a successful and beneficial debut season. Lord Peregrine is a fine young man."

For the first time, the sour expression eased but her words were barely audible. "Thank you, Lady Sculthorpe."

Judith looked up at Perry. "I most sincerely wish you both all happiness, Lord Peregrine."

He let out a sigh, and his color almost returned to normal. "I appreciate that, Lady Sculthorpe."

"I do hope you enjoy your stroll. I will leave you to it." Judith turned, motioned to Epworth, and resumed her walk. After a few moments, Judith sniffed. "Geese. I really should bring William to see the geese."

Epworth barked a laugh, then cleared her throat. "He'll be back."

Judith shook her head. "The man is simple but not even he is that daft. Infidelity may run rampant through the *ton*, but that does not mean I condone it. And he knows that." She paused. "I do feel sorry for her, though. He will be on the hunt for a mistress within the year, as soon as he is guaranteed an heir." Judith turned her steps back toward the gravel path of Rotten Row, where they had left the curricle. "I am starving. One more circuit and I will be in desperate need of an early supper."

Epworth readily agreed and fell into step, although slightly behind Judith as they approached numerous groups of the Beau Monde out to see and be seen. Judith knew most, greeting a few by name and nodding in deference to those of a higher rank. She had been Countess Sculthorpe for almost twenty years, dowager for the past few months. Most of the *ton* knew her by sight, as she had been in frequent attendance at Society events since she had come out of mourning, slowly slipping into the role of one of the *ton's* dragons—one of those women who held power behind the scenes of the aristocracy. She had been instrumental in Edmund's courtship of Margaret—she had secured a voucher for one set at Almack's for Edmund last year and had influenced two of the patronesses to offer one to Margaret and her mother as well. One waltz and one quadrille later, both had been smitten. Judith herself did not attend Almack's much anymore, but she knew all the players and who to discuss with whom.

Those two patronesses, Lady Jersey and Lady Cowper, in the company of a third woman Judith knew well—Lady Blackwell— approached her now. They looked at her closely, then exchanged glances. They looked again. More glances.

Something was amiss.

Judith resisted the urge to check her gown to see if some untoward stain had appeared. She knew better—Epworth would have raised an immediate alarm if anything about her appearance had gone awry.

Instead, as they grew closer, she heard Lady Cowper's whispered concern. "We should tell her!"

Judith slowed her steps, dipping her head, determined to let her friends take the lead. "Lady Cowper. Lady Jersey. Lady Blackwell. I hope you are having a pleasant outing today. It is a lovely afternoon."

"It is indeed." Lady Blackwell's expression tightened, although her voice remained calm, friendly.

More glances.

Judith let out a long sigh. "Apparently, you three ladies are only adept at keeping secrets from the gentlemen of the *ton*. Pray tell me, what is your concern?"

Lady Cowper's shoulders dropped a scant inch, even as Lady Jersey stiffened, as if facing the guillotine. She pursed her lips, as Lady Cowper leaned closer to Judith. "Because you are our friend."

Definitely serious.

"Then I am grateful." Judith waited.

Lady Jersey gave a single nod and squared her shoulders. "Would you consider yourself 'a certain fair widow of renown'?"

Judith stared at her. "I beg your pardon. A what?"

Lady Blackwell stepped closer. "Has anyone in your acquaintance referred to you as 'a certain fair widow of renown'?"

Judith scowled, confusion clouding her. "I do not think—I am not—"

Epworth cleared her throat, and Judith looked around at her. She mouthed, "The earl."

Judith's eyes snapped wide as she recalled the night. They had been in the withdrawing room after a congenial dinner with friends of Edmund. Two other couples. Playing cards. And he had teasingly called her . . . "my stepmother, a certain fair widow of renown."

The phrase had made its way through the servants to Epworth before the final hand of cards.

Judith looked back at her friends. "Perhaps. Why do you ask?"

More glances. "Do you know that the gentlemen keep a wager book at White's?"

Judith nodded. "This is a well-known fact, however much the gentlemen liked to think it a surreptitious item."

Lady Jersey looked around, as if searching for eavesdroppers. "We have it on good authority that a new wager has been placed in the book, concerning"—she cleared her throat—"Lord Mark Rydell and 'a certain fair widow of renown.'"

Oh, dear God.

"Of course," Lady Blackwell put in, "they would never include a lady's name. It would be too scandalous and dishonorable. But apparently a good many people believe it refers to you."

Of course they do.

Lady Cowper looked a bit chagrined, an unusual look for the patroness. "Surely, the earl would not—"

Judith sighed. "I would not bet on that. Edmund likes to gamble. And for some reason, he would like to see me involved with Lord Mark Rydell."

The three looked startled, and Lady Cowper's usual haughtiness returned in force. "Then let us hope he abandons that idea and quickly."

Odd. "I realize Lord Mark is somewhat notorious—"

"Notorious?" Lady Jersey's exclamation abandoned the pretense of secrecy. "Now we hear he is also a murderer. That he has killed his mistress!"

CHAPTER SEVEN

Monday, 18 July 1814
Embleton House
Quarter past six in the evening

"I S THIS WHY you summoned me? For pity's sake, Mother. I did not kill Stella. Matthew believes me. Even the runner believes me. Her maid saw me leave while Stella continued to screech at me. There are people who saw me after. Why can *you* not believe me?"

His mother paced before the receiving room fireplace, her black bombazine-and-tulle skirts sounding like a dog shaking rain from its coat. She thumped her fan against her palm, blithely ignoring the precarious hold her black-feathered bonnet had on the crown of her head. She had returned from the park in a full bristle, demanding to see him, and ranting about the world, the *ton*, and her sons in particular. Clearly, many of the pins had slowly worked loose from her hair, and now the bonnet ticked back and forth on her head as she strode, wobbling horribly whenever she changed directions.

"It is not about belief—"

Although Matthew had summoned their physician, he had not yet arrived when the duchess had demanded his presence. Even Howe had appeared cowed by the message as he helped Mark become more presentable. No one argued with Phyllida Rydell.

Except her second son, who now mumbled obscenities under his breath as he struggled to remain still, as every fiber of his being had begun to ache in earnest. He had barely made it down the stairs before collapsing into the chair. "It is for me."

"It is about the appearance of the thing." Phyllida pivoted, still giving the fan a good thrumming. "The rumors shredded through the park today like a wildfire, reaching me before I was ten feet inside the gate. I heard the rumor at least four more times before I could wend my way out, and Lady Cowper even hinted that we might be banned as a family from Almack's."

"Would that be so bad—"

Phyllida stopped short, glaring at him. "You may have abandoned society—"

"In truth, I have not—"

"But you have a sister—"

"I doubt that Daphne will want—"

"And your brothers may be off to war or school or out into the country, but they all still need wives. Respectable wives."

Matthew appeared in the doorframe of the room, pointing over his shoulder, a quizzical look on his face. "Stephens said you still have not rung for . . ." He looked from his mother to Mark. "Why are you out of bed? What has happened?"

Mark took a deep breath, then coughed, tugging at his shirt collar. Howe had not been able to persuade him to accept a cravat, as he was barely able to don trousers and a shirt with the valet's aid. "Command appearance. The *ton* is convinced I killed Stella." He coughed again, and his vision blurred, a ring of black appearing at the edges. He squeezed his eyes shut.

Matthew's voice held a note of confusion. "That was quick. How did they—ah, the servants. From Miss Ashley's maid to the drawing rooms of Mayfair."

"Are you surprised?" Phyllida snapped. "This could ruin us."

"She was alive when he left her, and he has an alibi. He was somewhere else when she died."

Phyllida huffed. "A brawl in the Rookeries." The fan slapped her palm. "That's no alibi. Those people would say anything for a halfpenny. No one would believe them."

Mark grabbed a breath. "Possibly because a ha'penny would put bread on their table for a week."

Phyllida's glare deepened. "Please do not tell me you have added 'reformer' to your list of iniquities."

Matthew stepped closer to Mark. "You looked like hell this morning. Now you look worse."

"A good scolding from Mummy always takes the wind from my sails."

The room fell silent, and Mark shuddered, a flash of chill seizing him. He slumped against the back of the chair as breathing became an issue. "I really do not—" He broke off, gasping as a roar of pain shot across his sternum.

Matthew swept into action, bellowing out the door for Stephens. Then he stepped to Mark's chair and slid an arm behind his shoulders. Pain speared down his back, and Mark gasped again. "That's probably not—"

"The doctor is on his way."

Mark heard rather than saw his mother leave.

"Can you stand? We must get you back upstairs."

Taking a deeper breath and trying to push through the pain, Mark put weight on his legs and pressed up from the chair. The deep pain in his back and side shot a sudden weakness down his hips, as the dark ring around his vision expanded. His voice vanished into a hiss as his knees buckled, and the world turned black.

Then darkness gave way to a riot of color.

Uniforms, crimson and navy. An azure sky, blotched by smoke, black, gray, and white. The gold of roiling flames. The march seemed interminable. Endless columns of French soldiers stretched before them, but they never moved closer. Just marching, churning the ground, firing endless volleys, the ends of their rifles belching . . .

The blast came from his left, and the compression brought earth, debris, and body parts slamming into him. His horse reared and he tumbled from its back, throwing out his arms and legs in attempt to brace for the impact of the ground. He hit hard, agony shimmering through his limbs. He called out to the faces that drifted through the smoke. Officers. Family. People he cared about.

"Mark!"

The urgent voice pierced the fading cacophony of the battle. Mark stopped moving, stopped fighting, trying to hear, but the roar in his ears made everything sound muffled.

"Mark." The voice held less insistence; more comfort. Reassurance. "You are safe. Mark. You are home."

He stilled, although the feel of the grime beneath him, the slickness of blood on his skin, the constant pressure on his limbs held him in thrall. The battering sound of cannon echoed in his head, and pain shuddered through him in constant waves, rolling over him in an unceasing repetition.

Something cool and bitter touched his tongue.

"He did not want laudanum."

Who was—?

"It will help with the pain."

Another voice. But one he knew. A man . . .

"He is afraid of its—"

"It is a small dose."

"So was the first one."

"He will not come to rely on it. We will see to that."

The bitterness passed over his tongue and down his throat.

"Is he always like this?"

"Almost every night. Not always this bad."

Ah. That one was Matthew.

"Does he sleep at all?"

The care in the man's voice soothed him. The battlefield faded. The hard ground beneath him turned soft, and the pressure on his arms and legs became warm, calming. Recognition settled into Mark's mind as the fog of pain lifted. *Dr. Oakley. His own bed.* Mark blinked, then squeezed his eyes shut against the light.

"Not much." A pause. "Seldom."

"Why did you not tell me?"

Another voice. A woman. Judith?

"He did not want you to wor—"

"Nonsense. I am his mother."

Ah.

"Would you have treated him any differently?" Matthew's voice almost sounded amused.

"Of course not. Do not be foolish. But he *is* my son."

Amazing how her words softened as she spoke. Yet still his mother. Mark cleared his throat. "I can hear you." His words sounded like boots on gravel.

A brief silence filled the room, and Mark opened his eyes. Slowly. Squinting.

"How do you feel?" Dr. Oakley laid a gentle hand on his wrist, fingers pressed against Mark's pulse.

"Like I have been beaten raw by ruffians in the Rookeries."

Matthew choked a laugh. "As you have."

"So . . . not a dream."

"You could only wish."

"How long?"

His brother sat cautiously on the opposite side of the bed. "Just over four hours."

"Ah. A nice nap."

"You were unconscious at the start. Asleep later." Dr. Oakley released his wrist. "You have at least two broken ribs and a great deal of internal bruising. You had a dislocated shoulder that apparently reset itself when your brother and your butler picked you up to bring you upstairs. They heard a rather ominous popping sound."

Mark glanced at Matthew. "Thank you. I think."

"Also a mild concussion, and possibly a crack in the bone around your left eye."

"And I thought the headache was just from Mother."

"Damn it," Matthew muttered, as he stood again.

Mark tried to force a grin. "Would you expect any less?"

Dr. Oakley cleared his throat. "There may be some good news out of this."

Mark swung his gaze back to the doctor.

"If the timing of events are as I've been led to believe, I can reassure the Bow Street Runner who is handling Miss Ashley's case that you could have in no way killed her. I will insist he make that well known."

Phyllida gasped, her hand covering her mouth.

Matthew's voice was a low growl. "How can you be sure?"

"Because with the injuries he has sustained, whatever the cause, he would have not had the strength or physical ability to strangle a healthy woman. They called me in before she was transported to the morgue. Miss Ashley had been a patient of mine, as is her mother and daughter, and Bow Street wanted to spare her mother or her young housemaid the duty of identifying Miss Ashley. I saw her injuries, and now I have seen yours."

Phyllida coughed. *"An actress* was your patient?"

Dr. Oakley nodded, then looked down at Mark, eyebrows arched.

Mark attempted a shrug, but it hurt too much. "I paid for it. I wanted her to have the best."

Phyllida turned away, hand still pressed to her mouth. Matthew's eyes gleamed with a question, and Mark merely nodded. Once. Then winced.

A smile flitted across Dr. Oakley's face, then vanished. He stood, addressing Mark. "I am leaving the laudanum, just in case. You know the dangers, so no more than twice a day, and for no longer than three days. I showed His Grace the dosage. After that, willow bark tea will help with the pain. Mostly you need a great deal of rest, preferably with no movement for a few days." He packed up a few instruments that had been spread across the foot of the bed, then left the room, leaving the three Rydells to stare at each other.

After a moment, Matthew took a deep breath. "I'll see the doctor out, then bring the servants up to date and ask for some of that tea to be sent up."

Phyllida scowled. "Why tell the servants?"

Matthew patted her arm. "Because rumors flow in both directions. Although I suspect the tale of his innocence will not be as enticing to spread along."

As Matthew closed the door, his mother moved closer to the bed, something akin to compassion and curiosity in her eyes.

"Do you believe me now?" he asked.

"It is not about belief—"

"Do you?"

"Yes." She stepped closer. "But probably not for the reasons you might think."

Mark studied her. As always, the two of them circled each other, with their banter, their thoughts, their devotion to the family. "So not because you think me incapable of killing?"

"You are a soldier. I know you can kill."

"And not because of what the doctor said? Or my alibi, which you so calmly brushed aside."

She shook her head. She moved to the side of his bed and slipped her hand in his. "You did not kill her because you did not love her. Nor hate her. To strangle someone takes a great deal of strength and anger. That kind of anger only comes from a deep love or consuming fear or blistering rage. You have shown none of those toward her." She paused and looked away a moment. When she looked back at him, her eyes glistened. "I think I knew that. I was worried about your reputation with her but not your heart. For a long time now, I have thought you would never love anyone, with your insistence on never marrying."

"Now you have seen why."

She shook her head. "You may think so, but that is not why. You did not call out for her in your anguish. Instead, your heart belongs to another. And not Lady Sculthorpe either, even though you did ask for her in your delirium."

Mark felt as if everything about him froze. "I did?"

Phyllida nodded. "You did."

"I—I thought you were her."

His mother's mouth twitched. "Well, we will discuss that later. For now, I have a different question. About the one whose name you called out most often."

"Which is?"

"Who is Olivia?"

Tuesday, 19 July 1814
Sculthorpe Manor
Quarter past seven in the morning

"MUMMY!"

William dropped a wooden horse and scurried toward Judith. She knelt and welcomed him into her arms for an enthusiastic squeeze.

Behind him, Nanny sauntered toward them. "You are definitely spoiling him, my lady."

Judith dropped a kiss on the top of William's curls, then brushed her fingers through his hair. "Good. Then he will think of me fondly when he goes off to join his brothers at school. He will not dread coming—" Judith chewed her lower lip a moment, squinting back the tears that suddenly brimmed over. *He would not dread coming home the way Daniel does.*

"My lady?"

Judith shook her head—not a concern for this moment—then kissed William again and turned him back to his toys. "Go on. Go back to whatever Nanny had you doing."

He grinned. "I was playing stable master!"

Her eyebrows arched. "Stable master?"

He nodded. "Mr. Robins was showing me. They are taking some of the cattle to the big auction place next week."

Judith glanced up at Nanny. "They are? Why—"

"Yes!" William pointed to a row of wooden horses. "So he said they had to figure out which to keep and which to sell. So I'm looking at all my horses to do the same."

"I see." An odd suspicion began to build in Judith's gut. "And how do you do that?"

William tugged at her hand. "Come see." As she followed him, he continued to talk. "With mine, as they are not real, I'm checking for chips, breaks, and splinters and such."

"Clever boy."

"Mr. Robins said if I tell him what I have done, then he will show me why he picked some of the horses over others."

"My! That is quite the"—*He's not quite four!*—"undertaking."

William nodded. "Mr. Robins says I have a—a good eye"—he glanced at Nanny for confirmation, which she gave with a nod—"for horses. And that I have, um, I have—" He looked up again at Nanny.

She bent slightly at the waist and whispered, "A fine seat."

"Yes! A fine seat! He showed me how one horse was going lame, although it was just beginning."

"Poor thing." *Why was Edmund selling some of their livestock?*

"I know. Mr. Robins said she would probably go to some farm to rest her leg, with big fields full of sweet grass and fresh hay."

"That would be a kindness." And probably was a lie to save William from knowing the real truth of what happened to lame horses. Judith had always had a fondness for the groom—now she remembered why. He had been equally kind with Robert and George as they learned to ride.

"I know. I want to go to where they sell them. To see *all* of them. I begged him!"

Judith stared at him. *My baby boy at the auction yard at Tattersall's? Over my dead—*

"But Mr. Robins said no." His pout returned. "I hate being too young."

Judith bit her lower lip to keep it from trembling. *Thank you, Mr. Robins! My baby!* She sniffed. "I am sure Mr. Robins knows best."

He tipped over one of the horses. "It's not fair."

Judith took a deep breath, knowing she might regret what she was about to say. "Would you like to go to the park to see the geese and ducks? We could ride."

Nanny turned pale. "Oh, my lady!"

William turned a startled face up at her. "Truly?"

Judith chewed her lip again, then nodded. "I will talk to Mr. Robins—"

"Mummy!" He threw his arms around her legs.

Judith struggled to stay upright, then stroked his head as she mouthed at Nanny, "I know. Spoiled."

Nanny merely shook her head. "Indeed, my lady."

Judith chuckled, then peeled her son away. "All right. Let me see what I can work out. I cannot promise anything, but I will make the effort."

He peered up at her, eyes gleaming and his bow-shaped mouth pursed, as he nodded furiously. "You will do it. I know it. You can do anything!"

Good Lord, this child is going to be trouble.

Judith did not care. She would do whatever she could for her boys. She had already seen what happened when she did not.

CHAPTER EIGHT

Tuesday, 19 July 1814
Embleton House
Half-past one in the afternoon

MARK DESPISED LAUDANUM for far more reasons than a potential dependence on the drug. Laudanum brought sleep. And sleep brought nightmares. Dangerous dreams that caused Mark to struggle, aggravating his injuries. The doctor had wrapped his chest to immobilize his broken ribs, but Monday night had been an excruciating round-robin of thrashing dreams and pain, chills, and sweats that awoke him with new levels of agony. By ten Tuesday morning, as he encased Mark's arm in a sling to rest the shoulder, Dr. Oakley had suggested either increasing the laudanum until Mark was truly unconscious or abandoning it entirely in favor of willow bark tea rotated with strong coffee, so that he could doze, but so lightly he would not dream.

Mark chose the latter, and his mother had ordered mounds of pillows brought to his bedchamber so that he could be propped up in a way that he could drink without choking and rest without hurting himself. She compared it to the nest she had made for herself as she recovered from her last lying-in, scowling as Mark reminded her that his pain emanated from a slightly different location.

But the change in his care seemed to be working. The soreness in his shoulder eased, and the last of the laudanum fog lifted. He had dozed, not deeply enough to dream, but in short bouts that found him resting more easily. The pain had returned, sometimes in waves if he moved too suddenly, but the willow bark tea made it reasonably bearable. He had suffered infinitely worse, he reminded himself, on the battlefield.

The violent dreams were, after all, reflections of a past he had survived, not imagined.

His family had also visited in pairs and groups, such as he did not usually see except on occasion at a holiday—or a funeral.

Matthew stayed nearby, of course, but his older brother frequently arrived with one of their four youngest brothers in tow. Peter, James, Theophilus, and Timothy had returned home from school for the summer and had been occupying themselves with their friends and their horses.

Luke, the next in line after Mark, remained on the continent with Wellington, even as their sister Daphne stayed ensconced with their aunt somewhere in Greece. Paul, the fourth of Phyllida's surviving oldest sons, had taken over their country estate following their father's death. Now he, too, had returned to the city, ostensibly to confer with Matthew about the estate.

Mark had his doubts about that last explanation. Paul had been a capable manager for some time, but his desire for a wife stood out from his and Matthew's reluctance. Mark did wish his brother luck in finding a young woman of the *ton* willing to abandon life in London for a permanent residence in the country. But Paul had hope—an admirable quality Mark did not share. And had not for some time.

At one that afternoon, Matthew and Paul had just left his bedchamber when a kitchen maid arrived bearing a tray with a salty broth, more willow bark tea, a cup of coffee, and a baked custard that tasted lemony enough to make his nose wrinkle. She stayed to stoke the fire in the bedchamber's grate, then curtsied and made her exit. Mark set aside the tea and lay back against the pillows. His mind drifted over his conversation with his mother about Olivia, still wondering if he remembered it correctly or if it had been part of a laudanum fog.

He had explained who Olivia was, and the duchess took with an unexpected grace the news that her second son had produced a by-blow on an actress. She merely expressed her surprise that he had not done so earlier and asked his plans for the girl. She agreed that Olivia was best left where she was for now. Then Phyllida patted him on the hand and left.

Possibly, facing the idea that her son might have killed his lover made any other scandalous news pale by comparison.

Although he doubted it. Mark suspected a return battle lay in store when his health improved. For now, Phyllida had executed a strategic retreat. For all his insolence toward her, his mother sometimes terrified Mark. Her ability to maneuver through and manipulate members of the *ton* had given her more strategic skills than a battle-hardened general.

"Are you still awake?" Matthew's voice came through a slight opening at the door.

Mark reached for the coffee. "I am."

His brother entered with two folded sheets of paper in one hand. He crossed the room, stopping to stare down at the tray on the bedside table. "That looks disgusting."

"The doctor thinks I should avoid anything heavy or solid for a day or two." He nodded at the papers. "Mail?"

Matthew gave a slight grin. "I have a meeting Saturday with a potential bride. Your suggestion turned out to be more beneficial than I expected."

"Excellent. Anyone I know?" Mark had connected Matthew with Mrs. Bessie Dove-Lyon, owner of a gambling hell called the Lyon's Den and a woman known for matchmaking among the *ton*, which would allow Matthew to avoid all the complications of doing a season of balls and soirees when he wanted to rejoin Wellington so desperately. A wedding with a suitable bride would allow him to settle his affairs here and return to France.

"No. But I will tell you more after the meeting." He gestured at the other note. "Smith wants to meet with us later this afternoon. Would you be up for it?"

"I am slightly more coherent than last night. But you might want to make sure I'm awake. Apparently, six months of not sleeping leaves one prone to abrupt naps."

Matthew sombered. "You should do something about it."

"I am considering investing in a boxing salon—"

"Mark—"

"Open all night. No one notices if you have not slept or have drunk a bit too much or scream too loudly—"

"You cannot—" His brother shook his head, glancing away.

"Matthew."

At Mark's solemn tone, Matthew stilled, studying him again.

Mark smoothed the covers beside his leg. "I am doing all I can. All I know to do." They fell silent, watching each other a moment. Finally Mark nodded. "The doctor is returning as well. Have Smith come at four. I would like to have an early supper, if possible. Or perhaps just tea. Real tea. Surely the doctor cannot object to a bit of clotted cream."

The doctor, who arrived at three, did not object and was cheered by Mark's returning appetite, although he advised continued caution about food and simple things—like moving. But Mark insisted on dressing before the Bow Street Runner arrived, and his valet, Howe, helped him to get out of bed and appear reasonably presentable, including a waistcoat and cravat—an intriguing process given the sling for his arm. Another cup of coffee provided a bit of fortification, and he settled into a chair before the fire just as the door opened and Matthew ushered the runner into his bedchamber.

Jeremy Smith's eyes widened as he entered, his hat-mussed hair adding to a slightly crazed look in his eyes. He stared around at the aspect of the room, pausing on each feature, as if memorizing the furniture.

Mark fought a sense of amusement. Laughing was definitely not recommended. "Is something amiss, Mr. Smith?"

The man swallowed hard and focused on Mark. "Forgive me, Lord Mark. I have never been in a gentleman's bedchamber before.”

Mark’s eyebrows arched. “Truly? A man in your line of work, I would have thought you would have been in every possible environment.”

Smith shook his head. “As you know, the aristocracy has their own rules when something untoward happens. I have been in many kitchens and a few drawing rooms, but the two unexpected deaths I was called to, the bodies had been moved to a more respectable room.”

Matthew cleared his throat. “That must not bode well for the investigation.”

Smith shook his head. “No. It does not.”

Mark motioned for the runner to sit in the chair opposite him. “Forgive me for not standing. My health does not allow for that at this time. What do you have for us today?”

The runner eased down on the edge of the chair as if afraid he would soil it. “I have a few questions for you, and I wanted to let you know that you have been dismissed as a potential suspect in the death of Miss Ashley.”

Matthew let out a long sigh and sat on the bench at the end of Mark’s bed. “So we are out of it.”

Smith shook his head. “Not . . . precisely.” He focused on Mark again, his fingers twitching a bit. “I found one man who had been a part of your . . . row . . . in the Rookeries, but he could not be considered a reliable witness. But Dr. Oakley’s information *is* reliable and without question your best defense. It lends credibility to the first, and my superiors think that is enough for me to pursue other possibilities. But I need to ask you a few more questions.” Smith took a deep breath but barely paused. “Do you know about any other . . . associations . . . that Miss Ashley had engaged in?”

Mark gave a twisted grin. “You mean other paramours.”

Smith glanced down but nodded.

“You need not glaze over anything where this is concerned, sir. There is little decorum about it. My arrangement with Miss

Ashley was supposed to be one of mutual benefit. I protected her, provided her with a decent place to live, and additional funds for amenities. In return, she was to provide me a safe and reliable place to bed a woman. The deal we struck meant that she would have no other lovers. In return, I paid for Dr. Oakley to care for her, her mother, and her child. 'Safe' meant she would stay free of disease."

"This is why you were upset when she violated your agreement."

"Yes. I only found out that night she had bedded another man. But I took my anger out in the boxing ring and in the Rookeries. Not on Miss Ashley."

"And who was that man?"

"Shropshire."

Smith paused. "The duke?"

"Yes."

"And you know of no others?"

Mark shook his head. "No, although I suspected there might have been." Then he scowled as a sudden thought crossed his mind. "Do you?"

Smith studied him for a moment, then pulled a folded piece of paper from his pocket. "Um, yes. I am afraid so." He unfolded it. "We talked to her maid, who led us to a diary in Miss Ashley's bedchamber. Apparently, there were several other . . . um . . . paramours. She only refers to them by nicknames, which mean nothing to us. Her maid was equally clueless. We thought you might shed a bit of light on them."

"What are they?"

"The falcon."

Matthew gave a quick cough, and Smith looked from him to Mark. "This means something?"

Mark fought another laugh. "You might wish to look at Lord Peregrine Gower. Two of our youngest brothers matriculated with him, and his name became an unfortunate source of ridicule."

When Smith looked confused, Matthew supplied a quick explanation. "Of birds of prey, of the falcons, the peregrine is one of the smallest and fastest."

A grin flashed across Smith's face. "Ah. Poor chap."

Mark's mind suddenly tripped back to the Huntingdale ball, and the way Gower had petted Judith with a far too familiar gesture, earning him a scolding look from her that should have sent the man fleeing across the room. *No. Surely not . . .*

"Lord Mark?"

Mark brushed the thought away. "It is nothing. Go on. Who were the others?"

Smith consulted the paper. "The badger?"

Nodding, Mark gave a dismissive wave. "That would be me. Because I wear mostly black and white."

The runner examined the paper a bit more closely, then his cheeks pinked. "Ah. Well. Um—"

"Whatever she said about me, I do not want to know."

"Wise choice," muttered Matthew.

Smith cleared his throat. "Of course. So. Merlin?" He looked up. "Another bird?"

Annoyance began to churn in Mark's gut. "No. King Arthur's mentor. Probably John Whatley. He's a member of her acting company. She complained that he had worked some kind of magic to get more pay. A wizard with the theater owners. She said she intended to find out how he achieved that. She did not mention her plan to gain that knowledge."

"The leprechaun?"

Mark swallowed a laugh. "Most likely Shropshire. Because she thought he had pots of gold instead of what he really had."

"Yes . . . well . . ." Smith cleared his throat. "The apprentice."

Mark jerked, sending a sudden pain through his gut. Even Matthew's face tightened as he repeated the name. Smith looked from one to the other.

"Gregory Penmore, Lord Harding," Matthew muttered. "Bloody rotter."

"Sounds as if he should be first on my list."

Mark took a steadying breath, his mother's words returning to his mind—love . . . and anger. "Miss Ashley would not have been the only woman to call him that. And if she called it to his face, he would have been exceptionally furious."

Smith's eyes narrowed. "Why would you think so?"

"Because he became enraged when *I* used it in jest."

Matthew sat a little straighter. "It refers to a certain lack of skill."

Smith needed no elaboration. "Ah. I see. I will talk to the gentleman."

"Tread carefully." Mark let out a breath as the pain eased. "He will not take kindly to being involved."

"Few gentlemen do." Smith consulted his paper. "Just one more. The raider."

Mark's brow furrowed. "I have never heard that term." He looked at Matthew, who shook his head.

"She also referred to him as the border raider. Apparently, a recent . . . um . . . acquisition. Her first mention of him appeared in her diary about a week or so before her demise. A brief notation, mentioning his desire to 'beg, barter, or steal, no matter the cost,' with no explanation, then the number one hundred."

Mark shook his head. "No idea. I never heard her use that term, even in relation to some item in the newspaper."

Matthew's eyebrows arched. "Stella read the newspaper?"

"Rather devoutly. While she definitely kept up with all the *ton* gossip, she also asked me about items regarding Parliament and the courts, occasionally the wars."

Smith made a note, then folded the paper and stood. "Thank you, my lord, Your Grace, for speaking with me."

Matthew stood as well. "Stephens will see you out." Matthew followed the man through the door, let Stephens take the escort, then closed it before gesturing toward Mark's bed and mouthing, "Now."

Mark nodded but continued to stare at the fire, in his mind

the image of Harding's face, beet red and nostrils flared, during their encounter at White's. Harding had intended to gloat, to flaunt Stella's infidelity, and he had become enraged when Mark outwardly did not seem to care. Had that set this all in motion? The idea that women, specifically Stella, would consider Harding inept in the bedroom. Was the man so fragile that he would kill a woman for holding such an opinion?

No. Not a woman. *An actress.* Harding would consider an actress of little more worth than a prostitute, and Mark could definitely envision Harding killing a prostitute who laughed at him.

Or perhaps gave him the pox.

Mark watched the flames, the irony of the encounter gripping him slowly. He had gone there to look at the wager book. Harding had initially approached him for the same reason—the "certain fair widow of renown." That the encounter had taken a dark turn for the worse had caught them both off guard.

Judith. Mark's gaze shifted from the fire to his escritoire, which sat in a corner near the door. A single silk stocking, tied with a ribbon, lay curled neatly inside a hidden cubbyhole, waiting. He had plans for that stocking—and its mate—plans he dearly hoped had not been derailed by a suspicion of murder.

He closed his eyes, a low desire stirring as he remembered Judith's scent of arousal—which had flowered as his fingers caressed her calf—the softness of her leg, the abrupt change in her face at his words, *I wish to own a part of you.* Her mouth had parted, her eyes wide and understanding. She had known exactly what he meant. And had been thrilled by it. The pure joy in that expression had taken some of the edge off discovering Stella with Shropshire. Had, in fact, tempered the anger he had felt. It had been a blessing, a promise. A dream.

But first, he had to heal. Slowly, he pushed up out of the chair and eased his way to the bell pull next to his bed. Time for Howe to earn more of his money.

CHAPTER NINE

Tuesday, 19 July 1814
Sculthorpe Manor stables
Five in the afternoon

JUDITH WAS NOT certain which terrified her more—seeing her four-year-old son sitting atop a gentle pony or the fact that he did, in truth, have "a fine seat."

Their time in the park had been short, yet they had still run later than Judith had wished. She desperately needed a wash and a rest before supper, but she could not break away from watching William as he learned to groom his own horse. He stood on a stool, with Mr. Robins within catching distance should he fall, and Nanny nearby, waiting to take him for a bath and supper. They had waited until early afternoon so that Robbie could join them, and he, too, stood nearby, brushing his own, slightly larger Highland Pony. Although they would seldom have to groom their own horses when they were grown, she—and Mr. Robins— felt learning to care for the animals an important part of becoming an adept and knowledgeable estate manager.

Tears clouded Judith's eyes. Her babies were becoming skilled and handsome young men.

"Oops!" The brush flipped from William's hand and hit the floor of the stable with a *thunk*.

"I'll get it." Nanny scooped up the brush and handed it to Mr. Robins. Their hands touched briefly, and they glanced at each other. Nanny's cheeks pinked and Mr. Robins cleared his throat, returning his attention to William.

She should be grateful, Judith told herself, that her boys were so loved and cared for by so many. But she did not feel grateful.

She felt afraid.

Judith took a deep, steadying breath and swept away the tears. She moved forward and brushed a hand down William's back. "Did you enjoy today?"

"Yes, Mummy! When can we go again?"

Everyone chuckled.

"Soon. As soon as I recover."

He scowled. "What? Are you hurt?"

She kissed his cheek. "Never you mind. I must go up. Will you be all right with Mr. Robins and Nanny?"

"Yes!" He rocked up on his toes, almost losing his balance on the stool.

Mr. Robins gripped him, standing him straight. "We've got him, my lady."

"I know you do." She touched the man's arm and turned, striding from the stable before the tears flowed again.

Her marriage to Edmund had not been one of tremendous love, but his loss had still hollowed Judith out, leaving her bereft, without an anchor. Her only grounding had been the children—all five of them. Now she felt that hollowness again as she watched her three boys edge away from her, just as Edmund and Daniel had, simply by growing up. Daniel, who had quarreled with his brother over some issue they had never explained to her, had become estranged from them all, and Judith missed him terribly.

They are all leaving me.

Although she wanted exactly that—she dearly wished to see them become healthy and happy young men, thriving in whatever they chose to do—but it still left that ache of emptiness. The curse, she supposed, of being a mother who adored her children. Maybe her peers who saw their children as little more than accessories had it right after all.

Never.

Taking another deep breath, Judith swept up the steps, pausing on the first floor as she heard voices from the receiving room, businesslike and strident. Edmund's . . . and a voice familiar but annoying. Not their steward. With apprehension, she stepped into the open doorway.

Their words stalled as they spotted her. A man Judith knew by sight—and reputation—sat in a wingback opposite Edmund and Margaret, who took up either end of the settee. The man—and Edmund—rose to their feet as Judith swallowed and spoke, her words coming rapid-fire. "My apologies. I did not realize you had a guest." She dropped her voice as she addressed Edmund. "Have I overlooked a visit at which I should have been present? Or am I intruding?" She gestured down at the flared skirt and coat of her riding habit. "I was riding with the children."

The man touched his forehead. "Not at all, my dear lady. We are discussing estate business, but you are welcome, if you like."

Ah. That explained why Margaret looked like a trapped fox, huddled against the arm of the settee, fingers digging into the arm. She had probably arranged for the tea and assumed it to be a social visit before the truth emerged at a point when leaving would appear rude if she suddenly bolted. Edmund gave his wife a quick glance, then sniffed and focused on Judith. "Ahem, um, Lady Sculthorpe, may I present Henry Tatlock, Marquess of Whitlow."

The marquess dipped a quick bow, the emerald-green skirt of his immaculate silk frock coat brushing with a soft whisper against his gold-embroidered waistcoat. A diamond-and-pearl pin anchored his cravat, matching his cufflinks, and his cheeks bore the telltale blush of a light touch of rouge. Kohl rimmed his eyes, winging outward from each corner. His trousers carried the look of silk, and his leather shoes shone with a high polish. He looked dressed more for a royal appointment with the Prince Regent than afternoon tea with an earl, and completely out of place. "Lady Sculthorpe, it is an honor."

Judith gave a sharp nod, trying to get a flash of irritation under control. "The honor is mine, Lord Whitlow, as I know well who you are." She glanced back at Edmund, then eased down into the wingback next to the one Whitlow had occupied, noticing that the early tea had been served and mostly consumed. Empty teacups and small, crumb-dusted plates of their finest set of china littered the table between the settee and the wingbacks. The silver urn and trays were from their most elaborate collection. The three-tiered tray had been divested of most of its scones, biscuits, and small sandwiches.

Margaret's grip on the arm of the settee tightened, her knuckles white. The mood in the room remained tense, and Judith was not convinced it was only because of her sudden—and apparently unexpected—arrival.

The gentlemen sat as well, and Whitlow gave a straightening tug on his starched white cravat. "The oversight is mine, I'm afraid, Lady Sculthorpe. I requested a visit sometime after noon today. Although Lord Sculthorpe graciously agreed, it did not leave much time for preparation." He waved a hand at the cluster of dishes. "Although the countess has provided a most luxurious respite." He patted his stomach. "My own supper will have to come much later."

"And you were already out at the stables." Margaret leaned toward Judith, her words *sotto voce*. "We thought you would be gone all afternoon."

Both Edmund and Judith shot her a silencing look. To her credit, Margaret pressed her lips together but commented no further.

"Which mounts did your sons ride today?" Whitlow did not meet her gaze. He instead focused on his forefinger, which tapped the arm of his chair with a relentless pattern.

The irritation in Judith's gut spread. She knew what Whitlow was about, including his reputation for swooping in to "rescue" respected and noble families who struggled with a changing financial situation. Now, thanks to an offhand comment from her four-year-old son, she understood exactly the reason for his visit—and his seemingly innocent question. She narrowed her eyes and opened her mouth, then noticed the warning scold in Edmund's eyes.

So it was true. Edmund planned to sell some of their cattle. How many? Which kinds? More importantly, *why?*

Judith looked down a moment, gathering her thoughts, then flashed a reassuring smile to Whitlow. "We have a blessedly gentle, older gray pony who has been ridden by all the boys as they were learning, even Edmund here. William is four but is already developing a fine seat. He will probably need the pony only a few more months. Robert is ten, and our groom has moved him to a delightful bay Highland Pony who is only fourteen hands."

Whitlow's eyebrows arched, but he still stared at his own fingers. "You still have Highland Ponies?"

Judith glanced at Edmund, who gave her no sign. "We do. Four. Two here and two on our country estate. My husband, the late earl, found them to be reliable and stolid, perfect for young children or work on the farms. We had sev—" Judith stumbled over the word, a sudden realization sweeping over her. *Still?* He asked if they *still* had Highland Ponies? *How would he know?*

They had had more than sixteen of the sure-footed beasts on the estate—breeding stock—until this past spring. Edmund had sold them, assuring Judith it had been because of their ages, and that he would exchange them for more powerful workhorses, perhaps a new breed that had been growing in reputation in Scotland the last few years, strong animals bred from Flemish stallions.

He had not. The ponies had gone, not to be replaced.

She snapped a look at Edmund, who barely met it. *What have you done with all our money?*

As if he could read her thoughts, he shook his head.

Judith forced a weak smile to her face. "Are you greatly interested in horses, Lord Whitlow?"

"Not greatly." A smile flicked across his face, and he glanced at Edmund, then back to his finger. "More for investment purposes, I'm afraid. I am not much of a rider."

"But surely you appreciate the magnificence of a well-formed stallion?"

"I leave such to my head groom. He advises me when to buy and when to sell. One does not have to be an expert on such. Just to know when to hire an expert."

"Ah. You should mention to him then a new breed I have been hearing about. It is a workhorse being bred from Flemish stallions that is growing in popularity in Scotland. Near the River Clyde. Heftier and much larger than a Highland pony. Of course, they would not be worth the same as a racing thoroughbred, but they are helping a great deal with estates that have been lagging in production from their tenancies. They can pull larger payloads and plows and work longer hours. They are bringing a goodly price in the markets and are helping some estates turn a profit for the first time in years. It is the primary reason for their spread. Landowners who have invested in them have found a remarkable return on their investment."

Judith ended by glaring at Edmund, who had the decency to blush.

The finger stopped tapping. "Indeed?"

Judith smoothed a wrinkle from her skirt and sniffed. "Oh, yes. If I were looking to invest in horse flesh, sir, I might look there instead of at an aging herd of geldings fit mostly for children and old women."

"Mother." The word held a low growl, a sign that Edmund struggled to hold his temper. He cleared his throat. "Lady Sculthorpe. Perhaps you should leave such a discussion to the men."

Judith snapped to her feet, forcing both men to do likewise. "Perhaps I should." She turned to Whitlow. "Forgive me, Lord Whitlow, but I have developed quite the headache. My apologies. It has been very enlightening to meet you."

"Of course, my lady."

Judith strode from the room and up the stairs. In her bed-chamber, she rang for Epworth and began stripping out of the riding kit, fighting the urge to rip it from her body and fling it into the fire. She truly wanted to spend her rage on some inanimate object, understanding for the first time why some women threw pottery at their husbands—and why men battered each other . . . or equally hard objects like walls.

Following a soft tap on her door, Epworth entered, stumbling to a halt when she spotted the crumpled kit, the fury on Judith's face.

"My lady?"

"Do they know?" Judith's voice grated with the demand. "Do the servants know?"

Epworth chewed her lower lip. "My lady . . ."

"How long?"

Her maid glanced down at the floor, then met her eyes slowly. "Six months ago, her ladyship—"

"Margaret."

With a nod, Epworth went on. "She gave instructions not to bring on any more servants nor to replace the ones who had left. And she told the housekeeper and butler to pick five each that the household could manage without. At the country house as well. We have also heard from one of the footmen in the country that some art has gone missing." Epworth took a deep breath. "We were warned—threatened—not to tell anyone. Especially you."

Judith squeezed her eyes shut. "I will kill them."

"My lady?"

Waving away her concern, Judith looked at Epworth again. "Two years ago, that boy inherited an estate that was self-sustaining, with a coffer stuffed for the next generation. Not only for Edmund and Daniel, but for my three boys as well."

A sharp thought struck her, and ice settled on her shoulders. "Is this . . . is this why Daniel left? Did Edmund drive his brother away?"

Epworth looked to the floor but said nothing.

"You should have told me." Epworth remained silent, and the chill settled into Judith's bones, slowly spreading a dark numbness. "My family is disintegrating around me." Her chest tightened to the point of pain, and her voice dropped to a whisper. "I have done this. I turned my back and they have floundered."

Then, after a moment, Judith let out a long breath and dropped down on her dressing stool, abruptly weary. "Now I know why he wants me out of the house. I have become a burden. A burden who knows far too much." She turned to face the mirror. "Help me dress for supper. I know it's early, but if I plan to confront Edmund, I need to look my best." She paused. "Preferably something that will not stain too badly if blood is spilled."

Friday, 22 July 1814
Stella Ashley's former residence, Bloomsbury
Half-past ten in the morning

STANDING IN THE narrow foyer of the Bloomsbury house, Mark leaned heavily on his cane as Stella's maid, Clara, trembled, the hem of her plain gray skirt quivering as she repeatedly clinched the fabric in her fists. Nothing he had said so far had eased her worry, no matter how much he had reassured her that she would not have to leave his employ. His patience wore thin as his morning dose of willow bark tea dissipated, and he reminded himself that this woman, barely more than a girl, did not deserve any of his ire.

"Clara, let me ask you plainly. Do you wish to leave this house? I know this cannot be easy for you."

She shook her head but could not meet his eyes. "No, my lord. I don't wish to leave. It's only that—I mean, the other maids on the street say"—she dropped yet another quick curtsy—"I mean no offense, my lord, but they all know what Miss Ashley is—was—and if it is to be only you living here, then they might think that I—" She dropped her skirt and clutched her hands in front of her. "I mean, *I* know that you would not, but—"

Ah. Understanding finally reached Mark's still somewhat addled brain. "You are concerned about your respectability."

She crossed her arms over her chest and gave a barely perceptible nod. "Even though the mistress was—what she was—no one thinks that I would be—but if—if you—" She could not finish the sentence, and the blush that had been building in her cheeks reached a surprising shade of crimson. Clara could not be more than seventeen and had worked for Stella at least four years. She had come to the house during Stella's lying-in. Her mother, a midwife, had helped with Olivia's birth.

Mark shifted his weight on his cane. "You can reassure your friends that there will be more than two of us in the house. My valet, Mr. Howe, will be here, and I intend to hire a butler, a groom, a cook, and another maid to help you with the work. Since Miss Ashley only used a small portion of the house, we will be doing some work on the other areas. I realize it has not been long since her death, but there is no need for you or the house to languish abandoned."

He again looked around at the foyer, at the cracked and peeling paper, the neglect that had begun to reveal itself, after only four years. He had not truly seen the house in the sunlight since he purchased it, and his tour of it today had left him aghast, as some rooms held only piles of trash and abandoned furniture. Stella had allowed a once-fine Town home to edge toward rot.

But making it his own residence had been Matthew's idea, presented yesterday when Mark turned surly following an afternoon visit from Phyllida. Why look for other lodgings when he owned a perfectly good house in Bloomsbury? Yes, moving in so quickly may seem a bit callous but delaying did not make much sense either. Although Mark still had difficulty breathing and moving easily, he had regained a great deal of his strength in the last two days—once he could eat solid food—and the time had come long ago for him to leave Embleton House.

"A team will arrive this afternoon to remove Miss Ashley's belongings—" He stopped, tilting his head to one side, peering at the girl. "Is there anything of hers you might want to keep for your own?"

Her amber-colored eyes shot wide. "I could not—I mean, where would I—"

Mark held up his hand. "Listen to me. Her possessions will be packed and delivered to her mother, who most certainly cannot use Miss Ashley's frocks or small clothes."

Clara's blush deepened, which Mark had not thought possible. But surely the girl understood. Rose Ashley dressed so primly folks frequently mistook her for a nun. "She will probably pass them along to some charity or other. I have gathered the jewelry I gave Stella, which will pay for the new staff and some of the renovations."

An understatement. Over the years, he had gifted Stella with jewelry suites worth hundreds of pounds, usually paid for by his winnings at cards. He would put those stones—now tucked in a cloth bag under his arm—to a more beneficial use. "But if you wish to keep some of her gowns for yourself"—Clara opened her mouth to protest, but he spoke over her—"or to *sell*, perhaps to her modiste—"

"Oh." This time Clara's rounded gasp revealed her recognition of his meaning. "Oh!"

"They might bring enough to provide you with a bit of a nest egg for the future."

"Oh, my lord!"

Mark, not entirely sure if she meant him or God in heaven, chose the former. "Can you read?"

She nodded fervently, the brown curls around the edge of her cap bouncing. "Mama taught me because she thought it might help me find a good place."

Wise mama. "Good. You will be senior housemaid, and you

will work with Cook on running the household. If all goes well—if you prove yourself—I will make you the housekeeper. I will give you a letter tomorrow, stating my permission for you to sell the gowns and anything else. Definitely speak with her modiste on the gowns. I'm sure she could help you find buyers if she does not want them herself."

Mark paused, took a deep breath, and checked his pocket watch. Though he was well on his way to healing, Mark still needed to rest frequently, and he had acquiesced to his mother's request to accompany her to another blasted ball tonight. He needed to get home. "It is almost time. The first people will arrive in half an hour to begin work on Miss Ashley's rooms. Let them in, serve them tea and supper, but keep an eye on them so they do not walk off with the silver. Go now and collect what you wish to keep or sell and tuck it away in your room. I will be back tomorrow afternoon."

Clara curtsied and fled up the stairs, looking happier than Mark had ever seen her. Stella had been a rather harsh employer, but Mark had tried to keep such thoughts to himself, since he did not live under the same roof. He was certain Clara expected the same from him, but she would soon find his attitude toward staff to be vastly different. Matthew declared their time in the military had changed them both in that regard. While they had been commissioned officers, they still served under others' commands and fought alongside all ranks of men. The closeness had given them a new perspective, and neither had quite returned to the view that those in service deserved little consideration.

Upstairs, a squeal burst from Clara, and Mark chuckled as he left the house and returned to the waiting carriage. Even with the aid of his cane, Mark needed the strength of his footman to enter the conveyance, sinking back against the squabs with a wince and a sigh. He pulled a handkerchief from his breast pocket to wipe perspiration, brought on by the pain, from his face. No dancing tonight. And as much as he hated lingering abed, a rest would be good, readying him for another night of vapid chatter and weak lemonade.

Unless, of course, Judith attended as well. That thought improved his mood, and his mouth twisted into his usual smirk as the horses jerked the carriage into motion.

CHAPTER TEN

Friday, 22 July 1814
Reddington Hall, Mayfair
Half-past ten in the evening

J UDITH DANCED HER anger, giving no quarter to awkward young
gentlemen, and snipped so soundly at one young lord during
their first few steps that he had remained silent the rest of the
dance. After the last bow, he scurried back to friends with a
terrified look over his shoulder. Perry, who had approached for
what he called a "farewell reel," retreated with a similar look
when she reminded him that she did not dance with men who
had other attachments. Looking more like a wide-eyed pup than
usual, he returned with haste to his new beloved and her
scowling mother.

Judith did not care. Other men remained to dance, some even
eager to match her energy if not her mood. A mood built of
frustration and fury—with men, with the *ton*, with herself, with
people in general. A wrath that threatened to consume her.

How could Edmund have been such a fool! How could I have!

She had been enraged for almost four straight days, since her
confrontation with Edmund at Tuesday's supper, barely sleeping
and struggling to keep from turning her anger on the servants,
who had hidden the reality of their situation from her. But them
she could forgive; they had done so in an attempt to protect her.
Edmund had done so to deceive her.

But faced with her outright statements about the signs their
money had drained away, he had collapsed under her furious

accusations, confessing that a series of gambling debts and fraudulent investments—including a heftily financed partnership in a Triangular Trade shipping company that proceeded to have three ships sink in the North Atlantic—had turned a legacy of financial soundness into an estate in tatters. *In two years!* The bottom line was that the burden of being an earl simply had been too much, and his unskilled attempts to outshine his father had pushed the family close to ruin.

In the end, Judith blamed herself. She had been so lost after her husband died she had been relieved to hand the estate over, not realizing that she herself had thrived at her stepson's age precisely because her experienced and gallant husband had been beside her. And her mother-in-law. And a wise housekeeper. Upon her marriage, Judith had been gifted with mentors, guidance, and help. But she had thrust all the duties at Edmund and Margaret without any advice or recommendations, blithely accepting that they neither desired nor needed her aid.

But she included them in her wrath as well. They had been prideful, even in the face of a downfall. They had rejected offers of help from the estate's stewards, land managers, and their man of business when those professionals recognized what was happening. And at even a mild suggestion that she could use some help, Margaret had puffed up, lording her position over the housekeeper and the staff, insisting that she knew best.

After her initial burst of rage, Judith had merely said, "Show me the accounts and let us get to work."

And they had, the three of them meeting with the people who could help them in a steady stream of appointments—encounters fueled by Judith's ire, which flared when either Edmund or Margaret complained of being tired, or in Margaret's case, bored. The boredom comment had provoked a tantrum in Judith that left Margaret sobbing in her bedchamber for a full day. As their examination of the estate turned up lie after lie, Judith's mood continued to sour.

She knew she had no real power to do anything—the title and

estate were fully Edmund's, and he could do as he wished with them. They all knew it. But she had landed on them like a hawk in full attack—wings flared and talons extended—and they had caved beneath her knowledge, her determination, and their own panic at a future with no income.

Harsh steps had already been taken. Margaret's allowance and clothing budget had been slashed, and Judith had surrendered part of her widow's portions to the estate in order to pay off some of the most immediate debts. They partitioned off two of the tenancy farms from their country estate to sell to a neighboring baron, as well as scheduling more of the artwork and furniture from the country house to be put to auction. Judith put a halt to the sale of their livestock, however. A breeding herd was an investment with great potential returns. Besides, she despised Whitlow and would rather starve than see her beloved horses go to him.

Other investments were turned over to their man of business for the next few months, and Judith and the housekeeper had reclaimed the household expenses, with the promise to train Margaret in how to best manage them—which did not include the younger woman's obsession with sugar and the finest teas, wines, and meats. They would recover, but it would be a long and difficult journey.

Now Judith turned her attention to those who had led Edmund down this path; they would face confrontation, as well as a demand for restitution.

Starting tonight.

Judith had searched for her prey all evening, finally spotting Mark Rydell—and his mother—when they entered the room a few moments after ten. Finding them only after so many fast and furious dances was probably fortunate for all three, as some of her anger had abated under the expenditure of energy. Yet she still fought the urge to march directly to them, skirmish in mind. That would be inadvisable in more than a few ways, including one that could leave her vulnerable—she no longer trusted Edmund to be completely truthful with her. He had hidden so much, lied so much to cover his failings that Judith had lost faith in his ability to be honest on any level. She had their account books to verify much of what he had told her—foolish investments, drained coffers—but nothing to back up his claims of who had lured and encouraged him to take such a dark path.

And Lord Mark Rydell had been named among the most prominent of the villains, along with one of Rydell's best friends, Sir Rory Campbell. At least according to her stepson. But as Judith danced, doubts swirled around her more freely than her skirts. She watched the Rydells even as Phyllida watched everyone else, her ubiquitous fan getting a thorough workout. Lord Mark sat next to her, looking abjectly miserable.

Good.

Any affection, any desire she may have had for the man had shattered under her stepson's explanations. Reportedly one of the worst of the corrupting influences, Lord Mark Rydell had lured Edmund into gambling establishments, introducing him to predatory gamblers and erstwhile business associates. It made sense as Edmund explained it. The man did have a notorious reputation, frequented infamous hells, and seemed to have a source of income no one could explain. It had been Rydell, Edmund proclaimed, who had encouraged him to invest in the Triangular Trade shipping companies, a chance to pay back money Edmund owed Rydell from gambling. That one decision had been the nail in their financial coffin, a substantial and risky investment now at the bottom of the Atlantic. Everything had cascaded from there.

According to Edmund, Rydell held all the cards, all the debts, all the vowels.

Although right now, Rydell appeared as if he held nothing but his mother's arm. The man sat gingerly beside the duchess, his face as pale as bleached muslin. He held his body at an odd angle, stiff and still. He had not danced, had barely even risen to greet approaching nobles, since they had entered the room. Any beverage had been delivered on a footman's tray, and when Rydell did stand, he leaned heavily on a solid, black cane.

What the bloody hell was wrong with him?

The man looked to be a shell. Not the bold and energetic dancer she remembered or expected. Nor the enthusiastic and commanding flirt who had stolen one of her favorite silk stockings.

That memory heated her face even more than the dancing. Had that been part of their ruination as well? Part of his schemes to destroy Edmund?

Why would Rydell want to destroy my son? My family?

It made no sense. None. And her mind, her determination, turned cautious.

The music ended, and when her partner turned her toward the edge of the crowd, she pulled away—gently but firmly—and gave him a wan smile. "Thank you, my lord, but I need to take a rest for the next set."

Judith acknowledged his startled expression with a pat on the arm, then turned toward a beverage table near the far wall of the ballroom. She scooped up a small cup of lemonade and sought out an elaborately decorated ficus tree as a refuge. She wedged her body and the skirts of her rose-colored gown between the tree's pot and the wall, peering out through the branches at the rest of the ball's guests, careful not to entangle the feathers and ribbons in her hair in the leaves.

The Reddington ball had always been a highlight of the season. Their hosts, Lord and Lady Brawley, Earl and Countess Reddington, spared no expense. Even the lemonade revealed the money behind the event—overly sweet and thick with lemon pulp—which made it, to Judith's taste, as foul as the normally weak and watery brew served at most balls. Congenial to all comers, Lord and Lady Brawley welcomed their guests into a room filled with Egyptian-themed decorations and champagne served early and often. Even her tree's pot carried the theme, hieroglyphics circling it like marching soldiers.

The room shone as bright as a summer afternoon, lit by dozens of candelabra and six 120-candle chandeliers. Guests, expecting the best in fare and décor, wore their finest garb. Gowns glittered and swayed with frills, metallic embroidery, and gauze. Men wore kits of bright colors and intricately designed waistcoats, their eyes fashionably ringed with lines of kohl and cheeks dotted with rouge. Even cravats varied from white into reds, golds, and indigos, all of them tied with the latest in unique knots and secured with jeweled pins. The wealth of the *ton* shone—even the dragons and spinsters in their rows of out-of-the-way chairs seemed to shimmer with gems and pearls. All of Society had gathered to see and be seen.

Judith, too, had arrived in a similar effort. Her modiste had spent a week refurbishing one of Judith's favorite and most alluring gowns—rose silk with a gold gauze overlay on the skirt and slits in the sleeves and bodice that allowed glimmers of gold silk to peek through. The original hem had been trimmed back and replaced with a weighted and ruched gold border. Gold silk embroidery on her décolletage drew every man's eyes down, and Judith kept her posture straight, shoulders back. Her gown—and her dancing, as vigorous as it had been—were means to an end: to locate and draw the attention of the two men whom Edmund had claimed as his friends—and nemeses: Rydell and Sir Rory Campbell, the latter a nephew and presumptive heir of a currently childless duke.

When her rage had first flared earlier in the week, she had craved confrontation and restitution. But as she reviewed her conversations with her stepson over the past few days, her desire had evolved into something else: a need for verification.

Edmund had lied to her for months. What assurance did she have he did not continue to do so?

Judith took another sip, wincing as she glanced down at the yellow swill in her cup. She pressed her lips against the syrupiness and forced a swallow.

"The ratafia is infinitely sweeter, Lady Sculthorpe, but equally as disgusting."

Judith coughed a laugh, then peered through the branches of the ficus tree to see Lord Anthony Blackwell, one of the more distinguished men of the *ton*, watching her with curiosity. Tall and lean with hair the color of platinum, Lord Blackwell and his wife also hosted one of the premier balls of the season and frequently attended the assemblies at Almack's, although they both circulated through the *ton* for reasons more political than social. They knew everyone—and apparently everything.

Judith dipped her head in acknowledgment. "Rather so, my lord. I had hope for the lemonade, but it has proved a disappointment."

"Much like seeing you lurking behind the decorations."

Judith grinned. "I needed a respite from dancing. I did not expect so many gentlemen to desire a turn with an ancient widow."

"Which would not be you, my dear lady. You may be a widow but are far from ancient. And anyone with eyes can see that while you are a lively dancer, you remain most intrigued by the one man who is not doing so this evening. Also that your energetic display on the floor has an ulterior motive."

Judith stilled and glanced down at her cup. "I am unsure—"

"He is injured. Seriously so."

She stared at the man. "I beg your pardon."

A slight smile creased Lord Blackwell's gently lined face. "Rydell. That is why he is not dancing. And why he looks like the apocalyptic horse of death. Most of the *ton* is surprised he is even here. Some altercation in the Rookeries left him with a few broken ribs and bruised innards. While he is much better now, the *on dit* has been circulating for a couple of days that this is why Bow Street dismissed him in the death of Miss Ashley. He would not at that time have been physically capable of rendering injury to her." He gave a quick smirk. "Of course, as is the nature of *ton* prattle, many are unwilling to pass on such a delectable idea. Yet."

Judith studied him through the leaves. "Why are you telling me this?"

Lord Blackwell shifted his gaze to the dancers, who were concluding a country dance. "Your late husband and I were good friends."

"I remember."

"I admired what he had endured, what he had built, and his ability to increase his fortune and his family after his marriage to you. His father and older brother were not entirely wastrels, but they were distinctly inefficient managers. Your husband turned that estate around through wisdom and care, building a rather impressive legacy. I would hate to see any of that tarnished because of foolish mistakes."

Judith stepped out from behind the tree to face Blackwell directly. "Apparently the *on dit* has been rather extensive."

He gave a single nod. "Apparently. And *you* are not being given the entire tale."

Judith's eyes narrowed as she spotted her next dance partner approaching from the far corner of the room. "How so?"

Lord Blackwell lowered his chin, speaking a bit more intimately. "You are an intimidating woman, my dear. It is one reason our Edmund cherished you so completely by the end. He trusted your cleverness and your competence. He knew you could manage the estate after his death. But there are those who fear your wrath—and your extraordinary ability to manage your own affairs—should you know all the gruesome details of what has transpired with your estate. This includes your pusillanimous stepson. So you are being misled." He glanced at Rydell. "I know you love the young Edmund but look deeper before you make any accusations elsewhere."

Judith scowled. "How do you know?"

The elder gentlemen smiled kindly. "You are hardly a stoic, my dear. And out of respect for my friendship with your late husband, I would like to see you resolve the issues his heir has stumbled into. For your sake, the sake of your family, and the health of the *ton*. We have always had rats and mice—minor vermin—in our midst. It does no one a fair turn to invite the weasels to our tables as well."

Her next partner had almost reached them. "So who should I look to?"

He cut his gaze toward Rydell again. "Despite what the man has claimed, he did not go into the Rookeries merely looking for a row following his disagreement with Miss Ashley. That he took to a boxing ring. But it was at that boxing ring that he discovered information about your stepson that sent him excavating for more information. He has some of the missing pieces you need. Also, I suspect he would enjoy chatting with someone other than his mother this evening." With that, Lord Blackwell bowed slightly and slipped away.

Judith watched him saunter toward his wife, even as she barely acknowledged her latest partner, a young baronet who had received his title only this past New Year's. The naïve gentleman, a kind sort who still often stumbled on his way to finding his place among the *ton,* waited patiently. Judith did not keep him waiting long, despite the turmoil churning within her, a miasma of emotions that tamped and fueled her anger at the same time. She knew now that her stepson would definitely lie to her without remorse or hesitation. Something Judith would make sure he would come to regret.

MARK WATCHED LORD Blackwell ease his way through the crush of dancers moving onto the floor, gathering for a quadrille. The statesman had been sequestered with Judith near a potted tree long enough for her face to move through a dozen expressions—surprise, annoyance, suspicion, and curiosity, among others—even as she had repeatedly glanced in Mark's direction. She had taken the arm of her newest partner with a continued look of anger, however, and Mark found his gaze slipping from Judith to Blackwell more than once as he studied them both.

Lord Anthony Blackwell had been a privy advisor for King George III and an important voice in Parliament—and he still had the ear of the Prince Regent. Although well past sixty, his posture remained perfectly straight, his frame trim, and his eyes bright and clear, like an old general with a military bearing and discipline. The ball he and his wife would host later in the season remained one of the most desired invitations, and the man could squire even the liveliest young women about the floor with ease. Yet he had not danced with Judith. Instead he had engaged her in a private conversation of obvious import, much has he would a fellow peer on a matter of political significance.

Why?

The unexpected feelings of jealousy that swirled through Mark's gut as he had watched Judith move from one handsome— and usually *young*—partner to the next throughout the evening had been eased by her conversation with Blackwell. Her presence at a Society ball normally meant a light, fun experience on the floor. But tonight she had danced with a fierce enthusiasm, intimidating most of the men. Even some of the Society mavens had noticed, dragons who watched her from behind flipping fans, their gazes following her through each set.

What are you up to, dear Judith?

"What are you plotting?" His mother's low demand came from behind her own fan.

He sniffed. "In case you had not noticed, I am rather incapable of plotting anything at the moment." He shifted on his chair, trying to give his aching ribs a bit more room. He felt stronger, more able to move about, but the lingering aches were sharper at times than others.

"You do not need to move to plot, and you have done so since you were a child. Observing your brothers and devising some prank or other to embarrass or humiliate them."

"They should not be so easily embarrassed."

"They were children. Some still are."

"So was I."

"You were never truly a child. I swear you arrived on the planet with a plot and a prank in mind, even as you had a thumb in your mouth."

"Timothy will reach his majority in six months, and he has been at school since he turned twelve. He is hardly a child."

"Scarcely my point—"

"You reared my brothers."

Phyllida gave a low growl. "My point is that your mind never ceases plotting about something. You watch and you plot."

Mark glanced at his mother. "Apparently, I am not the only one who watches and plots."

"I am a matron of the *ton*. That is my right."

He nodded at Lady Sculthorpe. "Something is going on with Judith."

"You mean other than that her stepson is in the process of bankrupting the family? And please do not use her Christian name with me. The implication disturbs me to no end."

"So you have heard?"

Phyllida huffed. "Of course, I have. I suspect most of the *ton* will have heard by now. So, from the look of her tonight, has your precious Jud—Lady Sculthorpe—despite the machinations of the earl to keep the information from her. Neither that blundering fool nor his shrew of a wife have been very discreet otherwise. And the implications of what he has been up to have been rather horrendous. I suspect that is why Lord Blackwell cornered Lady Sculthorpe. To warn her of the social, governmental, and financial ramifications if the situation is not resolved. The ruin of one family is not without much wider consequences." Phyllida lowered her fan. "You do know that your name has been bandied about."

Mark studied Judith as she whirled through a quadrille, the dance reminding him of how she had felt as his partner. Confident. Sensuous. Alluring. The feel of her skin . . .

His loins tightened.

Damn it. He shifted again. "I do, although the *on dit* about it has apparently been tempered by a murder accusation."

"You will be the death of me."

"True. But not for many more years, during which you can continue to torment me to your great pleasure."

"Not if you move into that brothel."

Mark stilled for a moment, unsure of precisely to which brothel his mother referred. "Mother, I do not think—"

She waved a hand. "Oh, I know it was just the one, and she's gone and you own the house outright, but I still think—"

Ah. *That* brothel. "Mother, one mistress does not a brothel make."

Another wave. "It is the profession, not the location."

"Her profession was acting."

"And you, of course, paid her for her 'acting' talents."

Mark's teeth clinched. He had to extract himself from this conversation before he added to the gossip already surrounding his family. "I believe you need a beverage."

Phyllida glared at him. "I most certainly do not—"

He pushed up on his cane. "I shall retrieve one for you."

"Now, just a moment—"

Mark did not wait. As much as he relished bantering with his mother—and he knew she did with him also—his mood had soured as the evening had brought little relief from her sniping and Judith's indulgent dancing with other men.

Young men.

The quadrille had ended, and the first notes signaled the beginning of a reel as the dancers milled and mingled. Judith had dismissed her latest partner with a quick curtsy before retreating back to the tree, new cup in hand.

Annoyance tugged at Mark's mind as he circumvented the dancers, his cane thumping on the floor. He had not been jealous of a woman since . . . well, never. Jealousy simply did not play a part in his dealings with fairer sex. If a woman preferred another's company to his, he wished her well and turned his interest elsewhere. Prior to following Matthew to the Peninsula, more than a few women had sought him out, some still did—he had no lack of interested partners. Any jealousy had stemmed from the ladies, yet another reason why his arrangement with Stella had made sense. He cared not for the dramatic antics of the *ton's* women.

So it made no sense for one he barely knew to stir this unexpected feeling of . . . *what?* Ownership definitely did not describe it—no man on this planet could ever claim such a thing of Judith Lovelace, Lady Sculthorpe. And without even investigating it, Mark knew any man who tried would risk life and limb. Which he might be doing even at this moment, approaching her from the other side of her tree.

But as he did so, Judith seemed inordinately fixated on the cup of lemonade clutched in her hand, as if the beverage held the answers of all the world's ills.

"Champagne"—Judith jumped, and Mark lowered his tone—"might be of more solace."

Her scowl deepened. "Why are men so fascinated by what I am drinking?"

"Perhaps if you were not studying that cup as if it contained the Elixir of Life."

"Hmph. Believe me, immortality is the last thing I would desire at the moment."

"Perhaps you might tell me what it is you do de—"

She glared through the branches. "Did you truly push my son into bankruptcy?"

Mark stared, blinking at her. Definitely not the greeting he had expected. Especially after their last encounter at the theater. "I do not think that—"

"It is a rather simple question, my lord. A yes or no should do nicely."

Mark studied her a moment, then allowed his tone to match her own. "May we speak without the bloody tree between us?"

Her chin rose and those emerald eyes flashed. Then she set the lemonade down in the tree's pot, stepped from behind it, and faced him. "Is this to your satisfaction, my lord?"

Mark shifted, trying to ease some of the discomfort in his chest, and winced. Judith's face mirrored the wince for a moment, then hardened again, even as her voice softened. "Would it not be better for you to sit?"

"In a moment. For me to sit next to you would create more difficulties for me than the pain is."

Her mouth jerked. "Your mother still has no fondness for me?"

"A generous way of putting it, but you are correct."

"Then we should conclude this as rapidly as possible so you can return to her side. Please answer my question. Are you the one pushing my family toward the brink of ruin? It is what I have been told."

Mark hesitated, his mind roiling through a half dozen answers, all of which would lead to more questions than could be answered on a dance floor. "I suspect Edmund has also led you to believe the situation is more simplistic than it actually is."

"Is that a yes?"

"No. It is not. The only person truly responsible for the current predicament is Edmund himself. But there are others involved whose advice to him has been less than well intentioned."

"Does that include you?"

"Not precisely. What did Lord Blackwell tell you?"

"That I should speak with you. However little good that is doing at the moment."

"Does that not convince you that this is not a simple situation?"

Judith let out a long sigh and clutched her hands together in front of her, as if she were trying to avoid hitting him. "Not since you are talking in circles."

"May I call on you?"

She blinked. "I beg your pardon?"

"A lot of elements are at play, more than I can detail on a Society dance floor, some of which I only discovered recently myself. And I greatly desire that you understand everything fully. May I call on you at a time when Edmund will not be in the house?"

Recognition seemed to register in her eyes, and Judith glanced around. Yet another young man approached from the far side of the room, and Mark resisted emitting a low snarl.

She straightened her shoulders. "I would suggest neutral territory."

Probably a good idea, especially if she truly wishes to hit me. "Any suggestions?"

She looked him up and down as if evaluating a lame horse. "I suspect you are not up for a stroll in the park."

He arched an eyebrow. "Hardly."

"Storey's Gate. St. James."

"Still a park."

Her mouth twisted. "Meet me there. There is a tearoom down the street, suitable for women but without the gossipy crowds of Gunter's. They have some private alcoves for quieter discussions."

"And you believe that you and I could have a quiet discussion in an alcove?"

Her eyes suddenly gleamed. "I believe, sir, that we already have."

Mark coughed a laugh, grimacing as yet a new ache arced through his chest. "Humor is not currently good for my health."

"Then we will focus on the truth instead. Meet me there Monday. At three. We will need tomorrow to recover, and the tearoom is not open on Sunday. Besides, I plan to have Edmund at St. George's on Sunday, for service and a chat with the rector." With that, she turned to the approaching young man and accepted his arm.

This time, Mark did snarl as the couple eased through the

crowd. They paused briefly as another man approached Judith, motioning at her dance card. She shook her head, her arm to her side, and the man moved away.

Mark's scowl deepened, but this time he was puzzled. The gentleman she had refused compared admirably to her other dance partners of the evening. Handsome, well-bred and well-known, and—as usual—*young*. So why would she . . .

Married. This one was married. Newly so.

Mark stood a little straighter. Most of the *ton* suspected that Judith took lovers—not exactly scandalous, as she was a widow in her prime. So having a man, any man, request a dance should not be unusual. Mark's gaze moved from Judith to her previous partner. Then another. And another. All of them, to a man, had two things in common. Their youth . . . and none were courting or married. Not one had made an attachment this season.

A smile worked its way across Mark's face. His ebullient "wanton harlot" had a distinctive moral streak to her character. Unmarried men. St. George's. "So, dear Judith," he muttered, "what will your reaction be when hearing exactly how far off the mark Edmund has strayed?"

CHAPTER ELEVEN

Monday, 25 July 1814
Storey's Gate, Whitehall
Quarter past three in the afternoon

J UDITH PACED BEFORE the stolid and plain block building of Storey's Gate, praying that Rydell would show soon and that her temper would have calmed enough by the time he arrived that she did not box his ears as if he were an errant child.

Because she dearly wanted to. And not merely because he had kept her waiting, although that annoyed her to the bone. His delay had left her to endure the obnoxious chattering of dozens of birds, all caged and in the trees lining the avenue leading from the gate. Most of the *ton* considered the birds to be a visual and auditory delight. Judith thought it cruel to keep such lovely creatures caged, and she regretted choosing the meeting spot from the moment she stepped from the Sculthorpe carriage and dismissed the driver. She had only been thinking of the tearoom, where they could have a bit of seclusion without actually being in private with each other. A quiet place but one with lovely people around. People she actually trusted.

Because she did not trust herself to be alone with Mark Rydell behind a closed door. The very concept sent her mind toward thoughts of silk stockings and bare thighs, firm hands and promises of far more pleasurable activities—all when she should be focused on rectifying her family's plunge toward financial ruin.

Another reason to box his ears. During yesterday's chat with the rector, Edmund had gone into more detail about Rydell's involvement, laying blame directly on him for some of the worst investments. Edmund had spoken of this before in more general terms, but yesterday he had provided more details—details that made sense—and included a scheme involving a gaming hell, fixed fights, and a web of outrageous bets. The deeper and more convoluted this became, the more Judith understood Edmund's desperation, the unrelenting panic of a young man in over his head with older men primed to take advantage of his youth, his money, and his status.

She did not need to be thinking about Rydell's kisses. Or the firm stroke of his hand on her thigh.

A clattering of wheels on stone interrupted her musing, and she turned to see the Embleton ducal carriage approach, the family crest a glimmer of gold on the door. It stopped next to her and a footman descended to open the door and lower the steps. But Rydell did not emerge. He remained still, his shadowed form backlit by the windows on the other side of the vehicle as he spoke. "Is there any reason we cannot ride to this tearoom of yours?"

She crossed her arms, her reticule bouncing against her stomach. "Other than I would prefer not to be alone with you in a carriage?"

His head bowed and he chuckled. "I assure you the entire *ton* knows that I am incapable of anything untoward at the moment."

They stared at each other a moment, then Judith sighed and gave the direction to the driver. The footman helped her inside, folded the steps, and closed the door. Once she had settled on the seat opposite him, Rydell rapped with his cane on the roof, and the carriage moved forward.

"Your injuries are the only reason I have not heaped bodily harm upon you."

He fought a smile, his hands twisting the cane against one palm. "I surmised as such. You have had a rather nasty shock."

"For which you are partly responsible."

He dipped his head. "I will admit to playing a part, although probably not as large a one as your stepson may have implied."

"Do you or do you not have part ownership of a gambling hell called At Wheel's End? A rather nonsensical name, I might add."

He stilled. "Recently acquired, yes. And it refers to the Wheel of Fortune. *Rota Fortunae.*"

"Apropos. How recent?"

"A bit over three weeks ago. Just before"—he gestured toward his torso—"this. A few days before Miss Ashley's murder."

A wave of annoyed confusion settled over Judith, making her head ache. *Only three weeks? But Edmund had declared . . .* "This is provable?"

He gave a single nod. "There are records of the transactions. The partial purchase of the gaming hell is an investment to help out an old friend."

"Sir Rory Campbell."

His eyebrows arched. "Yes, as a matter of fact. Sir Rory is set to inherit a title, money, and a rather large estate from his uncle. He wishes to divest himself of some of his less reputable properties before that happens. He foolishly desires to find a wife among the waifs of the Beau Monde and believes becoming more respectable will help those efforts as well as his position in Society as his uncle's heir. Eventually, I will buy him out completely."

"Because you are less concerned with reputation."

"I believe we have established that much already."

"And where did you get the money? You are a second son. I know your family is generous, but I cannot see your mother—or your brother, for that matter—approving such a thing enough to fund it."

"I have my own sources of income."

"Such as?"

He shifted uncomfortably as the carriage drew to a halt. "I believe, madam, that we are here to discuss your stepson's lack of fortune. Not the acquisition of my own."

Rotter. Judith really did want to box his ears. "As they are entwined with yours to his detriment, I find all related topics up for discussion. Do you or do you not hold most of his vowels? His debts? Have you not, in fact, called those debts to account, escalating his situation and desperation?"

The door opened, and they fell silent. After a frozen moment, Judith moved to exit, accepting the footman's arm. She stepped away on the pavement, turned . . . and her breath caught.

Mark Rydell's lips were almost as pale as his face, and fine beads of sweat dotted his forehead. Both footmen moved forward to help him down, and he leaned heavily on each until he could regain his balance. He walked a bit easier than he had at the ball, but his progress remained slow and calculated, with a great deal of weight on the cane. His mouth twisted into a smirk as he caught her expression. "As I said, I am not capable of anything untoward."

"You looked more healed at the ball."

"I am progressing. But it has been a rather eventful three days, and I may have overestimated the level of my recovery."

Judith paused as the footmen remounted and the carriage lumbered away. "Then you have not rested as someone in your condition should have?"

He held one arm wide, even as he braced on the cane with the other. "The life of a rake is never dull." He looked up at the brick-and-timber building before them, his eyes lingering on the name stenciled on a curtained window next to the door: *Le salon de thé d'Adélaïde.* "Who is Adelaide?"

"You will see." Judith suddenly ached to inquire whether he were truly up to this meeting, then decided that he would not have come if he could not manage it. And she thought he wanted answers from her almost as much as she did from him.

Rydell opened the door and held it for her. She entered, pausing inside to inhale the delicious aromas of pastries, teas, and seasoned meats, and to let her eyes adjust to the dimly lit room. Judith adored this establishment, with its low, heavily beamed ceiling, small tables, and ambiance of feminine rebellion.

Rydell closed the door behind him. "It does smell heavenly. And not at all like the normal ladies' tearoom. More like a pub for women."

"Wait till you taste her clotted cream."

"Lady Sculthorpe! My darling Judith!" Adelaide's clear alto echoed through the room as she approached, the shawl draped around her arms and tucked underneath her elbows flowing and weaving as much as her voluminous, multicolored skirts did as she made her way through the tables of customers.

Judith heard Rydell chuckle as Adelaide, her wild red tresses of hair ebbing and flowing about her head, engulfed Judith in a hug.

"My darling lady, it has been too long. I was so thrilled when I received your message. And this is the gentleman you referenced?"

"It is."

Adelaide gave Rydell a quick study, head to toe. "Well, he is much more handsome—and older—than I imagined, although he does look as if he has spent far too much time in the boxing salons." She turned and motioned for them to follow. "I have saved the best table for you, *ma chérie*. Come."

They did, moving through the small tearoom, whose customers—unlike those at Gunter's—kept their eyes on their own teacups and their voices low. Women with women, women with men not their husbands, men with men. A community of secrets. Adelaide led Mark and Judith to the back of the central room, then down a short hallway to an alcove with one table and four chairs. A fine linen cloth covered the tabletop, and two formal place settings lay waiting for an afternoon tea. Although no door closed off the entryway, the privacy of the space impressed Judith. Only one other alcove branched from the small hallway, currently empty.

"Please sit. I will bring sustenance." Adelaide bustled out of the room, muttering to herself.

Rydell waited for Judith to sit, then slowly eased down onto a chair facing the door, bracing on his cane and the back of the chair. "The lady is definitely not of the Beau Monde."

Judith grinned and shifted in her seat, smoothing her skirts and arranging them around her ankles. "She is and she is not. Adelaide is the youngest daughter of an earl. She ran away to stay with an aunt in Moravia before she could debut. Her father brought her back after the Battle of Austerlitz for safekeeping, but Adelaide had never been one to conform to the ways of the *ton*. She opened this tearoom for like-minded people. Her father has never disowned her, but you will not find her at many family gatherings or Society events. But the ladies of the *ton* value this tearoom far too much to ever give her a cut direct."

"My best! My best!" Adelaide sang as she entered the alcove, a much younger serving girl following close behind. Adelaide sat a silver tray before them, laden on one end and around the edges with a china teapot with a floral design, as well as matching cups and saucers, an empty bowl, a brimming pitcher of milk, and a bowl of brown, lumpy sugar. In the center of the tray sat a tall silver urn, steam rising from the narrow spout, and a small wooden tea chest. A strainer and spoons in a neat line rested near the chest.

The serving girl waited, holding a three-tiered display of pastries, small sandwiches, and meat pies, as well as small pots of jam and clotted cream. Adelaide took it from her and nestled it beside the silver tray. She leaned back and studied the arrangement, hands on her hips. "What do you think?"

Judith nodded. "It looks delicious."

"Should I do the tea or will you?"

Judith slipped off her gloves and draped them over her lap. "I will take care of it."

Adelaide nodded. "Very good. I will check on you later but will mostly leave you to it. Stay as long as you please. I can provide an early supper, if needed." Her voice dropped and she leaned closer to Judith. "Or a late supper, if you desire. Do not be too rowdy or you will arouse too much curiosity."

"I assure you we will be civil."

Adelaide left, shooing the serving girl in front of her.

Rydell, who had watched Adelaide in silence but with a gleam of curiosity in his eyes, nodded toward the departed hostess. "Are you sure about our civility? I have sensed some hostility in you this afternoon."

Judith poured a bit of hot water into the china pot and swirled it about before pouring the water into the empty bowl, resisting the urge to dump it into his lap. She then opened the tea chest and spooned leaves into the china pot. "And why should I not be hostile toward someone who is trying to both seduce me and ruin my family simultaneously?"

His mouth gave a sly twist. "I am not trying to ruin your family."

"Even though that appears to be the case."

"Appearances can most definitely be deceiving."

"Almost always. You, for instance, have been attempting to appear the reformed rake, without much success."

"I can assure you I am in no way reformed."

Pursing her lips, Judith added more hot water to the pot and replaced the lid. "And before we arrived, we were discussing Edmund's vowels. Do you or do you not hold most of his debts?"

"To be precise, At Wheel's End holds the debts."

"Of which you are the owner."

"Part owner. Recent acquisition. *After* the majority of those debts had been incurred." Rydell took a deep breath and twisted his torso a bit. "And Edmund, despite what he may have told you, has incurred substantial debt at several locations throughout the city."

"His shipping investments—"

"Are not ours."

"He said that he met—"

"One meets many people at a gaming hell. We do not screen our clientele for their legitimacy. That is not our concern."

"He said you encouraged him toward particular businessmen.”

Rydell paused and placed a pastry, a meat pie, and a small bit of jam on the plate in front of him. He picked up a pot of clotted cream, peering at it. “This is pink.”

“It is flavored with dried raspberries, which she grinds into a powder.”

“Curious.”

“But tasty. Try some.”

He did, dolloping a mound onto the plate and tasting it hesitantly. “Hm.”

Judith rested the strainer over a cup and poured the tea, then moved to the second cup. “Edmund.”

Rydell leaned back against his chair. “Your stepson has some intriguing proclivities. Not unusual in a young man who has lost the guidance of a father. He is exploring his world and its possibilities. He is also rather injudicious about when and where he indulges those.”

She set a cup and saucer near his plate. “This sounds as if you are changing the subject.”

He reached for the milk, pouring a few drops into the tea. “Not at all. His proclivities include a fondness for odd wagers as well as other . . . unusual activities.”

Judith froze, then slowly replaced the teapot on the tray. “He has betrayed Margaret?”

Rydell cleared his throat as he stirred his tea. “Not . . . in the sense you mean. He does not bed other women.”

“Then what do you—”

“He likes to watch. Others.”

Judith felt bile rise in her throat. “Does this affect his finances?”

“Not to any great degree, although he does pay for—”

“Perhaps we should focus on his debts.”

Rydell hid a smile with a sip of tea. “His shipping investments in that Triangle Trade company happened because he bet the owner that he could guess the number of ships currently set and ready for loading, without visiting the docks themselves."

Judith paused in adding sugar to her tea. She blinked, trying to register what she had just heard. "That is . . . madness."

"Indeed. And, yes, I introduced them, as they both had expressed a desire to play roulette, which is—as you might infer from the name of the establishment—our primary gaming option. We recently brought over two more wheels from Paris. As the afternoon progressed, they began to bet against each other as well as against the wheel. Edmund suggested the ships bet. The owner, who recognized Edmund for the fool he is, had been down on the docks earlier that afternoon. He took the bet, with the wager being Edmund's sizeable investment in three of his ships."

Judith set the sugar bowl down with a clink, staring at Rydell. "And if the owner had lost?"

"Proceeds from two cargos current waiting for unloading."

She closed her eyes. "And Edmund did not hear the hint in that?"

Rydell shook his head. "With the amount of ale in his gut, I doubt he would have heard cannon fire."

"Have all his bets been that outrageously spectacular?"

Rydell shrugged one shoulder. "Not all. He started with smaller wagers, for which he could easily pay. But he escalated quickly. The more he won, the more he bet—"

"And the more he lost."

Rydell gave a quick nod. "Indeed. And he would take no advice from me, Sir Rory, or any of the more experienced gamblers. He owes money to two other hells. And many of his substantial bets were placed at White's. Horses. Society affairs. Who would speak first on a given day at Parliament. He once bet on how low a top hat set on an earl's forehead. How long a particular gambler could balance a pint of ale on his head. They are on the wager book there, if you would like to—" He stopped, then took a bite of one of the pastries. "If you would like to ask one of the other members to check for you. I am fairly sure

Edmund would not tell you the truth about it, and I can see you do not entirely trust me. Perhaps Lord Blackwell."

Judith folded her hands in her lap, staring at the array of food before her, suddenly not nearly as hungry as she had been when she sat down. Anxiety about meeting Rydell had kept her from luncheon, but the treats before her now appeared tasteless. *What a devilish web!* Rydell was correct; she did not completely trust him on this. But she heard enough truth in his statements—statements she could check with other sources—that she knew Edmund's own deceit still had not been cleared away. Nor had the question that had launched this inquiry been answered. Still gazing down at the tea service, she whispered, "Why do you think—"

"Because he thought it would keep me from calling in his debts."

Her head snapped up, eyebrows arched.

Rydell swallowed a bite. "You were going to ask about why Edmund had introduced us, were you not?"

Judith nodded.

"You have money from your husband's estate?"

The irony did not escape her, and she grimaced. "Not as much as I did. I surrendered a great deal back to the estate to help with his . . . obligations."

"Ah. So he achieved his aim, only in a different direction than he had intended."

"I do not think he realized how I would react to his situation."

"Then he does not know you as well as he thinks, if he believed you would be a passive participant in your family's demise."

Judith finally took a sip of the now lukewarm tea. "Apparently not." She set down the cup. "You do know I will check your information."

"I expected no less. I will be glad to provide the name of the shipping—"

"I have it." When his eyebrows arched, she shrugged one shoulder. "Edmund did not realize I would tear into our accounts with the fury of a panther. He had not thought to hide anything before I ripped into his study. Invoices. Duplicates of his wagers. Receipts of payments. Invoices. All in his desk and not in the least hidden."

"Then I suspect he is fortunate that those ships went down carrying only crops and rum on their return to England instead of their cargo out of Africa."

Judith tasted bile again, but looked up at the unexpected awareness, oddly pleased that he had recognized that. "Indeed. His father had fought in the colonies. He had seen slavery up close. And despised it. Spoke out against it. If he had known his son would ever be involved, he would have disowned him." She took a nibble of a small biscuit, her gaze on her plate again. "I am a dowager with no legal power in any of this, and he took comfort in that as he deceived me. Edmund may not have realized exactly how miserable I could make his and Margaret's lives." She swallowed, the lump hard in her throat.

"But he is finding out."

"I suspect so." She gave a slight smile. "He keeps looking at me as if I have grown two heads." She pushed her teacup away and looked into Rydell's eyes. Even laced with obvious pain, those blue eyes entranced her. "Why is it men always underestimate women? Treat them as if they are part of the furniture?"

The smirk returned. "Because they are fools who do not recognize how truly remarkable women can be. How strong and powerful. How determined."

"And you do?"

"You will find, Lady Sculthorpe, *that* is an advantage rakehells and rogues have over other men. Most of us adore women. We not only take great pleasure in their sweet scents and soft skin but their conversations, the power they wield when their husbands are not paying attention. It is part of our charm."

"And how you managed to seduce so many."

"Enjoying the physical company of the fairer sex is only the beginning."

"I really do despise that phrase."

He tilted his head. "'The fairer sex'?"

"Yes."

"Why?"

"It implies we are kinder and weaker than men. We are not."

"Are you saying women are cruel?"

"We can be, even more so than men at times. And you are about to witness exactly how cruel I can be."

"How so?"

"You may be less to blame in this than Edmund implied, but others are not. And if I have to go to war to save my family, I will gladly do so, no matter the consequences."

⇶❯❯❯❮❮❮⇷

MARK HESITATED, STUDYING Judith, the set of her jaw, the dark expression that clouded her face. He had no doubt how seriously she took her own declaration—and at first, he thought she intended to turn her cruel streak toward him. Now, not so much. "Exactly what do you have planned, my cruel lady?"

Her mouth jerked, an attempted smile that failed miserably. "In all your worldly travels, have you ever come across a female wolf with cubs?"

Mark's eyebrows arched at the image. "I have. In one of my journeys to the American colonies. Do you see yourself in that way?"

She gave a quick nod. "Do you remember me telling you I believe all children to be precious?"

"It is seared into my mind." An image of Olivia flashed through his thoughts, but he pushed it away.

"That includes Edmund. And Daniel. Although we both have referred to Edmund as my stepson, I do not, in truth, see him as my husband's son alone. Nor Daniel. They are *my* sons as well. I married their father when Edmund had barely turned four. Daniel not even a year old. I am the only mother they remember, and I could not care more about them had I birthed them. And someone has tried to ruin them, ruin my family." Her eyes narrowed. "And if I have it in my power, I will destroy them, make them suffer until the day they die."

Mark believed her, every word. "So what is your plan?"

She paused and sipped her tea. "First, determine exactly how errant my son has been. You have helped with that, but I need a great deal more verification. Second, find out without a doubt who the miscreants are and what they have done. From there, I will examine what is within my power to wreak vengeance."

The calmness with which Judith made these pronouncements both unsettled and intrigued Mark. "Can I presume you no longer consider me one of those miscreants?"

Her mouth pursed a moment. "Let us say that I find your side of the tale somewhat more believable than Edmund's." Her expression smoothed and she took a bite of a small cress sandwich. "But I must ask. Why did you call in his debts?"

"A business decision, not a personal or social one. When I reviewed the accounts of the establishment before I bought in, it became clear that he had amassed debts greater by far than his annual income, and I knew his investments and possessions would begin to tumble next, especially when I discovered his debts to other organizations. Prudence dictated collecting while time remained on our side."

"Is that why you agreed to meet me?"

Mark shifted in his chair. "Partially. I was curious as to Edmund's motives. But you also intrigued me."

"How so?"

"Your reputation."

Her eyebrows arched and a smile played on her lips. "You mean as a wanton harlot."

Mark laughed, then groaned as his ribs ached.

"My apologies."

He grinned at her. "No need. Laughter may make my ribs sore, but it is good for my spirit. And not much has been these last few weeks." He paused for a sip, then went on. "According to my mother—and others—you came out of mourning like a racehorse freed from its stall. Balls, soirees, long discussions at Gunter's with some of the most prominent members of the *ton*. Visits to the Royal Society lectures. Afternoon calls on friends you had not visited in months. Everyone believed your goal was remarriage, but after a year and no acceptance of potential suitors—even turning down some admirable prospects—you seemed more keen simply to enjoy life than improve your situation. You are known to take lovers, with no obvious confirmation as to who any of them are. The mystery that remains woven in their certainties makes the *ton* most intrigued and speculative. And rather gossipy, if I may add. You are fascinating to those who conform to all social guidelines."

Her eyes gleamed as she ate a few more bites. "Indeed? I had no idea anyone paid that close attention."

"Bollocks. You know it and you adore it."

This time her laugh sounded genuine. "I have to admit I did. I do."

"And you would have continued had Edmund not pissed on it all. Another reason I despise what he has done."

She focused on him. "And why is that?"

"Because obnoxious bets aside, after only one dance, I truly wanted to know more about you. And to bed you, had the opportunity arisen."

Her eyes widened, the pupils dilating. "Somewhat presumptuous, do you not think?"

"Not at all. I had already made plans for our paths to cross often."

"By attending more balls with your mother?"

"As I suspected encounters in the theater would be more scarce, I intended to court you."

Her gaze turned sharp for a moment, then softened slowly. "And if I were not interested?"

He reached for her hand. She did not offer it but nor did she resist as he took it, holding it between both his own. "Then I would have had to convince you that the two of us have far more in common than we have with the young waifs and pinks of the Beau Monde. Experience that could make our time together enticing, arousing, and memorable."

She bit her lower lip. "You are not suggesting marriage."

He released her hand and leaned back. "No. Which I believe is something else we have in common. An extended courtship is allowable, as some of the patronesses of Almack's can attest."

She laughed, a low chuckle that sent a shot of heat into his chest. "You are quite incorrigible. Like a boy who can never quite surrender his toys."

"But *my* toys, dear lady, make a great deal more money."

Judith hesitated, a finger circling the rim of her teacup. "Did you really go to the Americas?"

Mark blinked, startled at the change in topic. After a moment, he nodded. "I did. And I plan to return. My father and uncle had their own involvement with a transportation company. I went several times on my father's behalf, and after my uncle's death, my cousin Gordon and I went over to survey that part of the company—and the country. We traveled through the colonies, down to the West Indies. I came home. Gordon stayed for almost ten years. Why do you ask?"

She pushed a sandwich around on her plate. "Edmund—my Edmund, the fifth earl—fought in the colonies." She gave a dismissive wave with one hand. "He was not the earl yet. Second son. Expected to always . . ." Her silence lingered a moment, then she took a deep breath. "He changed . . . he said it changed him. He couldn't sleep. Nightmares. I always wondered what he had been like bef—whether it was the Americas that changed him, or the fighting."

"It was the war." Mark's voice caught in his throat, sounding like a rusty wheel. He cleared it as he stared at the wall behind the table. "It changes men."

"Did it change you?"

He looked back at her, fear lingering in the back of his mind. How far would her questions take him? "Yes."

"Is it why you have only had one mistress since your return?"

CHAPTER TWELVE

Monday, 25 July 1814
Le salon de thé d'Adélaïde, Whitehall
Four in the afternoon

JUDITH WATCHED AS everything about Mark Rydell grew still. His usually expressive face, his often-fidgety fingers, the leg that had been bouncing under the table for the past half hour. His pupils dilated, making his eyes dark and a bit menacing.

But she did not withdraw the question. Instead, as his silence continued, she decided to up the ante. "Because one hears rumors of many kinds. You, too, returned from war a changed man. You roam at night. You acquired a single mistress, an actress, instead of a string of noble lovers as you did before you served. And now that your mistress has died, you are making plans to move into the house you purchased for her. Alone. With only a few servants."

Rydell pushed his chair away from the table. "Am I to presume that our business concerning your son has reached its conclusion?" He pushed down on the cane, as if to stand.

Judith took a deep breath, watching his face as she grasped his arm. The tension of his muscles beneath her palm told her exactly how far she had stepped over the line. "No. Please stay. I will press no more about anything that does not concern Edmund. But I hope you will listen to my reasons for asking. I will require no answers, if you will only listen."

After a moment, Rydell scooted his chair back under the table. "I will listen."

She released his arm, then hesitated as Adelaide poked her head around the door. "Do you need anything, my friends?"

Judith shook her head, and the hostess vanished. She gazed over the display of food, most of which remained untouched. "I am afraid we are wasting this delicious array of treats."

His face softened. "We have had other concerns."

"We have indeed." She pushed her teacup away and faced him. "After I found out about our loss of funds, I have not trusted Edmund to tell me the complete truth, a skepticism that has proven accurate time and again, including today. I do not understand why he cannot lay all the events out in the open, but he apparently believes I will think him less a fool if I do not realize the extent of his mistakes." She sniffed. "Although why he should care about what I think, I do not know."

"You are his mother."

She chuckled. "If that is the case, then it is something he should have been concerned about *prior* to diving into the deep end of his desires. However, since I did not trust him, I have spent my time talking to others. Blackwell. Servants. Guards at other gaming hells—"

Rydell's mouth twitched. "That must have come as rather a surprise."

She grinned. "More for them than for me, apparently."

"No doubt."

"I went with guineas in my pockets and questions on my lips."

"And what did you learn?"

"That guineas open many a door and surprises loosen many a tongue."

"But what did you learn?"

She peered closer at his face, waiting to see his response. "That I was not the only one asking questions about Edmund and his wagers."

His eyes gleamed but he remained silent.

"I went asking questions about you as the holder of his debts but found you had been there before me, asking questions about Edmund and his debts other than those of your club. And me. I was told that the night Miss Ashley died, you took your grief about her betrayal with Shropshire to the boxing ring, only to discover information about Edmund that sent you into the Rookeries in search of a particular person. A search that"—she gestured up and down at his torso—"led you into a bit of trouble on your own."

The gleam remained. So did his silence.

"Was it worth it?"

He nodded. "It was."

"You will not share this with me?"

"It will not be easy to hear."

"The past few days, I have discovered that my son pays to watch unusual sexual encounters, makes bets the king could not cover about ludicrous things, and believes I am an ogre who could skin him alive. Yet you believe what you have found will be harder for me to absorb?"

He tilted his head to one side. "Possibly."

"Tell me anyway."

"Edmund is being blackmailed."

Judith's chest tightened, and her voice fell to a whisper. "How so?"

"The holder of several of his debts, one Vincent Atkinson, convinced Edmund they could be resolved if he 'procured' a particular item from Devonshire."

Judith breath caught. "The vase."

Rydell nodded. "The vase."

Judith put a hand over her mouth as she fought to catch her breath.

This was indeed worse.

Tears stung her eyes. All the *ton* knew about the disappearance of a Wedgewood vase from the Duke of Devonshire's collection. Reportedly the design of Joseph Flaxman, the priceless vase had been a cherished part of the duke's family heirlooms. It had vanished after a grand ball and had been the talk of the Beau Monde ever since. Rumors had flown that it had been stolen by someone close to Devonshire, despite the *ton's* obvious preference it be a servant or other underling, which had been the first assumption. Even the mere suspicion that the thief came from within their own ranks had horrified the *ton*. Such a thief, if caught, would face dire consequences for himself and his family, socially if not legally.

"Do you think Edmund truly stole it?"

Mark stilled, on finger tracing along the edge of his saucer.

"So you do not."

His eyes narrowed. "Atkinson has intimated that *he* has it. He has also hinted that he has resolved your stepson's debt to him."

"However . . ."

"He is demanding more money from Edmund, ransom money, if you will, or Atkinson will spread the word among the *ton* that Edmund is the thief. But I believe he is holding something else over Edmund's head, although I am not sure what that is. Whatever it is, Edmund has acquiesced because of it. Atkinson has a go-between who is gathering the money and delivering it."

She lowered her hand as the news settled in her mind alongside all the other shocks about her son. "So no matter whether Edmund is guilty, Atkinson has set it so that he will appear so, the truth be damned." A realization settled over her and she stared at Mark. "This is why you went into the Rookeries."

"I wanted to verify the rumor. The go-between is a young man who lives there. He collects the money and delivers it to Atkinson."

"Delivers it where?"

"Atkinson is the owner of a small and exclusive but profitable club in Bloomsbury."

"You have been there."

"Many times. I consider him a competitor."

"So it would be in your interest to help me destroy him."

Rydell gave a low laugh. "I would be most interested in seeing you try, although I'm not sure that's possible. His clientele includes some of the most elite of the aristocracy."

She nodded, resolve settling over her. "You provide me with a list of that clientele, and I will do the rest."

He reached for her hand and brought it to his lips. "I will send over a list tomorrow."

Judith closed her fingers around his, squeezing gently, loving the feel of his skin against hers. "Meanwhile, I will plot. And I dearly wish an audience with your mother."

Tuesday, 26 July 1814
Embleton House
Ten in the morning

MARK RESTED AMIDST his nest of pillows, his eyes on the dying fire opposite, his mind on Judith—and his family. The last five days had been a whirlwind.

Against all odds, his brother Matthew had found a bride, a dowager countess who had agreed to a marriage of convenience that would benefit them both. He had met her on the previous Saturday and squired her around the park the next day. On Monday, yesterday, Mark and Phyllida had met the lady—one Sarah Ainsworth, Lady Creswell—and today the three Rydells would be escorting her to the park yet again, a show of familial solidarity for the sudden betrothal. And tonight, he and Matthew were to meet with yet another Bow Street Runner, this time about Sarah's relative, her late husband's heir, a nefarious man with a cruel and avaricious reputation.

Mark despised him already.

He took a deep breath, contemplating the coming day. His ribs ached and his muscles remained sore and stiff, despite a continued improvement, and sometimes a sudden movement reminded him that his insides had not fully recovered from their pummeling either. He glanced at the bottle of laudanum on his dressing table, the temptation tugging at him. The willow bark tea continued to give him some relief from the pain, but he had not been able to rest as he should. Sleep, even with nightmares, could prove beneficial at this stage.

Yet he dared not. He needed to keep his senses alert. It would not do to be seen stumbling about in the park as if he were a drunkard, much less meet with a runner. And he had far too much to do to laze about abed. Yet here he lay, annoyed. At himself. At his circumstances. At the world in general.

Mark shifted under the covers, trying to stretch his legs. He had achieved a few tasks this morning. After breakfast in his room and using the bed tray for a desk, he had made the list of Atkinson's clientele for Judith and sent it over by messenger. He had sent for Clara, meeting with her—with Howe standing in the open door as chaperone—about the progress on the Bloomsbury house. He had been impressed with the preciseness of her information, and he sent her on her way with more money and instructions. He had also sent Howe to the jewelers with the bag from Stella's room for an appraisal.

So the morning had not been a complete waste.

Mark made circles with his feet under the covers, virtually the only parts of his body that did not ache when moved. His restlessness made him itch to be up and moving, pain be damned. He craved seeing Judith again, and his fingers curled, remembering the way she had squeezed his hand the day before and the strength in her arm when she had grasped his, urging him to stay seated. His mind went over her every expression, including the one of shock when he spoke of the blackmail, followed by the determined resolve that turned her face hard and her eyes narrow. It was as if each minute element of her being had entranced him.

Bloody hell, how he wanted her! His loins tightened as his eyes drifted shut, his mind creating a vision of his hands in her hair, pulling her closer, his lips on hers. Not that his body would cooperate with such a move at the moment . . .

Which is why Mark looked at the laudanum bottle again. Perhaps a small dose—

A rap on his door brought him back to earth, and he let out a sigh. "Enter."

Howe opened the door, a rare smile on his ruddy face. He had the bag of jewels tucked under one arm and held out a paper to Mark. "Twice what you expected, my lord. Mr. Kingston was pleased but not surprised to see them." The smile faded and a lock of ginger-colored hair fell over the man's forehead. "Apparently, he had heard about Miss Ashley's unfortunate demise."

Mark glanced at the offer. "Apparently, the entirety of London has heard about Miss Ashley's 'unfortunate demise.'" He handed the paper back. "Good. Tuck it and the bag away somewhere in the dressing room—obviously not out in the open. I'll take it to the shop in a few days." He then gestured to the dressing table with one hand. "And take that blasted laudanum away before I drink it in my sleep. Hide it so that I do not have to look at it all the time." He took a deep breath. "You know Matthew wants me to join him and Mother on this absurd excursion to the park this afternoon?"

Howe pushed back the lock of hair and nodded.

"I wish to write a few letters before you have to drag my ass out of bed for dressing." He pointed to the bed tray, now sitting on the bench at the end of his bed. "Hand me that, along with quill, ink, and foolscap from the escritoire."

"Of course, sir." Howe disappeared into the dressing room a moment, then returned and fetched the items Mark had requested, placing them on tray. Helping Mark into a more upright position, he settled the tray across Mark's lap, then scooped the laudanum into his palm. "Would you like anything to eat?"

Mark shook his head. "If I continue to lay about like some wounded pigeon I will be as fat and useless as one before long."

Howe sputtered, glancing down at his own somewhat rounded form. "My-my lord, I do not think—"

Mark chuckled at the suddenly red-faced valet. "It is not the weight, Howe. It happens to most men sooner or later. Even Matthew is beginning to acquire a bit of a belly, and I am sure someday I will be as round as a king. Until then, I am merely cheap. I do not wish to have a whole new wardrobe made."

"Ah." Howe pointed at the door. "I-I should go."

"Please do. Return at two so that I can get dressed for this bloody outing."

Nodding, Howe left, and Mark began to write his first letter, to his business partner, Sir Rory Campbell. If Judith planned to declare war on some of the *ton's* gentlemen, Rory needed to be forewarned. Because Mark had little doubt that whatever Judith intended, a lot of their own clients would be impacted as well.

CHAPTER THIRTEEN

Monday, 1 August 1814
Sculthorpe Manor, London
Half-past ten in the morning

D O I HAVE *the right to ruin a man's family—or many families—just because he tried to ruin mine?*

The question had haunted Judith since her meeting with Lord Mark Rydell. Now she stared at the stack of missives on her escritoire, dozens of letters, sealed and waiting for her scheme to take flight.

Yet she had not sent them. And something deep inside told her not to. For the hundredth time, she fingered the list from Mark. Atkinson's clientele. Each and every one of the men was nefarious, and she had spent the past few days gathering proof of their outrageous peccadillos, proof that would keep their wives on edge and the *ton's* gossips busy as bees. Proof that had been carefully locked away in her escritoire, in a drawer that now felt like Pandora's box.

Did she dare open it?

At first, blackmail for blackmail had seemed the easiest way to ruin Atkinson, to resolve his hold on Edmund. Convince his clientele to abandon the club. Bankrupt the man. It had taken so little—a few quid and a sweet smile, in most cases—to persuade servants, merchants, and paramours to give up details that could shatter reputations and spread scandal.

How fragile we all are . . .

She had known corruption and more than a little depravity

ran rampant through the Beau Monde, but she had not realized the widespread nature or depth of it. And Edmund was hardly the only one Atkinson held at ransom. He had convinced at least two others that he would ruin them with tales of the stolen vase should they not pay him. Between them, they were paying Atkinson a king's fortune.

Four days. That's all it had taken to gather her own material for blackmail. But now Judith's very soul twisted with the idea.

There has to be another way.

Her mind settled, Judith stood, scooped up the letters, and dropped them onto the fireplace grate, where they landed with a whispery *whomp* before crisping as the flames licked at them, curling the edges and tingeing them brown. She watched them burn, an odd peace easing over her.

Judith pivoted and headed downstairs, finding Edmund in his study, his focus on one of the estate ledgers. He looked up, then leaned back in his chair, his eyes narrow. "What do you want now, Mother?"

She dropped into an armchair in front of his desk. "Tell me about Vincent Atkinson."

His jaw went slack.

Judith sighed. "Have you not yet realized there is little that goes on among the *ton* that I do not eventually get word about? I was countess for almost twenty years. Everyone knows me. Most trust me. And anyone with a tale they can't keep to themselves seeks me out. You were only able to keep your errant ways a secret for so long because I was not paying attention. Stop being so surprised by this. And, for god's sake, stop trying to hide anything from me. Now. Did you steal that vase?"

Edmund stared at her, eyes wide.

"Yes or no. It is not a complicated question."

He swallowed hard. "No. I wasn't even at Devonshire's ball when it went missing."

"So why does Atkinson believe he can substitute your debts with extortion?"

Looking down at the ledger, Edmund fingered the quill. "I have no proof I was somewhere else."

"Where were you?"

He remained silent, his eyes on the numbers in front of him.

"A brothel."

A nod.

"Watching women."

Edmund hesitated, continuing to stare at the page. "Yes and no."

Judith blinked as the implication sank in. Mark Rydell had said, "watching," but had not been specific. "Watching but not women."

A single, brief nod as color left his cheeks.

As Rydell had said. "This is the hold he has on you. Two-fold. You cannot tell Bow Street about the vase because of the second part. You pay him or he lets everyone know you stole the vase and prefer men. You might survive one but not both."

"I love Margaret." His words came on a bare whisper.

"I'm sure you do."

"She is with child."

"I know many women like her."

Edmund finally looked up. "I beg your pardon?"

Judith's heart softened, aching for this son. "She is hardly the only woman who will have children with a man who prefers . . . others. Does she know?"

He shook his head.

"Watching would be scandalous but not illegal. Have you broken the law?"

He shook his head.

"Where did these visits take place?"

He named an establishment unfamiliar to her, but she knew she would never forget the name.

"Does Atkinson have actual proof of your visits to this 'salon'?"

"No."

"Are you willing to tell Bow Street about the vase?"

"Mother, I cannot. If I do, Atkinson will tell them about . . ." He focused on his fingers again.

"The men."

"Yes."

"Why do you not let me take care of that part?"

He looked up, his eyes filled with confusion. "How—I mean, you cannot—"

"Do you trust me?"

Edmund hesitated.

"Have I ever failed you before when you needed my help?"

"No."

Judith gave a quick nod and stood. "Do not pay him again. When that young man from the Rookeries returns, have the servants bring him to me."

Edmund's mouth fell loose again.

She strode to the door but glanced back at him. "One day, you will learn. Dragons rule the world."

Monday, 1 August 1814
Embleton House
One in the afternoon

MARK GLANCED AROUND his bedchamber—his *former* bedchamber—more as a final farewell than to see if he had forgotten anything. "Shipshape and Bristol fashion" had been Howe's pronouncement earlier that morning, as the last of the trunks and crates had been hauled down the backstairs and loaded onto the wagon waiting in the rear courtyard. The phrase amused Mark, as the young and rotund Howe had never been near a naval ship in any of his few years on the planet. But his meticulous valet had been correct. Even the mattress on the bed where Mark had slept since childhood had been curled away from the edges, awaiting a good thrumming as the staff prepared to turn this room into a space for guests.

The Bloomsbury house too had been declared ready for its new occupant the day before—most of the repairs complete and staff in place. Howe would double as butler for the time being, and the new cook and housemaid were working well with Clara. Mark had waited until after Matthew's marriage to Sarah—which had taken place the previous Saturday—to announce the move to his mother, although it had never been exactly a secret to her or anyone else in the household.

The wedding preparations had provided some cover and explanations for all the activity of packing, but the now-*dowager* duchess, Phyllida, Lady Embleton, had never been blind or deaf to her children. She had become even more aware since, after his unfortunate encounter in the Rookeries, attempts to conceal his ongoing nightmares had been abandoned. And Mark had become increasingly exasperated at how the entire household stared at him come the dawn.

Mark tapped his cane on the floor. He no longer relied on it—he had certainly been well enough to stand beside Matthew as best man in his polished and pressed military regalia—but found he'd grown accustomed to having it handy. He took a deep breath, then turned, closed the door, and headed down the front stairs to one final luncheon with his family.

Yet he stopped in the doorframe, his gaze taking in the almost vacant space. The dining room table held only two place settings. His brother's place at the head of the table, as well as his new bride's at the opposite end, remained unoccupied—as did most of the others. His mother sat in a chair to the right of the duke's; an empty one awaited across from her.

"Where is everyone?"

Phyllida focused on a letter in her left hand as she sipped from a glass of white wine in her right. "The boys are off to . . . something to do with horses. Matthew and Sarah are meeting two of our stewards for luncheon in town." She glanced up at him. "To be truthful, I am grateful. You and I have a lot to discuss, and I'd rather the rest of the family not hear."

A deep feeling of misgiving tightened Mark's gut. Perhaps he should have skipped this meal as well. He pulled out the chair and sat, leaning his cane against the chair next to his as a footman appeared at his side, pouring wine. "As long as it does not have anything to do with a ball or another wedding."

Phyllida laid the note aside and nodded to Stephens, who stood patiently next to the buffet. The man disappeared through a servant's door at the back of the room. "No, it does not. Although you will attend the Blackwell ball."

Mark held back a sigh of frustration. Instead he sipped his wine, then muttered, "I am much too old."

"Your age is irrelevant."

"And when is this unctuous ball?"

"The nineteenth. A Friday. And you will not insult Lord and Lady Blackwell by refusing to attend. You will gather me here before the event and we will go in the ducal carriage." She put a finger on the note and moved on from what she obviously considered a settled issue. "Judith Lovelace, Lady Sculthorpe, has invited me to visit her this afternoon."

Stephens emerged from the servants' door with a tray holding two bowls of soup. He placed one in front of Phyllida, then Mark. A fish and potato concoction that smelled heavenly. He hoped his new cook had the talent of the Embleton one. "Why?"

"She does not say. She asks that I come at four."

"Are you going?"

"I am. I admit I am rather curious."

"Are you not afraid to be seen in the company of a—what did you call her—ah, yes, a 'damnable hussy'?"

Phyllida sniffed, then tasted her soup. "She is still a member of the *ton*." She paused for wine. "And I have been hearing some most intriguing rumors about her."

"Oh?"

Phyllida set down her glass, scowling at him. "Do not play

coy with me. I happened to know a letter for you arrived at the same time as this one, and that you have been down with the servants, asking all kinds of questions while you pretended to be moving."

"I am, in truth, moving, Mother."

She gave a dismissive wave. "But you were not, however, discussing your relocation with the servants."

"I attempted to hire most of them away from this house. They would have been tempted but for fear of repercussions from you."

"Nonsense. They adore Matthew, despite his surly nature, and most have already developed a fondness of Sarah. What nefarious request did Lady Sculthorpe have of you?"

"She wanted to know the name of the Bow Street Runner who has been looking into Stella's murder."

Phyllida Rydell froze, wine glass halfway to her lips. After a moment, she set it down. "Intriguing. The rumors I have encountered say that she has been spending a good deal of money—money I do not believe her family has at this time—gathering reprehensible information about various male members of the *ton*. Apparently in some misguided attempt to salvage her stepson's reputation." She lowered her chin and peered at Mark. "You are not involved in these efforts, are you?"

Mark scooped up the last spoonful of his soup and focused on keeping his expression stoic. "We both know the activities of the *ton's* gentlemen are usually above Bow Street's purview. I cannot image how the two would cross paths."

"Hm." His mother motioned for Stephens to remove the bowls, remaining silent as the soup disappeared and an entrée of lamb and potatoes appeared, the fragrance speaking of pungent summer herbs. The white wine goblets vanished, replaced with broader glasses, which Stephens filled with a deep-red Bordeaux. "I also hear the name of Mr. Vincent Atkinson being bandied about."

Mark stared at the wine, his fingers caressing the stem. "I doubt—"

"I know who he is. What he does. With that degenerate establishment of his."

"If you plan to meet with her this afternoon, why do you not ask her?"

"I absolutely will."

"I would not think otherwise."

Phyllida paused as she cut into the lamb and took a small bite, chewing thoughtfully. "I suspect that Lady Sculthorpe and I do have one thing in common."

"And what is that?"

"We would do almost anything to protect our families." She dabbed the corner of her mouth with her serviette. "I have been a duchess for a great many years. She a countess. It would be unwise for anyone—*anyone*—to challenge that."

A truer statement Mark had never heard.

Chapter Fourteen

Monday, 1 August 1814
Sculthorpe Manor
Quarter past four in the afternoon

JUDITH STOOD BY the fireplace of the receiving room, relishing the warmth from the low fire in the grate. The unusually cool temperatures, which had started with a winter so frigid the Thames had frozen over, had continued, even into August, and this Monday had turned surly, with a harsh breeze bringing in low clouds and a chilled mist off the river.

Yet Lady Embleton, Phyllida Rydell, now the dowager duchess following her son Matthew's recent marriage, had accepted Judith's invitation, arriving a few minutes after four in a snug linen-and-wool afternoon gown, the deep-purple color accented by a black collar, black stripes on the sleeves, and embroidered black spirals around the hem. A small black bonnet topped her gray-and-blonde coiffure, and curls of black and purple ribbons circled it and flowed down the back of her gown. Black turned most women pale and wan, but it seemed to highlight the rosy glow in Lady Embleton's cheeks and emphasize the pure blue of her eyes.

So like her son's.

As the butler announced her, Lady Embleton swept into the room, her hem weighted with moisture. Judith greeted her, then motioned toward an armchair near the fire. "You might be more comfortable here. This room seems to have held a chill most of the year." She looked at the butler. "Please bring tea for Lady

Embleton."

He nodded and left as the dowager duchess settled in the armchair, snuggling her reticule in her lap. "Thank you."

Judith sat in a matching armchair on the other side of the grate. "I appreciate you accepting my invitation."

Lady Embleton gave a slight wave of her fingers. "Lady Sculthorpe, if my son's descriptions of you are accurate, then I suspect we share a disdain for the trivial niceties of Society conversations. So let us speak plainly. Why am I here?"

Judith repressed a burst of laughter. "Indeed. I suspect you are correct. I have invited you here because I need an ally and advice, and of all the women I know or know about, I believe you would be the most helpful, if you are willing."

"I will not help you with that vulgar bet concerning you and my son."

Judith's eyebrows arched, her chin lowering. "Nor would I ask you to."

"Then what are we discussing?"

"Mr. Vincent Atkinson's attempts to ruin my family—and those of at least two other men. I believe he has declared himself to be at war with the Beau Monde and is in the process of using our own foolish natures as ammunition against us. He is, in particular, mired in competition with your son's new venture, and he hopes to further his own ambitions by smearing Lord Mark's name as well as that of the others."

"And what do you wish to do?"

"I think the *ton* should fight back. More precisely, I think you and I should fight back. These men are our family and find themselves unable to combat Atkinson on their own. But they are men. I believe you and I have other resources at our disposal."

Lady Embleton sat completely still, her gaze wavering from Judith's face only when the tea arrived. Both women remained silent as the butler prepared and served it. Lady Embleton sipped, still watching Judith, as the butler left the room, pulling the door closed.

"You have a plan." It was not a question.

Judith nodded. "I do."

"It involves my son."

"It does. Lord Mark's new venture puts him in direct competition with Mr. Atkinson, and I believe this can be useful."

The duchess's eyes narrowed. "Competition. How so?"

"Lord Mark is part owner of a gambling establishment called At Wheel's End."

Lips pursed. The cup and saucer clinked. One hand fisted, opened, fisted. "Why would my son purchase such a business? An aristocrat does not hold employment."

"He claims the purchase was to help a friend become more respectable. And I suspect he intends for his role to be more in ownership and management, not actual day-to-day operations. In addition, while I could not say for sure, I suspect he no longer wishes to be a soldier nor develop a calling to the church. He seems to have a rather independent nature."

A long sigh. "And has since he emerged from the womb. No matter what his father or I did to combat it."

"He suggests obstinance is a family trait."

Her mouth twisted, but the eyes gleamed. Like her son. "He seems to have mastered that as well." She took another sip. "Tell me your plan and how I can help."

Judith smiled and leaned forward, taking up the challenge. For the next half hour, she described Lord Mark and Sir Rory's involvement in At Wheel's End, as well as Vincent Atkinson's machinations against Edmund and the other men in his grasp. She also laid out her investigations into the debts and peccadillos of the *ton's* men, her original plan to use blackmail to bring all this to heel, and her decision not to pursue that course.

Lady Embleton shook her head. "Men and their games. Their love of risk will one day bring us all to our knees. You burned the letters?"

Judith nodded. "I did."

"But not the evidence?"

"No."

Lady Embleton sniffed. "Good. One never knows when such information might prove useful."

Judith's eyebrows arched, but Lady Embleton merely shrugged. "For instance, should we receive word that a man is maltreating his wife, children, or servants."

"Ah. True."

Lady Embleton shifted her reticule. "What do you wish of me?"

As Judith explained her plan to the duchess, Lady Embleton's hard expression softened even as her eyes narrowed with apparent curiosity. A dozen questions later, and Mark's mother gave her a single nod. "I believe this will achieve the success you seek. I, for one, would prefer my son's name to be less involved with the whole matter, but I have resolved that he will, in some form or fashion, always be a source of concern and indigestion. And the name of the gentleman you need to speak with is Mr. Jeremy Smith. We are agreed that I should set the meeting?"

"I believe so. Mr. Smith is already seeking and providing information about Miss Ashley's death to your sons, whereas this house has had no dealings with Bow Street at all. It will be less suspicious than if he arrived here. My information is that Mr. Atkinson is a cautious man with informants all over the city. And that he is certainly dangerous to cross."

Another sniff. "Arrogant pup. He will be on the watch for men. Not gentle and demure ladies of the *ton*."

"He seems rather dismissive of women." Judith gave a low laugh. "They really have no idea, do they?"

"None. Fools." She stood, and Judith rang for their butler. The door opened promptly, and the man waited with Lady Embleton's cloak. "I will arrange it and send word. I will also speak with our housekeeper and butler about the appropriate rumors."

"Thank you. I will do the same."

As Lady Embleton left, Judith returned to the fire, suddenly aware that the room had grown chillier and her toes were suddenly cold. She held to the mantle as she edged her left slipper toward the grate.

Her left foot. The one he had massaged. Caressed, his fingertips slipping gently up her thigh. Judith closed her eyes, feeling his kiss, the whisper in her ear . . .

I wish to own a part of you.

"You wish to see us, Lady Sculthorpe."

Judith's foot snapped to the floor and she pivoted, blinking. The butler stood in the doorframe, the housekeeper peering around his shoulder. Judith swallowed and motioned them in. "Yes. Please close the door. I need to inform you of a few rumors about the house. Rumors I wish you to spread among the other servants."

They looked at each, eyes wide, then entered.

Tuesday, 2 August 1814
Lord Mark Rydell's Bloomsbury residence
Half-past ten in the morning

MARK CLOSED THE door of his study to reduce the noise from the workmen on the upper floors of the house, then poured another cup of coffee from a setting on a table near the door. While most of the work on the house had been completed, he had discovered upon moving in and rearranging the furniture that a great deal more needed attention. Irritating but necessary, given his plans for the third and fourth floors of the house.

He settled at his desk and began to sort the correspondence before him on the blotter. Many of the correspondents had already found him at this new address, but some of the older mail had been addressed to Stella, arriving after her death from people either unaware of her demise or missives caught in slower mail routes. Jeremy Smith had searched the house in the days following her murder, taking all of her correspondence, so these had appeared later and been left for Mark, who had ignored them during his recovery. Even now, he set those aside while looking to those addressed to him directly, including one from Judith, which he opened first.

The meeting with your mother went well. We have reached a pact, such as those common amongst allies on a battlefield, since we have a mutual aim in mind. We have set a plan in motion, which I will provide more details about later. Meanwhile, do not be startled by anything you hear from your servants. News will break in a few days that will surprise many and rumors will be flying through the ton *in front of it.*

Part of our plan involves me being seen surreptitiously entering your home alone from its back garden tomorrow evening. Would you be willing for that to happen? If so, please send me the safest route you think a certain fair widow of renown would take.

It is also vital that we all attend the Blackwell ball on Fri., 19 Aug. Please plan to escort your mother.

You may also hear from her soon. Part of her involvement will entail setting an appointment with Mr. Jeremy Smith at Embleton House in a few days. If possible, you might consider attending.

I will also need a dear favor from you and Sir Rory prior to the ball. We will discuss this later.

Yours gratefully,
Judith

Mark reread the letter, both amused and intrigued, a smile spreading over his face. She obviously knew about the wager listed in White's book, but most of the *ton* did at this point. The mere thought that she might act on it, that she would come to him here in his own house set his imagination—and his loins—afire with longing. He shifted his rear, adjusting his trousers to accommodate the sudden fullness there.

As he settled back into his chair, Mark realized he had not had such an unexpected arousal in several months. The waif-like debutantes at the endless number of balls his mother had dragged him to over the past season most definitely did not engender such desire. He could not have had less interest in them, often feeling more protective toward them than flirtatious—as if he were their older brother. Or worse, a favorite uncle.

Dear God in heaven, he was getting old.

Even thoughts of Stella had not created such an erotic sense of anticipation, not in many months.

Stella.

Mark took a deep breath. It had been almost three weeks. He had seen no signs that he had contacted the pox from her, and he had examined himself daily, the fear of the disease driving his constant checking. Dr. Oakley had also examined him but told Mark that a firm declaration that he was free of it could not be had for at least a full month without symptoms. However, Dr. Oakley could not confirm Stella had truly contacted the disease— she had no sores or obvious symptoms upon her death. Neither had Mark noticed anything or he would have ceased contact immediately. Dr. Oakley also told him contact did not always mean infection, an attempt to reassure Mark without going into much further detail. With his own knowledge of the disease, however, Mark realized the doctor was being more kind and hopeful than truthful.

You have to tell her.

Judith. The very thought terrified Mark. He knew Judith probably did not have an intimate evening in mind, but such knowledge did not keep his desire at bay—which escalated his reluctance to possibly end their time together on a sour note. He could, of course, welcome Judith into his bedchamber without consummating a sexual act. Mark had long ago learned to behave properly when in the company of women, and his time with Stella had underscored that he did not always end an evening between a woman's legs, no matter how enticing she might be.

But he did love women and loved bedding them, adored how they looked as he brought them to the height of arousal. As he had told his mother, he was far from a monk in mind as well as in deed.

And he truly wanted Judith, in every way possible.

You still have to tell her.

Mark swallowed hard. This would drive him mad. He took a deep breath and pushed Judith out of his mind. Instead, he turned back to the correspondence. The second missive he opened was from Rory, minor details about the financial well-being of the club and the latest *on dit* about some of their clientele. Unlike Atkinson, Rory—and now Mark—did not engage in anything as sordid as blackmail, but they did keep abreast of all the gossip, lest some gamblers got too far in debt to be worthy of ongoing credit. One paragraph in Rory's note did catch his eye.

There is word that a concerted effort is being made to pull Sculthorpe back from the brink. The primary attempts seem to come from his mother, but the estate's managers are also involved. Apparently some property has been sold along with a great number of the fine artworks from their country house. A substantial payment was made here in the last few days by one of them, and I have heard from some of the smaller establishments that they have been paid off entirely. That would leave him only owing Atkinson, who, as we both know, will not relinquish any prey without a battle.

Mark set the note aside, a slight worry nagging at his gut. He hoped Judith knew how dangerous Atkinson could be. If not, he would definitely tell her. Pulling ink, a quill, and two sheets of foolscap from his desk, Mark composed two messages. One to Judith, explaining how and when would be the best time to access the back garden of his house, and one to Rory, acknowledging the information. Then, almost as an afterthought, Mark asked his business partner to stop by White's and make a wager in the betting book.

Setting aside his writing supplies, he finally picked up the letters addressed to Stella. Once again, Mark searched his soul for a modicum of grief for the woman who had been his bedmate for more than four years, the mother of his daughter. But her betrayal had lit afire any affection he had for her. In its place lay a smoldering emptiness, like a house gutted by a fierce conflagration. As almost every remnant of her presence had been removed from this house, so had whatever tenderness he had held for her.

Olivia.

Mark sighed. He had sent condolences to Rose, along with some money, but he had not dared show his face at the house. Not yet. Rose had returned a note of thanks, along with information about Olivia and her latest garden adventures, as well as information about her own health, which had declined again. Afterward, a new resolve had set in about what to do next, thus the newest changes to the house.

No matter what his family thought, he wanted Rose and Olivia here. Here they could be cared for as they deserved.

Mark sat a little straighter and used his paper knife to open the first message to Stella. An overdue bill from the milliner. Of course. The next one was a bill from the butcher, also overdue, and with a rude note. A particularly fragrant one—Mark picked up a whiff of tobacco smoke and cheap cologne—held a plea for marriage. The florid words of the declarations of undying love reminded Mark of a drunken poet, and he noted the signature with amusement before setting it aside for the fireplace. Two more bills and several more love notes awaited. Apparently, the men attending the Haymarket were easily entranced.

Then came the missive that caused Mark to still, a slight chill slipping down his spine. It contained five twenty-pound notes and one line:

If this does not keep your tongue quiet, I will find a permanent solution.

No signature followed, and Mark checked the wax seal

again—plain and flat. But the amount of money stood out, making him remember something Smith had said. He folded it up, included the bank notes, and set it aside as well. Obviously, he would have something to speak with Smith about, in addition to whatever Judith plotted out.

Mark drained the rest of his coffee, his mind caught up in all that needed to be done in the meantime. He pulled the necessary cash from a bottom drawer and sorted it out for Stella's outstanding bills. He wanted to pay these in person, in three cases to confirm they knew about her death, and to make sure that the butcher remained on good terms with the new household staff. A task normally left to the cook, but Mark wanted to get a measure of the man for himself. He folded the cash into each bill, tucked them into his coat along with the threat toward Stella, and stood, ringing for Howe and ordering a cloak and chapeau.

Time for a walk.

CHAPTER FIFTEEN

Wednesday, 3 August 1814
Lord Mark Rydell's Bloomsbury residence
Quarter to eleven in the evening

JUDITH STARED AT the rear façade of the redbrick townhouse, noting that lights still shone through only two windows—one on the third floor and one from a low, ground-floor room, probably the kitchen or housekeeper's sitting room. In her mind, Judith envisioned the woman, harried but catching her breath as she concluded the day's accounts and began plans for the morning. Pulling the hood of her black woolen cloak a bit tighter over her hair, Judith waited in the shadows of the hedge surrounding the back garden and kitchen yard, listening for the slightest sound.

Judith knew exactly the extent of the risk this was. *This is madness.*

But it had to be done. And Judith truly wanted to. Craved it, even.

Despite what the *ton* thought they knew about her, despite the gossipy whispers that circulated whenever she was in a ballroom or the park, nothing could have been proven without a doubt. She and her lovers had been discreet in that way. Any hint that a young man might be injudicious, and he would never find his way to her bed.

This, however, would be openly declaring her liaison with Lord Mark Rydell. There would be no turning back if this went awry. And Judith could not entirely claim this was about her family, about securing their future. Not if she were honest with herself.

Because she wanted him. Her desire for him had deepened the more she had looked into Edmund's business dealings and gambling debts. Rydell had been a thread through it all, and from her distant perspective, she could see that he had done what he could to safeguard her son—not ruin him, as had been claimed— but Edmund had been too foolish for anyone's aid to make much of a difference. Whatever his reasons, Rydell had tried. That she could achieve her aim of being with him while at the same time helping Edmund added a scintillating thrill to this evening's adventure.

Judith shuddered a bit inside the cloak, and not only because of the night's chilled air. She had never engaged in this type of skulking about, and she wondered if this is how blackguards and robbers felt—or maybe illicit lovers destined for a tryst. Shivery, chilled, and anxious, jerking at the tiniest noise.

She found it all rather exhilarating.

The sounds of the night varied distinctly from the ones of the daytime—the distant rattles of hansom cabs, the horses clopping lethargically this time of night. The yowl of a cat. The clunks and clanks of last-minute chores before bed echoing along the mews and alleyways. But all the clamor seemed far away, muffled by a fog that had begun swirling through the streets, moist and gray, carrying with it the smells of the gutters and the river—smoke, horses, tar, and unwashed flesh.

How different from the streets of Mayfair after a ball, with the rush of carriages and the chatter of happy, if somewhat inebriated, voices. This was the London nighttime everyone warned children and young ladies about—everyone from the press to the politicians to the fretful mamas trying to keep their children safe at home.

Judith knew she should be afraid. Instead, she found it allur- ing, almost addictive.

The light in the ground floor window went out. It was time.

Glancing around again, Judith gathered the hem of the cloak and picked her way along a strip of gravel beside a lower hedge that separated the landscaped flora of the garden from the kitchen yard—her destination. As she closed on the house, the gravel gave way to a muddied area around the steps leading down to the ground floor rooms. In the dimmest of light from the moon overhead, she closed her hand around the door's latch and eased it open.

On the other side, Lord Mark Rydell waited, holding a single candle. In only his shirt and trousers, his hair unkempt, he loomed like a sinister presence—except for the gleam in his eyes as he watched her, an expression of pure mischievousness. He put a finger to his lips and motioned her inside. He shut the door behind her, then glanced over his shoulder. When he spoke, his words were slightly louder than she expected, making her jump.

"Did anyone see you?" He pointed down the hall toward the kitchen and mouthed, *Cook is still awake.*

Understanding—she needed to appear secretive but not so much that the servants would not notice—Judith answered in the same volume. "Your neighbor, I think. I saw someone peering out the window. Also two cats, but I doubt they will tell anyone."

"Cats never give away their secrets."

Judith put her fingers to her lips, stifling a giggle. This all felt so deliciously naughty, so different from the discreet visits to her own bedroom, that she could not contain a touch of glee.

Mark pointed upward, taking her elbow. "Come with me."

In silence, they climbed to the third floor of the house, the light of the candle casting stark, dancing shadows on the bare walls of the servants' staircase. Judith tiptoed to keep her boot heels from clicking on the treads, relieved when they entered the corridor with its thick carpet and silk-papered walls. Lord Mark opened a door near the rear of the house and ushered her inside.

His bedchamber. Judith stopped, straightened, and stared. She had never been in a bachelor's rooms before. Even her husband's had been tempered by the tastes and influence of his first wife.

This room, however, looked like the heart of pure masculinity. The bed, wardrobe, and shaving stand had been polished to a fine sheen, the deep grain of the rosewood striking in the way the three pieces matched in design and construction. The rich colors of the curtains and bedcovers held deep reds and browns with an occasional touch of gold. Near the fire grate a single wingback chair with an ottoman waited next to an accent table stacked with books, while one tome lay open on the ottoman, a small, intricately carved wooden block holding the pages down.

A second door near the fireplace remained closed, which Judith assumed led to a dressing room. The golden glow of several lamps flickered and gamboled around the room as the ormolu clock on the mantel gave a gentle chime at the eleventh hour. Lord Mark stepped close to Judith's back, his presence strong and warm as he touched her shoulders, his low voice even softer than the chime. "Let me take your cloak."

She nodded and released the clasp, and he slipped it away from her, disappearing briefly behind that second door as she continued to look around. The heavy bedcovers had been peeled back, and thick, luxurious pillows had been piled up against the arched headboard, which had a center post topped by an acorn-style finial. Judith smiled, wondering exactly how far he was willing to take their charade.

She gave another shiver as she realized exactly how far *she* was willing to go.

He returned, holding his arm out toward the wingback. "Please. Sit." As she did, he scooped up the book and block from the ottoman and placed them next to the clock, then he straddled the ottoman facing her. He leaned forward, bracing his hands on his thighs, which caused the V-neck of his shirt to drop away from his chest, revealing the soft prominence of his collar bone and a few tufts of dark curls. "Now. Explain your plan to me. And tell me what this favor is that you need from Rory and me."

Judith swallowed hard, then glanced at the fire, chewing her lower lip. "They may not work, neither the plan nor the favor.

Vincent Atkinson is not a foolish man."

"But he is an arrogant one, is he not? And that is what you are relying on?"

Judith focused on Lord Mark again, studying his face, which seemed alight with curiosity—eyes wide, eyebrows arched. She nodded. "Mr. Atkinson is holding something over Edmund, beyond the vase. And unlike the theft of the vase, this . . . issue . . . has truly happened. Are you familiar with an establishment, a private salon of sorts, in the Strand, a . . . um"—she swallowed hard—"a molly house run by an organization called the White Stallion."

All curiosity drained from Mark's face along with the color as he straightened on the ottoman, his voice hoarse. "What do you know of this place?"

She took a deep breath. "Edmund has been frequenting it—"

"Bloody hell—"

Judith put up her hand. "He says he only watches."

"Of course he does. Please tell me you have not been there yourself."

"No, of course not. Even if I wanted to, I would not dare."

"Do not. The owners are dangerous. Edmund is more of a fool than I believed."

"He promises he will stop."

"Of course he does. Judith—"

"He insists there is no proof. That Atkinson has only heard rumors. If someone approached the . . . establishment . . . with the proper incentive . . ." As her words trailed off, Mark stared into the fire.

"You think Rory or I could provide the incentive."

"Or provide it to me. I could—"

"No!" He looked at her. "I will see what we can do. But do not ever go near that place. Or that organization. They will kill without—"

"How would Atkinson know? If he does not go there himself?"

"Atkinson has informants all over the city, just as I do. He probably has someone inside who provides him with the names of every member of Society who frequents the place."

"So dangerous for anyone."

"That particular activity is treacherous on every possible level. How do you think Shropshire acquired the pox?"

Judith choked. "I thought he liked women!"

Mark smirked. "Shropshire likes sex. Any port in a storm."

"I may be ill."

He leaned forward again. "I highly doubt that. You are one of the strongest women I know."

"I am not sure that is a good thing."

"It most definitely is, given the current circumstances. Now. Tell me your plan for Atkinson."

"You are persistent."

"You would know."

Judith fought back a grin. "All right. Your mother and I have been trawling the gossip mills the last twenty-four hours, putting our nets out wherever possible."

"I take it you caught something?"

"Many somethings, as a matter of fact. Mr. Atkinson, from all outward appearances, holds the aristocracy in complete disdain, with little regard for their status or bearing, except for what it can earn him at either the tables or with blackmail. The underlying truth is, however, that he truly desires to be considered among them, as an equal. He hides this well but is not always entirely sober when he is with his closest friends. Friends who also drink and talk, at White's and other, less noteworthy, establishments." She paused with a scowl. "A man with as many secrets as he does should develop more friends with discretion."

"And what have you done with this information?"

"Your mother has persuaded Lord Anthony Blackwell to issue Mr. Atkinson and his paramour an invitation to their ball on the nineteenth."

Those eyes brightened, and Judith's stomach clenched as he

went on. "Do you plan some sort of trap to be sprung?"

She nodded. "At the supper. He will be separated from his companion at the table and placed between the wives of the three men he is currently blackmailing. They, of course, have been informed that they are not uniquely in his clutches—and obviously the three men cannot all have stolen the vase—this is one spot in which Mr. Atkinson's arrogance has overstepped. The wives will begin to chatter to each other about the blackmail and their husbands' desperation, engaging Mr. Atkinson and asking his advice—which he, amused in his arrogance—will provide. At the appropriate moment, one will confess that her husband knows who has the vase, has gotten Bow Street involved, and they are currently in the process of retrieving it, as the miscreant in possession of it is currently out at an event."

Lord Mark scooted forward on the ottoman, leaning a bit closer to Judith. "Delicious. What do you foresee happening next?"

Judith inhaled deeply, a slight mistake, as she took in his scent of soap, pine, and mint, with a slight tinge of the wood from the fire. Her face heated as she gazed at his eyes, and for a moment, words failed her.

Finally, she cleared her throat. "Most likely one of two things. He, being the smug and arrogant bastard he is, will assume the vase is secure wherever he has stored it. And he will not react. The other is that he will find some reason to excuse him and head directly to wherever he has hidden the vase."

Lord Mark reached down and grasped her left ankle, lifting her foot into his lap. "And someone will follow him." He slipped off her boot and cradled her foot between his thighs. His gaze never left her face. "Your foot is cold."

Judith swallowed hard, the heat in her cheeks now spreading down over her breasts. "It is rather chilly outside."

"Go on. What happens from there?"

"Yes. Um . . . yes. Mr. Jeremy Smith will be brought up to date when we meet with him. We will be requesting one of his runners be waiting outside the ball, but also one at Mr. Atkinson's house as well as his warehouse near the river. If they cannot accommodate that, your mother plans to hire her own men."

He reached for her other foot, his hand warm as it closed around her ankle. "Mother always was the most resourceful woman I have ever known." He removed her other boot, setting it on the floor, and tucked her foot in beside the other.

Judith gasped and fought to control her breathing as his hands then moved under her skirts, caressing both calves, the fingertips grazing lightly over the silk of her stockings before tugging loose the ribbons at the top. "In the"—she swallowed—"the meantime, we have set the gossip mills flowing with tales of Mr. Atkinson's nefarious activities—some true, some not so much—that will flood the Mayfair ballrooms with rumors about his attempts to blackmail the very men with whom he desires to join ranks. He will be greeted at the ball askance, his welcome not to his expect—" Judith's breath caught as the ribbons fell away from her stockings and his fingertips grazed the flesh of her thighs. "Lord Mark, I do not think—"

He leaned back, his hands sliding down her legs, pausing at her ankles, and he lifted her left foot, his lips brushing the arch. "I suspect you may dispense with the title," he whispered, "given our current situation." He tugged at the silk, and one stocking eased down her leg. He pulled it free, dropping it on the floor. "So where does this visit fit in with your scheme to upset Mr. Atkinson?"

Every touch of his skin against hers sent a new wave of desire through Judith, and she quivered as he repeated his actions with her right foot. Whatever the night might bring, she wanted this man.

"It doesn't," she whispered, wondering how he would take her next words. "This is because I want you. I have almost since the moment we met." She took a deep breath, letting it out with the next sentence. "But it is also about making more money to pay Edmund's debts."

Lord Mark Rydell froze. Every part of him stopped moving—his hands, his breathing, his expression. Even the gleam in those blue eyes faded for a moment. Then his brow furrowed and his lips tightened. "What did you—" The words cut off, then the gleam returned with a wild fierceness, and he began to laugh as he let her feet fall to the floor. "You wicked woman!" He stood and grabbed her hands, pulling her up and into his arms. "You bet on us!"

The sense of relief that flooded Judith almost made her weep, and she threw her arms around his shoulders, pressing against his chest. "I did!"

He released her, taking her face in his hands. "How?"

"Lord Anthony. He thought the wager crude and vulgar, but when I asked if he would place the bet for me, he found it all quite amusing. Then insisted he wanted to know no more about it." She touched his cheek. "I think it rather embarrassed him. True gentleman that he is. Apparently, there is quite a bit of money wagered on this event. The first few bets were made closer to the initial placement, but then they dropped off, given your injuries and Edmund's difficulties. They have picked up lately, surging somewhat after Lord Anthony placed his bet. But no one thought it would happen this quickly. I knew it would be to our advantage to meet sooner rather than later."

Mark stroked her cheeks with his thumbs. "You clever woman." He kissed her, a tender and brief caress of lips.

Judith tried to pull him closer, but he resisted, easing away from her. She scowled as he looked away from her toward the fire. "What is wrong?"

After a moment, he took a long, deep inhale and looked back at her. "Before we go any further, there are two things you need to know."

Worry tightened her stomach. Had she missed something? "What?"

He held her hands, bringing them up to his chest. "Before I say more, please know that I truly admire you, and you have awakened something in me I thought long dormant. Never doubt that I want this"—he glanced quickly at the bed—"but we will wait, if you think that is the wisest course."

Judith hesitated, afraid to speak. What was he talking about?

"First, you should know that I also placed a wager on tonight, through Rory."

Relief pushed a tiny snort from Judith. "I certainly cannot hold that against you."

Mark fell silent, his mouth a tight line.

Her worry returned. "There's more."

He nodded. "Before she died, Stella bedded Shropshire."

This time, Judith's sense of relief was more understanding than humor, and her hands moved up to his shoulders, squeezing them. "I know."

His eyes widened. "You do?"

Judith brushed a hand through his hair, pushing the curls from the edge of his face. "You know that kind of gossip does not stay a secret for more than a minute. My maid told me about the goings-on in her dressing room the next morning. By noon, Rotten Row was abuzz with it."

"I swear to you I did not know before that night, or I never would have been intimate with her after she had . . ."

Ah. Now she understood. "But you were."

Another nod. "The night before you and I met at that ball."

Judith frowned as her mind ran through the passage of days. "Almost three weeks ago."

"Yes. But if you—"

"Any symptoms?"

His eyebrows arched. "You know about—"

She pressed a palm to his cheek. "My dear gentle man. I was married to a soldier and raised his two boys. I have run a household full of randy maids and footmen, and I have birthed three boys of my own. A woman does not get to be my age and maintain the innocence of a debutante without some serious effort to remain naïve and sheltered. Even if Edmund had desired it, that is not my nature. I learned early to be blunt with our sons as their father would often shy away from discussing the risks of being off to school with friends and ambitious young women. I assume you have spoken with your doctor. So . . ."

Mark shook his head, then covered her hand on his cheek with his own, grasping it and turning to kiss her palm. "I find you more remarkable each time we speak."

"Symptoms?"

"Persistent as well." He chuckled. "None so far. And, yes, I have talked to Dr. Oakley." His smile faded. "Which brings me to the point. He will not give me a clean bill of health for at least a month with no symptoms."

Judith fought a rising sense of disappointment. "You wish to wait?"

"I would rather spend a year in a pillory than give this to you."

Judith eased her hands away from his face, studying him. Mark waited, somber. Making up her mind, she slid her arms around his body, pressing her cheek to his chest, holding him tightly. She could hear his heartbeat, rapid but steady, and felt his breathing, also rapid but not so steady. "I will not put that worry on you," she whispered. "As much as I want you"—she tilted her head to look up into his face—"as much as I want to feel you inside me, we can wait until you have that cleared from your mind." She released him. "But I do have one favor to ask."

"Anything."

"May I stay the night?"

MARK FELT EVERY inch of his body go still. The woman in his arms—so beautiful and tempting, so clever and willing—had eased behind every guard he had ever raised. Since he had returned from the battlefield, he had held every person, even his mother and brothers, at a carefully curated distance, mostly through humor but also physical distance and a reluctance to engage in more than casual conversation. But his desire, his admiration for Judith had made him careless.

Judith, shrewd as always, sensed his hesitation, his tension. "You would rather I not?" The confusion in her voice speared him. "But I thought . . . it would add to the perception that we—"

Mark tightened his arms around her. "No. I would very much—" He shook his head. "I do not sleep much."

"So I have heard. Is it the war?"

He stared down at her. "What did you say?"

Judith eased out of his arms and took his hand, urging him toward the wingback. He sat, and she settled down on the ottoman. "Remember? I also asked this at Adelaide's, to which you took great offense. But it is no secret that men who have returned from the continent . . . many have been changed, even those who were not wounded physically. As I have said, rumors about you have swirled since you and your brother came home. Of course, most of those had to do with him becoming duke, his sullen nature. But you were a favorite of the women of the *ton*, especially the young widows, and greatly missed. They were eager for your return." Her face suddenly flushed crimson. "They were rather free with tales of your . . . um . . . prowess."

Mark grinned. "Is that why you want—"

She gripped his arm, and her strength startled him. He looked down at her hand as she spoke. "No." Her hold lessened. "Not . . . precisely." She released him and leaned back. "I married a few weeks into my first season, as much out of necessity as interest." She sighed. "I immediately fell into the marriage, helping with Edmund and Daniel, and within a short time, running the household as duchess. I had no plethora of suitors, no flirtatious dances, not even a visit to Almack's. After my marriage, I no longer attended many balls or Society events, as so little time and energy remained for those things. And I missed them terribly. Or I thought I did. So when Edmund died, I sought out all the young men, all the balls and soirees. All the fun I believe I had missed."

Mark listened as he had to other young widows in the past. He had heard something similar so many times, reminding him that the lives of the *ton's* women were far from their own choosing. Most—even his own mother—adopted an attitude of acceptance and forbearance. It simply was the way the world was, and the best path meant coping with whatever hand had been dealt.

But a few sought something outside their confining lives. And Mark had gladly helped them in the past. "But it was not what you remembered."

Judith smiled, but it was a sad expression. "No. I had forgotten that, like so many young women of Society, young men can be . . . empty-headed. My world had changed dramatically. Theirs had not. Even though I had no desire to marry, I found myself craving something more substantial."

Mark smirked. "You consider me substantial?"

She scooted forward on the ottoman, and he gasped as her knees forced his apart. She rubbed her palms firmly up and down his thighs. "I consider you enticing."

Loins tightening, Mark closed his hands around her forearms. "Judith—"

"Shh. You want to know what else I learned from my husband, the former soldier?"

Mark did not trust himself to speak.

She bent, kissing the inside of his thigh. "That there are many ways to please a man besides having him between your legs."

He tried to breathe. "You cannot use your mouth on—"

"Shh. I know." Her hands on his legs became firmer, the fingertips digging in, massaging the muscles with short strokes. "Scoot down a bit."

Every muscle, every nerve tensed as he pushed his rear forward, watching as she lowered her head and pressed her face on the fall of his trousers. His cock stiffened, pushing against the cloth as the heat of her penetrated the fabric. Her hands moved upward, slipping beneath his shirt, and the feel of her skin against his sent a spike of arousal down across his stomach and loins. His back arched as the pressure of her face against him grew firmer, warmer, and he groaned from the pure pleasure of the sensations flowing through him.

Judith eased away from him, tugging at his arms. "Take your shirt off."

A split second later, the linen tumbled to the floor, and she grinned, her hands scrolling firm circles on his chest, spirals around his nipples, and long traces with her fingernails down his stomach, pausing only as she began to release the buttons on the fall of his trousers, peeling it back and pushing down his small clothes.

His cock slipped free, and she gave a low moan, her eyes shining. "No wonder you have pleased so many."

Mark reached out to stroke her face, bending forward to kiss her. From any other woman, the compliment would have sounded vulgar to his ears. From her, it sounded like the admiration of a beloved partner. He slid his hands into her hair, cupping her head as he deepened the kiss, exploring her lips and tongue with slow, gentle caresses.

She responded in kind, her hands stroking his stomach and thighs even as she plundered his mouth with her tongue, sucking on his lower lip. As the kiss broke, Mark pulled combs and pins from her hair, dropping them on top of his shirt as her chestnut tresses fell free, framing her face and breasts with their curls.

Judith took his hands, kissing the palms, then pressed them down on the arms of the chair. "Leave them here. Do not let go." Then she raked her hands through her hair, parting it at the back of her skull and bringing the long strands forward. She entwined her fingers in them, then leaned forward, cupping his cock between her palms and twirling her hair around it.

The effect was immediate; the combination of strength and silken hair rubbing against him sent deep waves of arousal through Mark. His hands clenched the arms of the chair, fingers digging in, as he fought the urge to pull her to him. He bucked his hips up, his head grinding backward against the chair, his growl of pleasure resonating around the room. Judith did not let go—her grip becoming long strokes against his cock, strokes that seemed endless, time slowing to a stop as they continued. She lowered her head, adding long hot breaths to the mix, as she slid one hand into his crotch and under his balls, caressing them, one finger finding the golden spot just behind them.

His growl became a low roar of infinite pleasure as his body arched and jerked, finding its release, his seed erupting from deep within, spurting over his stomach and chest. Judith did not relent until his body slowed its gyrations, then she eased her hands and hair away. She brushed the long strands behind her shoulders, then reached for his shirt, cleaning his chest as he slowly extracted his fingers from the arms of the chair.

In pure awe, Mark watched Judith's ministrations as he fought to regain his breath, waves of ecstasy still coursing through every fiber. She used his shirt as if she were a highly skilled nurse, thorough but with a gentle touch. She focused solely on whatever spot she cleaned, following each with a soft kiss. She cleaned his deflating cock with a touch like fine cotton, as if she expected him to be sore, then pulled his small clothes back up as a cushion. She finally returned the shirt to the floor and looked up at him, waiting.

"Come here." He reached for her, and she complied, her body soft and pliant as she settled in his lap, resting her head on his shoulder.

"I hoped it would please you."

He raised one of her hands to his lips. "You please me."

She sighed and tucked her head down against his chest, her body becoming even more limp against him.

"You know I will return the favor."

She giggled. "I hoped so. When you recover. Perhaps after a nap."

He gave a low chuckle. "You do know men."

"I am a wanton harlot, remember."

He tightened his arms around her. "Definitely neither." After a moment, he released her. "Stand up."

She did, and he pushed out of the chair, a little annoyed at exactly how wobbly his legs remained. He turned her away from him and began to unlace her dress.

She looked over her shoulder at him. "Surely, not yet."

He laughed. "No. But you asked to spend the night. I thought you might be more comfortable without the dress and stays."

Judith nodded, releasing a long deep breath as the dress, then the stays, dropped away from her. "I do hate those bloody things."

"They are, however, rather entertaining to remove."

She turned to face him. "Oh?"

He took her arm, urging her toward the bed. "I can find all sorts of uses for those laces."

Red spots tinged her cheeks, and she shivered. "Do you promise?"

An odd spark of hope bloomed in his chest. "Do not tempt me."

She rested a hand on his bare chest as they stepped closer to the bed. "I am tempting you."

He stumbled, catching himself against the post.

Judith giggled again. "Perhaps after that nap." She turned and mounted the mattress, easing toward the center.

Mark doffed his loose trousers, blew out the candles—leaving only two oil lamps lit—and got in beside her. "Perhaps."

As he lay back against the pillows, Judith curled on her side, tucking herself beneath his arm, one leg draping over his. Mark pulled the covers up, snuggling them both in, relishing the feel of her heat against his side. He had no intention of sleeping, but he did need to rest, lulling in the exquisite joy of having this woman in his arms. He watched as Judith's body softened in slumber, her breathing evening out, her hair a glorious cascade down her back. As the last of his pleasure leeched out of him, he closed his eyes, imagining, wishing for a time when each night could be just this blissful, just this peaceful.

CHAPTER SIXTEEN

Thursday, 4 August 1814
Lord Mark Rydell's Bloomsbury residence
Half-past three in the morning

A MOAN JOSTLED Judith's slumber. A wistful dream of a broad meadow filled with wildflowers and dozens of Highland Ponies dissipated in a vapor as an almost instinctual urgency, a sudden spike of fear, pierced her sleep. Judith jerked awake and pushed up on the pillow just as a wild kick from Mark threw her leg off his. That urgency seized her again, and Judith rolled away, throwing aside the covers and bounding out of bed on the far edge away from him.

Mark screamed, a wild sound of terror and pain, as his hands clawed the air. Then one fist thudded against the headboard as the other slammed into the mattress. His eyes snapped open, but their stare was of unseen horror. Another bellow of fear blasted through the room, although Judith doubted he heard it.

Because Lord Mark Rydell was still very much asleep.

Memories of Edmund's violent nighttime fits flooded Judith, and she looked around, desperately searching for anything that would help. There. On top of his wardrobe, a thick quilted blanket lay neatly folded. Rushing to that side of the room, Judith bounced up on her toes several times until her fingers snagged the heavy cover, and it tumbled down on top of her. She gathered it, doubled it over, then held it in front of her and waited for a small moment—a second—a breath of calm in the chaos.

He continued to thrash for what felt like an eternity, his eyes staring into the unknown, but finally that moment came, a brief interlude as he panted, his body trembling as if pain consumed him.

Judith took her chance.

PAIN SEARED THROUGH him as his body slammed to the ground, the rearing, wounded horse looming above him. He screamed as another explosion sounded, the compression throwing the horse off balance, its hooves skidding as its body fell toward Mark, the ominous shadow of its bulk growing ever larger as it fell towards him. He flinched, then stilled, unable to move away from the collapsing beast.

A solid weight suddenly covered him—but not the horse, which fell to his left, shrieking in pain but alive and struggling to regain its feet. It writhed ever nearer, but the weight over him held him down. He pushed against it, but his arms felt clamped to his side.

Then he heard his name.

Distant. From within a thick fog of smoke.

Again.

Then the confinement around him tightened. Firm but soft. Not a weight of war, of danger.

Comforting. Safety.

"Mark."

His body shuddered as darkness overwhelmed him. The fight left him, and he relented, going limp. Surrender.

"Mark."

He opened his eyes.

JUDITH WATCHED HIM carefully. He had come to himself, awake, but she could see in his eyes the confusion and uncertainty of what he saw. Her, on top of him, having wrapped him in the thick blanket, mounting him and encircling him with her arms and legs, holding on as if he were one of her wild ponies, bucking to throw her off.

But he did not.

She had called his name, quiet but persistent, until he had gone limp beneath her.

They stared at each other. As his breathing eased, Judith slipped off his side of the bed, her feet cushioned by the thick carpet of the room. She peeled the heavy blanket away and draped it over the bench at the end of the bed. Mark watched every move, silent. Judith looked around and, spotting a glass and pitcher of water on the shaving stand, filled the glass and bought it to him.

"You should try to sit." She held out the glass. "Water will help with the dry mouth."

His eyes still on her, Mark pushed up in the bed, bracing his back against the headboard, sweat coating his face and neck. He reached for the glass, drinking as if he had been a week without. She brought him another.

"What did you do to me?" His words, low and hoarse, held more curiosity than accusation.

She crossed her arms, hugging herself against the sharp memories. "Edmund. He had those nightmares. The flailing fits. The doctor suggested that heavy bedclothes had helped some of his other patients—also veterans of war—something they had discovered by accident during one particularly cold winter. I had my maid sew two quilted blankets together, filling several of the quilted pockets with buckshot. It took a bit of experimentation to get the distribution and weight correct—so that he didn't roll out of bed or suffocate—but we finally found a combination that worked." She shrugged. "It helped most nights. He slept under it in the winter and kept it handy during the summer. It was not a solution—the nightmares persisted to the end—but it was . . . an aid."

"You got on top of me. You held onto me."

Judith gestured toward the foot of the bed. "I did not believe that blanket would be enough." A sudden thought occurred to her. "I did not hurt you, did I?"

He shook his head, still looking somewhat stunned. "You were not afraid?"

The question puzzled her. "Why would I be? Afraid of what?"

He blinked, his mouth tightening. "I can be . . . violent."

She shrugged. "Fighting demons usually is. But you were not fighting me." She smiled. "And, if you remember, I can be rather quick on my feet."

That smirk flitted across his face but did not linger. "Judith—"

She stepped closer, understanding. "This is why you did not want me to stay."

He nodded, a touch of normalcy returning to his face. "I did not intend to sleep, but sometimes, I drift off. I have no desire to hurt you. Or frighten you."

Judith reached and brushed his hair away from his face. "My darling, it takes a great deal more than a thrashing nightmare to frighten me." She kissed him, a butterfly caress of his lips. "Do you take to the streets to stay awake?"

"The theater. The gambling hells. To see Stella."

"So the problem is not that you *cannot* sleep. It's that you do not *want* to."

"It is rather treacherous territory."

"Ah. Perhaps we can discover other entertainments." Judith clambered over him, plumped pillows against the headboard, and snuggled in next to him. He watched every move, and as she took his hand and entwined their fingers, that smirk returned.

"Has anyone ever told you how retiring and demure you are?"

Judith laughed, squeezing his hand. "No. Not even in my first season. My only season. My mother considered one of her greatest failures to be that she could not convince me to keep my mouth shut. I learned the strictest posture and a mincing walk. I learned to play the pianoforte—somewhat—and to dance. I can tell the difference between a teaspoon, a soup spoon, a bullion spoon, a cream-soup spoon, and a dessert spoon, and where they go in a place setting. I have read Shakespeare, Plato, Defoe, and the novels of Mrs. Burney. I have studied Locke, Hume, and the writings of Mary Wollstonecraft and Mary Astell. But I can barely thread a needle and have a serious distaste for being bored. I could never play the coquette. Despite Mother's best efforts, I found the innocuous chitchat encouraged for young women to be nigh on intolerable. She once called me a harridan. But how often can you discuss the latest hat style before becoming as mad as the king himself?"

Mark shifted on his pillows to face her more directly. "I can honestly say I have never discussed hat styles with anyone but my hatter."

"As it should be."

He studied her a moment, his eyes narrowing. "Is that why you think you were Edmund's second choice? Because you are clever and outspoken?"

Judith closed her eyes. The question took her breath away. How could he have possibly remembered that? "I was not his second choice."

"Nor should you have been."

"I was his fifth choice."

A sharp intake of air made Judith open her eyes. He seemed truly surprised.

"You cannot possibly know—"

"He told me. Our first years were . . . unpleasant. He had been a second son, a widower with few prospects. He was far more interested in a bedmate and a mother to his sons than a wife who could manage his house. I know whom he courted and who rejected him because he made me aware of each name. No one thought he would be the earl, and he often threw up to me that if he had waited another year, he could have had his pick of eligible women." Judith looked down at their clasped hands, unsettled by how much saying it had caused a deep ache in her chest.

"Then he was a fool."

Mark's kindness eased that ache a little, and Judith shrugged, looking at him again. "I made an excellent countess, and we grew to care for each other. I threw myself into running the household, and he grew to see value in that, if nothing else."

He shook his head, then sat abruptly sat forward, twisting toward her and taking her face in both hands, pulling her close. "You are so much more than that." Then he kissed her, pressing his lips against hers in a firm, determined way. His fingers curled into her hair, tugging the locks as his tongue pressed into her mouth.

With a moan, Judith surrendered into the kiss, the pressure on her scalp igniting a fire deep in her belly, and heat bloomed between her thighs. She thrust her tongue against his and wrapped her arms around him, her fingertips digging into the muscles of his shoulders.

Then he was gone—his absence so sudden that Judith cried out as he pushed off the bed. Mark stared down at her, his breath coming in deep gasps.

"What are you—"

He held out a hand. "Do not move." He looked around, then scooped up her stockings from the floor and tossed them on the end of the bed. Then he opened the dressing room and pulled the sash from a banyan hanging on a peg behind the door. He disappeared inside a moment, then returned with the sash and one of his white ascots, both gripped in his left hand. His smirk returned as he came to the side of the bed, those blue eyes gleaming.

Judith wondered if she looked as confused as she felt. "What are you doing?"

"Do you trust me?"

Her eyebrows arched. "A little late for that question, do you not think?"

The smirk became a grin. "Depends." He mounted the bed on his knees, holding the ascot and sash in front of him. "Do you trust me?"

Judith's breath caught as his meaning seared through her, and she looked from his face to the fabrics in his hand, then his face again. Did she?

"Yes."

Mark moved closer, placing the sash on the pillow next to her, then brushing her hair away from her face, tucking it behind her ears. His gaze never left hers as he raised the ascot and placed it over her eyes. Judith held her breath as he wrapped the fabric around her head, tying it on one side near her temple. She could still see shadows and movement through the fine silk, but she closed her eyes, waiting for his next move, already intrigued—and aroused—by his actions. And his words from the theater echoed again in her mind: *I wish to own a part of you.*

She shivered.

Mark kissed her forehead. "Are you cold?"

"No. I think it is the anticipation."

He chuckled. "Good. Put your palms together."

She did, and Judith felt the satin of the sash loop around her wrists, the bond tight but not uncomfortable.

"Lean back. Easy." Mark braced an arm behind her shoulders, easing her back and slipping another pillow beneath her head and shoulders as they found the solid wood. He then lifted her hands above her head, apparently tying the sash to the acorn-shaped finial in the center of the headboard.

Judith shuddered again. The lack of sight, the confinement of her hands left her feeling exposed, uncertain. In all of her affairs, she had taken the lead and controlled how the evening had proceeded, how and what had happened in her bed. She swallowed hard, trying to stifle a tinge of fear—and an unexpected sense of arousal. In her moment of anxiety, her legs shifted and stretched.

Mark made a low tsking sound. "Ah. We must do something about those."

Judith was not sure she understood. "What do you—"

"Shh."

She felt his face close to hers, the heat of his breath on her cheek.

"Try, dear one, to feel with your heart, your skin, your nipples, your cunt. Not your mind." He kissed her again, tugging her lower lip between his teeth as one hand stroked across her shoulders, then down over one breast, which tightened with arousal, the nipple peaking as he toyed with them through her chemise.

She sighed, another wave of arousal sending warmth spreading over her. His hands drifted down her body as he moved toward the foot of the bed, where he spread her legs, kneeling between them. Something silken and cool circled her right ankle, then grew tight. He pushed her leg closer to the edge of the bed, holding it down a moment. But when he removed his hand, her foot stayed in place, tethered.

Judith fought a moment of panic as she realized he planned to immobilize her, and her left leg kicked involuntarily. "Mark!"

He caught her foot and lifted it to his face, kissing the ankle, the blowing a cool stream of air across the bottom of her foot, which both tickled and enticed. "I promise I will not hurt you. Do you believe me?"

Judith sorted through her racing, panicked thoughts, swallowing hard, finding a core of the truth she knew deep in her being. "I do."

"Do you want me to stop?"

A logical, fearful part of her mind wanted to call a halt to this, to regain her sensibilities. A feral part felt the deep arousal his touches had brought to her, enjoyed the sensation of being at his mercy. Once again, his words sent a thrill through her senses. *I wish to own a part of you.*

Other words pushed out of the fog as well. Harridan. Wanton harlot.

Fifth choice.

"No."

He kissed her ankle, nipping at the tender flesh above the

bone, and Judith gasped.

He chuckled. "Ah. Teeth are such wonderful tools." He pushed her leg even higher, his teeth scraping lightly against the inside of her knee, followed by a kiss. Then he secured her ankle with a similar silken bond as the other.

My stockings!

She felt the bed shift as he moved higher, his fingertip tracing gentle patterns up and down her calves and thighs, each stroke moving closer to her core. He paused only to push her chemise high on her chest, exposing her breasts as he tucked the fabric up under her shoulders.

"You have the most remarkable beauty."

Judith chewed her lower lip.

"You do not believe me?"

"I find it hard—"

His hands closed around her breasts. "These," he whispered. "Perfection." He kissed one nipple, then the other, pulling each into his mouth, sucking lightly at first, then his tongue pressed the tender bud against the roof of his mouth, rubbing it back and forth. As he tugged on one with his teeth, he rolled the other between his fingers, the force growing tighter and harder, almost to the point of pain.

Pure ecstasy shot through Judith, from her breasts to her groin, and her body stiffened, arching against the bonds. Heat flushed her face, and she felt a growing wetness between her legs, an increasing need. She tried to writhe, but the ties held her tight.

One hand still on a breast, he kissed his way down her torso, lingering just above her mound, as the other hand patted the inside of her thigh. "Your legs," he muttered, his words hoarse. "Glorious, a shape a queen would envy." His hand left her breast as he shifted. His fingers traced up one thigh, across her swollen cunt, and down the other thigh. "Hips made for childbearing. And the luckiest of men."

Judith's breath came in gulps, her muscles tensing under his touch, her arousal building as moisture slipped from her. She whispered his name.

He kissed the top of her slit. "But this." He licked from the top all the way to the bed. "Heaven."

Judith cried out, a fiery need consuming her, her entire body struggling against the bonds.

He slid both hands under her buttocks, raising her, tilting her hips, blowing streams of cool air over her aching cunt.

"Damn you!" What had meant to be a cry, a curse, emerged as a harsh and barely audible beg.

His tongue found her then, separating her tender folds as a chef would carefully open a ripened fruit. He pulled one hand free and held them apart as his tongue worked the swollen flesh, pushing, teasing, withdrawing, until Judith found herself begging him in earnest.

"Please!"

A finger entered her, circling. Then two. Three. Thrusting and twisting, searching for the sweetest spot, as his mouth focused on the engorged bud at the top of her sex, sucking.

The shattering jolt of her climax raced through her, hot waves of ecstasy as she cried out, her body bucking, jerking hard against her ties. He did not relent, continuing to lick, the thrusting of his fingers slowing inside her, until her body eased into the tiniest of spasms, her breath finally returning to its regular rhythm. Then he eased his hand out of her and made unbelievably quick work of releasing her bonds, legs first, then a quick pull at the sash holding her hands that freed them both. He pulled down her chemise, smoothing it over her stomach and legs. Then he moved over her, his groin against hers, and braced himself on his elbows. His cock had hardened again, and its pressure against her felt as warm as a comforting hug.

Judith pushed the cravat off her eyes to find Mark gazing down at her, his skin coated in a fine sheen of sweat, his eyes wide with adoration. Silently, gradually, he lowered his weight against her, and she wrapped her arms around his shoulders as he buried his face into her neck. "You are remarkable," he whispered.

Without reason, Judith sobbed with relief and joy, tightening her grip on him. Mark entwined his fingers in her hair, kissing the side of her face. He held her until she calmed and her breathing became even, then he murmured, "Are you all right?"

"I am"—she stopped, her throat raspy, and swallowed—"spectacularly all right."

Mark raised his head to look at her, then let more of his weight rest on her body, pressing her into the mattress. "Is this too much?"

It was not. In fact, Judith relished the feel of his body against hers, the heaviness making her feel protected. Cocooned.

"It is not. I want all of it. All of you."

With a slight smile, he straightened his arms, and his full weight rested on her. "Do not let me hurt you."

She shook her head. "I like it. It makes me feel . . ." The word would not come.

"Claimed."

I wish to own a part of you.

She kissed his cheek. "Are you claiming me? Am I one of your many?"

He shook his head, propping himself up again on his elbows, easing some of his weight off her. "I may have been with many women in the past, but I have only claimed one. You. My first choice."

CHAPTER SEVENTEEN

Thursday, 4 August 1814
Lord Mark Rydell's Bloomsbury residence
Half-past four in the morning

MARK STUDIED JUDITH'S face, waiting to see how she would take his words. He had not meant to say them—not yet—but as she had accepted his full weight on her, his heart had soared with a bizarre, somewhat twisted hope—one borne of his wonder of this woman in his bed, her understanding, warmth, and practicality. A hope that her reactions, her words, were not a pretense but all too real. He had never experienced a stronger sense of pragmatism in any woman, and he had never believed to find one. Yet his own life and lifestyle demanded it.

The smile that had flitted across her face vanished. She touched his cheek with two fingers, resting her thumb under his chin. Her eyes narrowed, but more in curiosity than anger. "What does that mean to you?"

"That of all the women I have met, you are the only one I wish to spend time with. To share a bed with. To hold near me in a way I have no other."

"Not marriage?"

Mark slipped off her and rolled to his side, tugging her with him, sliding an arm around her waist. "No. I do not think marriage is in the cards for either of us, if I am honest."

This time, she did smile. "No. I think not."

"But it also means that you are mine and mine alone. Mind, body, and heart."

Judith placed a palm against his chest. "So no more young blades tripping in and out of my bedchambers after balls, keeping me warm and happy at night?"

"I will buy you a puppy."

She laughed. A full-throated, body-shaking laugh that began with a startled bark and descended into girlish giggles. Mark held her, charmed, as she quivered against him, although the way she curled her fingers into the hair on his chest tested his every resolve to not pin her to the bed and take her for all they were both worth. "It is not that amusing."

She nodded, her hair flowing over her shoulders and trailing down his body, then gulped for breath. "It is if you know how often I think of them as untrained pups."

A sudden image of young Gower as a lanky young hound made Mark squeeze his eyes shut as he snickered.

As they calmed, Judith stroked his shoulder, testing his resolve once again. "Judith—"

"Yours alone?"

His hand slid from her waist, down along her hip, coming to rest mid-thigh, his thumb caressing her. "Mine alone."

"You would pit me against Edmund? My boys?"

Mark scowled. "No. Family is too important, especially children. But otherwise, your loyalty would be to me."

Judith remained silent a moment. "You say that almost as if you had children of your own."

Mark's mouth thinned, feeling almost as if he were being tested in some way. And perhaps he was. Given what he asked of her, perhaps it was time he extended the same . . . what? Trust?

Taking a deep breath, he pushed up and off the bed, holding out his hand. "I need to show you something. Let us get dressed first—no need to startle any unwary servants."

She smiled and slipped from the bed, straightening her chemise and reaching for her stays, which he helped her lace up, along with her dress. He pulled on his trousers but reached for the banyan instead of his soiled shirt. He picked up one of the oil lamps, then led her out the door and up the back stairs. Judith followed, his hand grasping hers, without a word. On the fourth floor, he paused, his hand on the door of the room his workers had been focused on for more than a week.

"If, after I show you this, you wish to pursue your own course, I will understand."

Her brow furrowed. "Then you must show me now."

With a nod, he opened the door and led her inside, closing it behind them. He released her hand, urging her farther into the room, as he lifted the lamp to cast more light around the room.

Bright moonlight streamed through the windows of the room, adding a silver sheen to the golden glow of the lamp, both casting stark shadows over the furnishings and bare wooden floor. The room held a moist chill, and it smelled of fresh paint and recently sawed wood. Judith looked around, her eyes slowly growing so wide he could see the white around the emerald-green of her irises. She turned, taking in each element of the room as if viewing a museum exhibit.

The room, once that of a servant, had been transformed into a child's room with study and play areas. In one corner, a tiny table sat flanked with a low bookcase filled with children's lesson books and an armchair for an adult. Against the far wall, a rocking chair and a variety of toys clustered near a child's bed.

Judith circled the room, touching a few items such as a rocking horse and a shelf full of painted rocks and dried flowers. Completing her circuit, she looked at Mark. "Who is this for?"

"Olivia. My daughter. She is almost four. Stella is—was—her mother, and she now lives with her grandmother, Stella's mother, Rose. But Rose is not in great health, and I want to bring them both here to live."

Then he waited.

Twin spots of red tinged Judith's cheekbones as she turned to survey the room again. She walked over, her fingers gliding along the head of the rocking horse. "Do you plan to hire a nanny? A governess?"

Mark blinked at the unexpected question. "Not yet. Rose has cared for her until now. But she should start her education soon, which I do not think Rose can handle. I hoped to hire a governess to handle her at that point."

"Why have you not . . . claimed . . . her before now?"

"Because I could not protect her."

She snapped around to stare at him. "What do you mean by that?"

"I was a soldier against the French, and I am now the owner of a gambling establishment. To say that I have a few . . . nefarious . . . acquaintances would be putting it mildly. I could not bring her into the family home prior to Matthew producing an heir. But I can bring her here."

"But you acknowledged her?"

"To Stella and Rose, of course. And my family knows now. I told them recently."

"Do they accept that she is—even though Stella—"

"Olivia looks like me." He shrugged. "Exactly like me. And my brothers when they were younger. And as far as I know"— another shrug—"Stella remained . . . faithful . . . during the months before Olivia was conceived. I have no doubt that I am her father."

"Does she know?"

"No." At her frown, Mark went on. "I believed it might be too confusing for her, especially since she did not live with her mother either." He glanced at the rocking chair. "Stella did not agree."

Judith's frown remained. "She lived here, but not her daughter?"

He shook his head. "Stella did not want Olivia around the . . . her . . . um . . ."

"Livelihood?"

Mark smiled. "More or less."

The frown turned sad, and she rubbed her hand along the horse again, her gaze distant. "It is hard to be away from your child."

Mark waited, somehow aware that Judith spoke of more than Stella's distance from Olivia.

After a moment, she released a deep sigh. "My George is at Eton. Robbie will go in the next year." Her eyes narrowed and she faced him again, her voice harsh. "I do not like it, but I do not want them to come home because the estate is in tatters."

Mark went and stood by her side, touching her arm. "Then let us hope your plans for Atkinson and ours for tonight"—she looked up at him, a slight smile on her face—"will pay off with the desired results."

She nodded, then glanced around the room again. "I want to meet her."

He blinked. "You are not off put by the fact that I have a child?"

"All children are precious." She tilted her head to look at him. "And, truthfully, given what I have heard about you, I am rather surprised there is only one."

"As far as I know."

"When can I meet her?"

"Give me a few days to sort some things out, including that wager at White's. You still have the meeting with the runner to work out. After that, I will arrange something."

"Excellent."

"Now. Let us get you fully dressed and home. Cook is probably already awake and baking, so it will be clear to her that you stayed the night."

Judith slid her arms around him, pressing her body against his. "Thank you," she whispered, "for all of it."

He held her. "And my claim . . ."

"Is accepted." She peered up at him. "Let us see what comes next."

CHAPTER EIGHTEEN

Tuesday, 9 August 1814
Sculthorpe Manor
Ten in the morning

JUDITH STRUGGLED TO remain still as her maid braided and twisted her hair into a tightly knit updo interwoven with a royal-blue silk ribbon and a half dozen matching feathered pins. Epworth had started with a psyche knot at the back of Judith's head and expanded the style with looping braids as well as the ribbon and pins. It made her scalp itch from the tightness, but she bore it silently, wanting to look her best for today's meeting with the Bow Street Runner.

But not for the runner. While important to their scheme—vital, even—Judith had no desire to impress him with her looks or style. Instead, her goal was to make a clear impression on the Duke of Embleton and his family . . . including his brother.

Mark.

Judith straightened her shoulders even as her thighs tightened.

"Almost finished, my lady. Only a few more minutes."

Judith smiled into the mirror, not wanting to admit the true reason she had squirmed a bit. "It looks remarkable. Thank you. And the bonnet will not hurt the feathers."

Epworth spoke around one of the said pins, currently held between her lips. "No, my lady. They point downward and will be below the brim."

"Excellent." Judith's hand rested on her right leg, her fingers tracing the outline of the white silken ascot currently tied around her upper thigh. Her mind lingered on the moment when Mark had tied it there. After visiting the room he had prepared for his daughter, they had returned to his bedchamber to fully dress. She had sat on the bench at the end of his bed to replace her stockings, and he had snagged the ascot from the covers, kneeling in front of her. He had pushed her skirts up and wrapped it about her thigh, tying it as if it were around his own neck, kissing her, his fingers stroking lightly between her legs.

"Wear it whenever you go out. To remind you that you belong to me."

And she had. Although she had not been out of the house much over the last five days. Most of Friday, she had been ensconced with Edmund, reviewing their accounts to check the progress of their efforts. Saturday, she had stayed in her room most of the day, as Edmund had received word from White's that his wager had been declared resolved. The payout that had accompanied the certification of the event had been lovely—several hundred pounds each to Edmund, Sir Rory, and Lord Anthony—but Judith had no desire to face either her son or his wife with the knowledge of how the wager had been declared and certified. It was one thing to have him *think* his mother had lovers—another entirely to *know* with certainty and have it declared in a public forum.

But when the money had arrived from Lord Anthony Saturday evening—as well as a note from Sir Rory as to how his winnings would be applied to Edmund's debt at At Wheel's End, her son had sent for her, any embarrassment set aside by gratitude. They noted the funds in the ledgers, and Edmund had delivered in person a good portion of their winnings to one of his creditors, closing off yet another debt.

Sunday had been set aside for church—Judith felt a touch blasphemous wearing the ascot under her clothes but did so anyway—but they had all skipped a promenade along Rotten Row. They had had their fill of being gawked at and whispered about for the moment.

Monday, Judith had met with the three wives involved in the scheme, including Margaret, and over tea and biscuits, they had discussed the topics to be raised with Atkinson. All three were young and far too giggly for her comfort, but those qualities could easily work in their favor, as Atkinson would be less suspicious of three flighty girls than experienced dragons of the *ton*.

Although, since Thursday, Judith had felt less like a mature woman than she had since her marriage. When not wearing it, she had slept with the ascot under her pillow, her hand resting on the fine fabric. Judith had scolded herself at first, feeling rather childish, as if she were a young girl with her first infatuation. But she also realized that what she and Mark had exchanged had been anything but childish. The very power of it sometimes took her breath away.

Judith also had Epworth retrieve Edmund's unique bed cover from the attic, cleaned and boxed, and delivered to the house in Bloomsbury. The return note of thanks had been ebullient and heartfelt, with a touch of naughtiness, as if the witty man with the gleam in his eye she had met at the Huntingdale ball had finally recovered from his injuries.

Epworth placed the final feather, then stepped back and took a deep breath. "That's it then." She glanced toward the array of garments on Judith's bed. "Let's get you dressed."

With a last touch on the ascot, Judith stood. Epworth expertly garbed her in Judith's finest summer day gown, a royal-blue linen with black embroidery around the puffs of the upper sleeves. It had been her favorite from two seasons before, and Epworth had added a broad black band at the high waistline, which anchored a pale-blue gauze overlay of the skirt. Epworth had added a ruched black smocking to the hem, a finishing touch to the gown's refurbish.

Black kid gloves and boots completed the outfit, and Judith sat long enough for Epworth to gently settle a blue linen bonnet amongst the feathers.

"You look magnificent, my lady!"

"And I am grateful for your skills." Judith glanced at the clock on her mantel. Almost time.

As if hearing her thoughts, their butler rapped lightly on the door, opening it to announce that the carriage awaited her at the front entrance. Judith took a final deep breath, touched her right thigh, and left the room.

Tuesday, 9 August 1814
Embleton House
Quarter to eleven in the morning

MARK STOOD AT the receiving room window, staring out at the pavement in front of the house. He felt rather than heard Matthew's presence behind him.

"Smith is downstairs. I told Stephens to have him wait in the servants' hall until we send for him."

Mark continued to watch the street, but his hand smoothed over the pocket holding the letter to Stella with its one hundred pounds. "Probably a wise idea."

After a moment, Matthew cleared his throat. "It is hardly time for her yet."

"She is punctual."

"And how do you know that?"

"Ask Mother."

"Ask Mother what, pray tell?" The question accompanied a rustle of bombazine and silk as Phyllida entered the room.

Mark and Matthew turned as their mother settled on one of the settees in the room, fluffing her purple-and-lavender skirts around her.

"About Lady Sculthorpe's punctuality."

Phyllida clasped her hands in her lap. "It is well known. When

I visited her, I arrived only a moment after the appointed time, but she was ready and waiting for me. A perfectly reasonable characteristic to expect of someone of her station."

Matthew sat in a wingback. "So she is no longer a hussy?"

Phyllida sniffed. "I suspect that is more a question for your brother."

Mark turned back to the window. "I am sure I have no idea what you mean."

"Not according to what I hear from my maid."

Matthew snorted as Mark smothered a laugh. Fueling the gossip trains of the *ton* did run the risk of wielding a two-edged sword. The news of his late-night meeting with Judith verified the completion of the wager, but it also meant the accounts of it— some more true than others—made their way around the kitchens and drawing rooms of Mayfair. "You should not believe everything you hear, Mother."

"If only some of it is true, you are treading on the edge of scandal, even if she is a widow. And this wild scheme of hers could push us all over that edge."

"Not if it works," muttered Matthew.

"*If* it works."

A carriage pulled up in front of the house, and Mark's chest tightened. "They have arrived." He turned toward the door, but a short bark of his name called him to a halt. He looked around at his mother, whose face held a storm, and Matthew, whose eyebrows had arched into his hair.

Phyllida's voice grated. "You will wait here. Stephens will announce her. Them."

Mark swallowed, then nodded as he went to stand next to Matthew's chair.

His brother looked up at him, eyes narrowed. "What has gotten into you?"

Mark crossed his arms. "Nothing."

But something had, and Mark knew it to his core. From the moment he had shown Judith the room he had prepared for

Olivia and had seen her reaction to it—curiosity and acceptance, as well as her desire to meet the girl—something had shifted in him. And when the buckshot-filled blanket had arrived at his home two days ago, that something had cracked, and he doubted he would ever be able to seal those cracks completely. Cracks that had revealed an unexpected need, almost a craving, that Mark could not quite put a name to.

Stephens appeared in the doorway, blandly announcing "Lord Edmund Lovelace, the Earl Sculthorpe, and Judith Lovelace, Lady Sculthorpe."

Matthew stood as they entered, exchanging nods with the butler, who retreated. He greeted Judith and Edmund, then presented his mother to the earl, to whom she had never been formally introduced. "Mr. Smith is also here and will join us momentarily."

Mark watched closely as Judith, who barely glanced at him, settled next to his mother as the earl sat in the other wingback. Mark and Matthew remained standing until Stephens announced the Bow Street Runner, who eased down on an armchair, his eyes wide as he looked from one to the other as introductions were made, before focusing on Matthew.

"Your Grace, I have to admit surprise at the invitation, even more at this gathering."

Matthew gestured toward Edmund and Judith. "Mr. Smith, this meeting is at the behest of Lord Sculthorpe and his mother. They have a series of events to relate to you, which I believe concerns work you are already doing on behalf of the Duke of Devonshire."

Smith physically jerked, turning his attention to the earl. "How do you know—"

Phyllida interrupted. "Mr. Smith, we kindly ask you to listen first, questions to come later."

The runner stopped, mouth open, and Mark tightened his lips to keep from laughing and cleared his throat, stepping from behind Matthew's chair. "We do realize that you are the one who normally asks the questions, but this is an unusual circumstance. You are here, Mr. Smith, because the revelations in the story include the possibility of physical danger to the earl, thus the need for a slight bit of misdirection and skullduggery. The tale sounds somewhat ludicrous, but as a party who is involved on a tangential level, I assure you there is truth in the words." He paused. "And it may be connected with Miss Ashley's death."

They all stared at him. Matthew scowled as Smith shifted in his chair. "How so?" his brother asked.

"I will get to that shortly." Mark nodded at Edmund. "Begin with how you became involved with Vincent Atkinson and the resulting blackmail."

Smith almost leapt from his chair. "Blackmail?"

Phyllida sniffed, and the entire room fell silent.

Then Edmund took a deep breath and began to speak.

As he did, Mark watched Judith, not bothering to disguise that his sole attention remained on her as her son wove the tale of his debts, the disappearances of Devonshire's vase, the attempts to work out a resolution with Atkinson—only to be black-mailed—and the discovery by Judith of Atkinson's scheming against two other noblemen.

Judith listened intently, her focus seemingly on Edmund. But as Mark studied her, he realized that one hand rested on her right thigh, palm down, her index finger tracing a line back and forth. That's when he noticed that in the slope between her index finger and thumb, a distinct bulge protruded beneath the fabric.

His breath caught. *She is wearing it!* She had his ascot tied around her thigh. The thought spiked through him, and Mark almost lost the thread of Edmund's tale, blinking as the earl paused, took another deep inhale, and finished by explaining that the *on dit* among the servants was that Devonshire's vase remained in Atkinson's possession, hidden away in a secret cubbyhole in his dressing room.

Smith seemed to take it all in. "But you have no evidence."

This time Judith spoke, her hands clutched together in her

lap. "Which is why we need you. Our plan is to goad Mr. Atkinson into revealing himself." She spelled out the plan in the same way she had for Mark. "I have coached the three women, who fully understand what they need to do. They know the risks, and none of them are indeed as flighty and brainless as they appear to be"—she glanced at Edmund—"in the presence of men. They all three run substantial households, and I can assure you that is not an easy or brainless undertaking." She sat a little straighter. "It is merely how most women have been taught to behave around men. An unfortunate social construct, but it is what is expected of us. And it will be what Mr. Atkinson expects of them. He will not believe them to be capable of a scheme of any sort."

Smith nodded. "And you expect him to take this gossipy bait."

"I do." Judith moved her right hand back to her thigh, and Mark felt his cheeks heat. "According to his servants, he is not fond of nor particularly respectful of women. Or, apparently, his servants, whom he treats as furniture without brains . . . or tongues."

Smith muttered, "Sounds like much of the British aristocracy."

Phyllida arched her neck. "I can assure you, sir, that he is not one of us, no matter what he wishes or desires."

Smith coughed. "Of course not, Your Grace. I meant no offense."

Matthew leaned forward. "Are you willing to work with us on this?"

The runner sat a little straighter. "Given the demands we have been given to locate that vase, I am willing to take any chance I can." He looked at Mark. "But I do not understand how all this connects to Miss Ashley."

Mark pulled the note from his inside coat pocket and handed it to Smith. "Miss Ashley received this anonymous threat after her death. Do you remember mentioning to us the nickname of one of her other . . . paramours? The border raider?"

Smith nodded, his face darkening as he read the note and counted the bills. "With the notation of one hundred beside it."

Matthew gave a low growl of recognition.

Mark gave his brother a nod. "Border raiders are most notorious for—"

"Blackmail," Smith muttered. He folded the note up and tucked it into a pocket. "Do we have any evidence that Atkinson had visited Miss Ashley?"

"No physical proof, although Miss Ashley's maid, who now works for me, has confirmed it. She described him as, and I quote, 'the nastiest sort of randy bloke.'"

Smith stood. "Would she say that before a magistrate?"

"I suspect so. She can be quite the persistent young woman."

"Then let us get on with bringing this man to heel."

CHAPTER NINETEEN

Friday, 12 August 1814
Sculthorpe Manor
Four in the afternoon

JUDITH TOOK A deep, steadying breath against the pain in her lower back, annoyed and grumpy at the changes that had happened over the past twelve hours. Last night at midnight, her world had appeared one of sweet moonlight and lovely anticipation of the day to come. Then it had all been upended in the hours before dawn, leaving her gritting her teeth and staying upright by a sheer force of will. She rolled her shoulders against the tension in her muscles, then looked over the two notes spread on the worn wooden surface of her escritoire for a third time. They had arrived a few hours ago, in the midst of Epworth's care for her, and Judith had only now looked at them, fighting the unexpected fit of nerves they had brought on. The tips of her fingers quivered as she ran them down the lines again, which aggravated her to her very core.

She, Lady Sculthorpe, Judith Lovelace, did not have nervous fits. She had never had nervous fits. Ever. Not as a debutante, not as a bride, not as a widow. And certainly not at the idea of sharing her bed with a man.

What she did have was monthly courses, which had arrived in the wee hours of the morning with a conflagration of deep-seated cramps and a heavy flow. A once-a-month season that she despised so completely she had to remind herself that it meant the fertility that had brought her three remarkable young lads.

Three blessings in her life. In the long view, the pain was worth it.

While this thought brought some consolation, it did not make the current moment any easier.

Judith took another deep breath and touched the note on the right again, one almost blank. It had been a carefully folded and sealed piece of foolscap, with no greeting or signature. It featured only seven words.

After ten. As you wish. With caution.

Her throat tightened as she read the words once again. But then so did her thighs. And the muscles across her lower back, sending a shooting pain through her hips.

Damn him. Damn being a woman. And damn their timing.

Judith had issued an invitation to Mark last night after supper, when her body had craved his touch so much her mouth went dry and her stomach clenched. Her own fingers on her body had been woefully inadequate, only further driving a need almost beyond bearing. So she had beckoned him to her bed tonight. Judith had completely befuddled the poor hall boy who had sleepily received the missive she had hastily scribbled, sending the lad off to the Rydell residence with the request and the instructions to her home, her bedroom, with final guidance to be provided by Epworth.

His acceptance—those lovely seven words—had arrived later this morning, not long after Judith had awakened in intense pain, ringing for her maid. Epworth, who tracked Judith's schedule almost better than she did herself, arrived bearing ginger-and-yarrow tea without being asked. She ministered to Judith with tenderness, bringing the thick rags from the basket in her dressing room and helping position them, then fetching a hot brick for the bed.

When the messages had arrived, Judith had ignored them until now, when she had managed to emerge from her bed—but barely—the constant, rolling aches making it hard for her to sit straight. But it had to be done: she faced rescinding the invitation to Mark in the most delicate, discreet, and least hurtful manner possible. Judith reached for the teacup resting near the edge of her escritoire to find the heavily sweetened but still abysmal liquid had gone cold. "Damn it." Her muttered words accompanied a wince of pain as another cramp gripped her abdomen.

The abominable nature of being a woman. She knew not every female had such a difficult time—her mother-in-law had made her well aware of that fact. Her midwife assured them both that some women did but had once promised that having a child would ease the intensity of Judith's monthly courses. They had not. The intense pain had lessened for a few months after each birth but eventually returned in full force, often crippling her for two or three days, much to her frustration.

Epworth always responded with extraordinary care, usually arriving in mere minutes with a heated and linen-wrapped brick or bottle of hot water along with a round-robin of teas made from ginger, yarrow, willow bark, or motherwort. They all helped, but nothing truly resolved the agony but time.

Blinking, with another ache clutching her belly, Judith turned her focus to the other note, one almost as short but equally exciting.

Well . . . *almost* as equally exciting. And without a new layer of dismay.

Bait cast. Attendance ensured. Requested seating in place. B.

Blackwell. Dear God in heaven, how in the world had he pulled it off? When Judith had requested that he invite Atkinson to his and Lady Blackwell's ball, he had been unaware of Atkinson's ambitions toward the aristocracy. Once Lord Anthony understood, however, he had ensured Atkinson's attendance by casting the ultimate bait for any man desiring admission to Society's elite: the presence of the Prince Regent. An introduction to the prince would put Atkinson one step closer to a possible grant from the king. Atkinson would not miss the opportunity except under dire circumstances.

Now there was little to do but wait for the ball. And perhaps coach the three women a bit more. The three younger women seemed to act as if silliness were an artform to be coveted and embraced rather than controlled and focused. But they could wait.

Mark was the most immediate concern. Judith pulled a piece of foolscap from its cubbyhole, opened her inkpot, and began to compose a brief note. Not an easy effort as desire warred with pain that warred with propriety. But satisfied with the results, she blotted, folded, and sealed it.

Judith leaned back in her chair and released a long sigh. At least by next Friday she would be past these awful aches. Judith pushed up out of the chair, forcing her body to straighten as she hobbled to the fireplace. Epworth had sent one of the kitchen maids up to build a nice, constant blaze—every female in the house understood Judith's agony, even if they did not experience the severity themselves—and to explain the situation to Nanny, who would provide a reasonable excuse for the boys as to Judith's absence, as she did each month. Judith turned her back to the flames, letting the heat soak into her muscles, as a light tap sounded on the door.

"Enter."

Epworth pushed the door open a few inches, then alarm lit her face. "My lady? Why are you up?" She entered carrying a tray hold a steaming teapot and fresh cup and saucer, along with a small bowl of sugar. She hurried to set the tea tray on the bench.

Judith gestured to the escritoire. "Please see that the missive to Lord Mark is delivered as soon as possible."

Epworth moved to her side. "You must sit, my lady. I brought fresh tea."

"Might as well. What is it this time?"

Epworth eased an arm around Judith's waist and guided her toward the bench. "Motherwort and ginger."

Judith winced.

"The sugar will help." Epworth's voice held a low soothing tone. "And I have the maids bringing up hot water."

"I needed to respond to Rydell. Obviously, he cannot come here tonight. Will you see to it?"

Epworth, who knew about most of Judith's late-night visitors if not the details, helped Judith ease down on the bench. Epworth then picked up the now cold brick from the end of Judith's bed, unwrapped it, and used the fireplace poker to slide it into the coals. As she tended to the tea, she glanced at Judith. "Are you sure the gentleman's presence would not bring some comfort?"

An image of how Mark had held her flashed through Judith's thoughts, but she pushed it away. "The gentleman is not expecting to come watch me moan and gripe like a wounded animal."

Epworth added sugar to the tea, paused, then added more. "I doubt you would hiss at him."

Judith snorted a laugh, then winced at a spiked pain. "I am not completely convinced I would not."

Epworth smiled, then handed the tea to Judith. She then retrieved the cold one from the escritoire and slipped Judith's note into her pocket. "I will take care of it, my lady. If he is a worldly gentleman, he should understand."

Judith gave a low cough. "Even worldly gentlemen are not always aware of or comfortable with the ways of women. They often act as if it makes us an exotic species of animal."

"I find that most curious." Epworth placed the cup and saucer on the tray. "I suspect it is different for us, my lady."

Judith peered at her. "The servants?"

Epworth shrugged one shoulder. "We do not live such separate lives as the aristocracy do, with bedchambers apart. The men, they know us, we know them. The good ones, they help when they can. My da, he would hold mum, especially at night after he came in from the docks. He'd curl around her, keep her warm. Mum said he put out more heat than any brick ever could. He'd also tend to the little ones, either him or me. Not all men, of course. Some are clods." She paused, looking at the flames in the grate a moment. "Absolute clods."

"Ah." Judith sometimes wondered if the lives of servants were not somehow simpler, easier to manage, but she dared not say so. She also knew far too much about what went on in other households to truly believe that. In her experience, "a simple life" did not exist. For anyone.

Another knock on the door revealed two of the housemaids, one bringing in a low wash pan and an empty bucket, the other a kettle of hot water and a stack of thick towels. Judith cocked an eyebrow at Epworth, who directed the maids to place everything in front of the fire.

Epworth then faced her directly. "You will feel better once we get you and the bed cleaned up, resupplied with fresh rags, the hot tea in your belly, and the brick at your back." As Judith started to speak, Epworth held up a hand. "Do not argue. You know this to be true."

The two women stared at each other, then Judith let her shoulders sag. "I hate feeling weak."

Epworth went into action, pouring hot water into the wash pan and retrieving Judith's soap from her washstand. "You are not weak. If men hurt this often and this badly, society would crumble." She motioned for Judith to stand so she could remove her dressing gown and night rail. "Let us make quick work of this before you catch a chill."

Friday, 12 August 1814
Mark Rydell's Bloomsbury residence
Seven in the evening

MARK PEERED DOWN at the woman who had delivered the missive a few moments before. They stood in the small front parlor of the house, where Howe, with a scowl of suspicion on his rosy face, had led her after she had arrived at the same back door where Judith had stood only last week. Howe had announced her only as "Lady Sculthorpe's lady's maid" and backed out of the room, hovering in the foyer, glowering.

The woman had handed Mark the foolscap without a word. He read it twice as she waited, expressionless, her austere, black muslin dress as still as her body, and now he looked from it to her and back, a little puzzled.

Yesterday's late-night message had been delivered by a sleepy hall boy who had barely stood upright, and it had left Mark exhilarated. This, however, was no hall boy. Her posture and her uniform indicated her much loftier position. Mark read the note again, any sense of anticipation withering into disappointment and confusion.

Unfortunate change of plans. A visitor, expected but forgotten about, arrived two days early during the night. Will send word soon for resumption of plans. Apologies.

He cleared his throat. "Epworth, I presume."
A single nod.
"You might have sent a messenger."
"Forgive me, my lord, but I suspected Lady Sculthorpe may have been more self-sacrificing and discreet with her words than she needed to be."
He glanced at the foolscap. "I am not sure what—"
"I realize I am speaking out of turn, with a liberty I have no right to, but I have cared for Lady Sculthorpe for more than twenty years. She has a long history of putting others first, carefully guarding those around her from any sort of . . . embarrassment . . . even when she should give her own feelings a priority."
Mark felt as if he were circling a muddy drain. If Judith's note had not been confusing enough. "I am quite unsure—"
"She is in a great deal of pain, which I doubt she mentioned in her note."
That got his attention. He stiffened, on alert. "She did not. Why is she in pain? What kind of pain? Is she taking any remedy?"

"Ginger-and-motherwort tea. Yarrow. A hot brick to her back."

Mark stilled. He had grown up in a household consisting mostly of men, but even he knew why women took those teas. Stella had been an advocate of them—along with some more potent cures—as had some of his previous mistresses. "Women's troubles" were not foreign to him—nor women's wariness about men during their courses. "She does not want to see me."

"Because she does not wish to embarrass you. But I know my lady well. She could use some plain comfort." She cleared her throat, twin spots of red appearing on her cheeks. "If you are willing. Simple comfort. Not, my lord, the kind her gentlemen visitors usually provide."

"Yes, well . . ."

"And she has clearly missed you. I can see it in everything she does, the way she speaks about you."

"If she knew you were speaking to me—"

"I might lose my position. Yes."

"Epworth, my connection with Lady Sculthorpe—"

"She needs something more."

Mark's eyebrows arched.

Epworth swallowed hard, her posture sagging somewhat. "I do understand, my lord, how out of line I am being. But in twenty years, I have never seen Lady Sculthorpe work so persistently to save her family, nor have I seen her so close to her wit's end. To feel so . . . alone. Nor have I seen her respond to anyone, *anyone*, the way she has to you. It's as if you have injected some sort of hope into her being. Something she has never shown before. Ever. I have prayed it is something she could give to you as well. If you both can see it."

Hope.

Not a word common in Mark's life. And that craving within him seemed to expand, clutching his very soul. "You have risked rather a lot in coming here."

Epworth nodded. "Much more than I had planned to when I

decided to bring the note myself."

"Why would you do this?"

The red in Epworth's cheeks spread, and she swallowed hard. "Because I am in her debt."

"How so?"

Her hands clenched at her side. "My loyalty is and always has been to Lady Sculthorpe." Her gaze darted away to some far spot, then back to his face. "She has been my first priority most of my life. But I"—her voice faltered—"I failed her, when I did not tell her about her son's . . . iniquities."

"You knew Lord Sculthorpe was in trouble."

A single nod. "We all did. The servants. They—the earl and countess—threatened our positions if we spoke out."

"Or if you told her."

Another nod. "Even to her. When she realized the . . . duplicity . . . she was furious with me. Rightfully so. I am only telling you because—"

"Because I already know."

"Yes, my lord."

"And what 'plain comfort' do you think I can bring to Lady Sculthorpe?"

She studied him a moment, then cleared her throat. "Women sometimes find a hot brick or a hot water bottle to the back or belly or feet eases the pain. But a brick cools quickly. It cannot provide an ongoing heat. Or pressure. Or soft words."

Ah. "You think I should return her gift to me in kind."

"It was a thought."

"An uncommon one."

Epworth remained silent.

He glanced down at the note again. "You know her original plans?"

Her hands relaxed at her sides. "I do."

"And your role in them?"

Another nod.

"Then let us proceed this evening as nothing has changed."

Mark folded the note and tucked it into his pocket. "However, if she expresses any displeasure at my presence, I will leave immediately." He paused. "This will be a risk for both of us."

"Yes, sir."

Mark took a step back. "Howe."

His valet, now butler, instantly appeared in the doorframe. "Please escort Miss Epworth back to Sculthorpe Manor."

Both servants looked startled, exchanging quizzical glances that almost made Mark laugh. "It is late, clouds are beginning to gather, and Miss Epworth is a respectable woman. Pretend for the next half hour that you are a gentleman, one who has an umbrella."

Howe's face turned almost purple as he cleared his throat, gesturing for Epworth to move ahead of him and glanced once over his shoulder as he closed the parlor door.

Mark retreated to the fireplace and dropped into a wingback chair. He pulled out the note and looked at it again. *Madness. This is pure madness.* He had seen Judith angry, but this ran the chance of having her push him out of her life entirely. Insanity.

Still . . .

He wanted to do it. If he could offer her comfort of any kind, he wanted to.

And there was a possibility that he could offer more than his presence . . .

CHAPTER TWENTY

Friday, 12 August 1814
Sculthorpe Manor
Half-past ten in the evening

JUDITH SHIFTED, TRYING to push the brick at her feet farther down under the covers. It had gone cold, and her legs threatened to cramp from being curled up against her belly for so long. She twisted her hips, groaning as another spike of pain moved across her back. Although she had been in bed for almost twenty-four hours, drinking so much tea she had almost floated to the chamber pot, she had not been able to sleep or even find a position that remained comfortable for more than a few minutes. As she lay there, Judith tried to imagine what it would be like for all this to stop permanently, dreaming of a time her mother-in-law had referred to as "a saintly relief."

She also tried to gather the wherewithal to get out of bed for a few moments, to stretch aching muscles, and she lifted her head to peer at the fireplace, wondering if a miniscule flare remained among the embers.

A soft tapping on the door preceded it opening a few inches. "My lady?"

Judith sighed. *No more tea, please. I'm swamped.* She had also had another cleansing and new cloths less than an hour ago. She should be good for the night, although she did not expect to get much rest. "Enter."

Epworth pushed open the door, bring in yet another tea tray, although she left the door standing open as she placed the tray on the bedside table. Judith watched, eyebrows arched, as she looked from her maid to the open door, then to the tray, where the sugar, teapot, and cup had been joined by a small brown vial.

"What is that?"

"A helpful gift."

Judith jerked toward the baritone voice, pushing up in her bed as she stared at Mark Rydell, the last person on earth she wished to see in that moment. "What in God's name are you doing here? Did you not receive my message?" She gave Epworth an accusatory glance, then winced as her stomach gave a sharp cramp. Judith pressed a hand to the pain. "Damn it."

Mark closed the door but came no closer. "I did. But I became convinced I should come anyway."

"Why in hell would you do that?"

"Because I am in your debt, and I believe I know a way to repay you." He gestured toward the tray behind her.

Judith turned as Epworth added sugar to the cup. "Please, Epworth. I do not think I can take another sip of those blasted teas."

Epworth nodded, stirring. "This is just regular India tea, my lady." She picked up the brown bottle, uncorked it, and added a few drops to the cup. "Plus Lord Mark's gift."

"Which is?"

Mark cleared his throat. "Laudanum."

Judith stilled a moment, her mind a bit fuzzy, then murmured. "Laudanum?"

"I figured if it would help my innards, it might help yours. I understand the teas bring some ease but not full relief."

Judith tried to push back against the headboard, without much success. "True."

Mark moved around the bed. "Let me help."

Before Judith could react, he slid an arm about her waist and pulled her backwards, his strength like a warm massage against her aching back. He braced her with one arm and plumped a pillow with the other, slipping it between her and the headboard.

"Nicely done," muttered Epworth, standing back with the tea in hand.

Judith's eyes narrowed as she looked from her maid to Mark. "You really should not be here. Have the two of you have conspired on this? My note said nothing about my actual ailment." She winced. "Which is not an actual illness, so to speak—"

"Only in that Epworth was startled enough by my appearance that I was able to persuade her to present you with the laudanum." He stepped away from the bed, and Epworth moved up, offering Judith the cup and saucer.

Judith took the cup, eyeing both with suspicion but aching too much to truly care. She took a small sip, relishing the taste of real tea, even if it were overlaid with a bittersweet tanginess. She licked her lips, then nodded at Epworth. "The brick is cold."

Epworth blinked, then moved quickly to pull the heavy square from beneath the covers, as Judith glared at Mark again. "You should not be here."

Mark stepped to the side of the bed. "Ah, and that brings us to another reason I decided to come, despite your admonition."

Judith sipped the tea. "And that is."

"To deliver to your aid a regenerative source of heat and pressure that does not need to be inserted into the fire grate every hour or so."

Epworth snorted but did not look around. Instead, she busied herself stoking the fire and pushing the brick into the embers.

Judith heard his words, but her mind did not truly register their meaning. She blinked, playing them over to herself, her brain attempting to sort through all the scientific lectures she had heard at the Royal Academy or information from any of the books she had read about any device that created its own heat. Her thoughts swirled in confusion. "You mean like Thomas Savery's engine?"

Epworth stared at her as Mark laughed. He moved closer, his gaze focused on her face. "You really are the most remarkable woman. I had something much simpler in mind. And more at hand."

Judith drank more tea, which began to have a warm and calming effect on her stomach. "Such as?"

"A human body. Specifically, mine."

Judith's eyes widened. *He could not possibly want me to—* "You cannot mean for us to—"

He held up a hand. "No. Not that. At all. I only propose to hold you. To talk, if you are able. There are things we should discuss."

"Such as?" Judith swirled the tea in her cup, then took several sips. The taste did not seem as bitter now, and she could see a few grains of the brownish sugar in the bottom.

Mark rested his hand on the covers near the top of her thigh. Judith could feel the warmth of his palm through them, and it seemed to spread upward toward the heat growing in her abdomen. She nodded slowly as he answered.

"The Blackwell ball. Your plan."

"Our plan."

He smiled. "The plan. The three ladies. Olivia."

Judith snapped a look at Epworth, who still busied herself with the fire, which now blazed brightly.

Mark's smirk returned in full form, as did the gleam in his eyes. "If you do not think the servants know everything in our lives . . ."

Judith relented, give a low chuckle. "Oh, I know they do." Judith drained her cup. "Epworth?"

The maid turned. "My lady?"

Judith held out the cup. "Thank you."

"Of course." Epworth took the cup, then gathered the tray, pausing at the door. "I will wait for you to ring, my lady."

"Please do so."

Epworth gave a slight curtsy and left, pulling the door firmly closed.

Mark began to untie his cravat. "Where do you hurt?"

Judith rolled her shoulders. "Pretty much all over. Mostly my back and hips. Where you would expect." Judith studied him. "How much do you know about women's ailments?"

He shrugged out of his coat and draped it over the chair near her dressing table. "Probably more than most men."

"Another advantage of being a rakehell and rapscallion?"

He sat down on the bench at the end of her bed and pulled off his boots. "Most likely. I know some women struggle more than others. I know certain acts can prompt an early arrival. I know some teas help, but I also know some potions can more effective."

"Thus the laudanum."

"Stella and the other actresses used it frequently, especially when they had to perform."

Judith felt suddenly weak. "Women who cannot take to their beds, like I have?"

Mark stood and unbuttoned the fall of his britches, slipping them off. "Some months were harder, even for her, than others. And I know a certain duchess, one of the strongest people I know, who cannot hold down food for the first two days." He folded his britches and laid them on the bench, smoothing out the wrinkles. Still wearing his small clothes and shirt, he went to the other side of the bed and peeled back the covers, then stopped. "Let me help."

After a moment, Judith nodded, watching as he slid in beside her. She scooted down in the bed to lie flat again, then winced as the cramps moved through her again.

"Turn on your side, away from me."

She did, a groan escaping from her unbidden as she drew her knees up again.

"I am going to position you."

Judith nodded, biting her lip as he pulled her backwards toward his body, lifting her shoulders, plumping pillows, and settling her into a nest of covers.

"Are you all right?"

"More or less."

Mark moved over her so that most of his body rested against her, his knees pulled up to parallel hers. He wrapped an arm around her, his broad hand pressing against her stomach. Judith tucked her hand beneath her face, her breath slowing as the warmth of his body eked into her, the heat spreading through her like a hot bath. He held her, silent for a few moments, as the tension in her muscles, the aches that had crippled her, flowed away.

Mark kissed her temple, his calming voice a bare whisper. "The laudanum takes about a half hour. You may fall asleep after that."

"I have not slept in two days." The gravel in her own voice surprised Judith, and she swallowed.

"I am not surprised. Pain is not conducive to slumber."

"Speaking from experience?"

"Quite recently, as a matter of fact."

Judith coughed a laugh, then groaned.

"Ah, that, unfortunately, sounds familiar. Laughing is not recommended."

She almost laughed again but choked it back. "Stop."

Mark brushed her hair away from her face. "How do you feel?"

Taking a deep breath, she murmured, "I think it may be working." Indeed, her muscles had grown lax, the heat of their bodies enveloping her in a soothing cocoon. "Tell me about Olivia."

Mark paused, then his voice became low, rhythmic, as if he were a master storyteller. "I have moved Olivia and Rose into the house."

"Already? How did that go?"

"Smoother than I anticipated. Rose had told Olivia about Stella's death right after it happened. We kept my first meeting with Olivia brief. And the second. Then Rose brought Olivia for a visit, and they examined the rooms. Olivia only wanted to know if she could bring her own toys and to see the garden. They moved in two days ago."

Judith stroked his arm, and his hand pushed a little harder against her stomach. The warmth and weight felt so comforting, she found herself worried he might pull away. She covered his hand with hers.

"Were your servants startled?"

"The servants were startled when I added a nursery. They knew some plot lay ahead."

Judith felt herself drifting, her thoughts jumbling. The laudanum. "Are they settling in well?"

"Olivia has already made fast friends with Clara, my head housemaid, and has convinced Cook that treats should be given after ever visit to the garden."

Judith yawned, closing her eyes. "Children can add such joy to a home. I am surprised the servants did not start a rumor that you were about to marry, once they saw the nursery."

Mark fell silent.

"But I am glad they have welcomed them. That is not always the case with a"—Judith swallowed, searching for a word without an insult built into it—"an unexpected child."

"True. And Howe would have squelched any rumor about marriage. He knows well how and why the institution would not suit me."

Judith felt herself fading, the grogginess of sleep overwhelming her as the pain in her body vanished. "Never?"

Mark remained quiet as Judith's breathing evened out and the peace of sleep ended the conversation. Only barely did she hear his last three whispered words.

"Only with you."

MARK HAD NOT meant to say those last three words, and he held onto the idea that Judith had been fully asleep when he said them.

He had not meant to *say* them.

But he had *meant* them.

Mark had once dreamed of marriage, as he supposed most young men did, before being thrown into the Marriage Mart at the age of twenty, where he discovered most of the young debutantes differed from his mother and sister Daphne in the same way that fine wines differed from ciders. Wine and cider both delighted the palate and quenched thirst but in vastly varied ways. He had grown up bantering with his mother and Daphne, wits sharpened by sarcasm and education. Daphne had been a dedicated and determined reader, consuming books on every possible subject and driving her brothers as well as her governess mad with questions. Mark's dance partners at various balls could not compare, and his sharpest questions and wickedest barbs often met with blank stares or expressions of pure confusion.

This woman, whose soft, tortured body now lay so close to him, had conjured up Thomas Savery's invention of the pistonless steam pump in the midst of her pain. On the dance floor, no matter how hard he pushed, she met him step for step, barb for barb. She enjoyed their sexual play and seemed ready for more. She had met his announcement of a daughter, a by-blow, with grace and openness. She had understood his nightmares, showing no fear at all.

Yet she had come at him, claws bared, when she thought he had harmed her family.

He did not want to live without her.

But too much lay ahead, too many problems yet to be re-solved, for either of them to consider marriage. While the quilt she had sent helped, the nightmares still plagued him. Her family's finances still lay in tatters. And the Blackwell ball awaited them, with its fragile scheme that could risk both their worlds. At that thought, a line from *Richard II* crossed his thoughts, and he whispered. "'But time will not permit: all is uneven, And every thing is left at six and seven.'"

Judith stirred but did not waken.

Mark smiled, watching her sleep. *I bet you would know where that came from.* She probably would have read Shakespeare's play, even if she had not seen it. *We must get through this. We must.*

With that thought in mind, Mark snuggled a little deeper beneath the covers, pulled Judith closer, and rested his head against the pillows. It would be a long night.

❦

CHAPTER TWENTY-ONE

Saturday, 13 August 1814
Sculthorpe Manor
Seven in the morning

"WHO ARE YOU?

Two bright and wide brown eyes stared at Mark over the foot of Judith's bed. He blinked and so did those eyes. Mark waited, swallowing hard and trying to clear the grogginess of sleep from his brain.

He had merely drowsed now and then through the night, never sleeping deep enough for the nightmares to appear—he had drunk far too much coffee before coming to Sculthorpe Manor the night before for that to happen. He had also gotten up and moved around some, once Judith's laudanum-induced slumber seemed deep and secure. He had stoked the fire, wrapped the heated brick for her bed when he was not in it, found the chamber pot, and discovered one of Mrs. Burney's novels to keep him entertained as he watched Judith rest. At the least movement from her, Mark had returned to her side, holding her, sometimes dozing. Enough, apparently that he had not heard the bedchamber door open or soft footsteps enter.

"Why are you here?" The bright eyes came with a mass of dark curls and a sweet boy's voice.

Mark put his finger to his lips and pointed to Judith.

"Nanny said Mummy was sick. Is she still sick? Are you the doctor? You do not look very much like a doctor. And not like our doctor at all."

Mark pressed his finger hard against his lips, even as his shoulders quivered with repressed laughter.

"I want her to get well. She needs a doctor. I miss her."

Persistence, thy name is child. "I am sure she will be better soon," Mark whispered. "Right now, she is asleep."

"Not any longer," muttered Judith.

"Mummy!" The boy clambered down from the bench and trotted around to the side of the bed. "Are you awake?"

Mark shifted as one of Judith's arms snaked from beneath the covers, her hand cupping the boy's face.

"My jammy boy." She cleared her throat to push away the gravel in those first words. "What are you doing here?"

"I missed you! Nanny said you would only be sick a few days, but it's been three whole days!"

Judith shook her head. "Barely a day."

"It seems a lot longer. I wanted to make sure you were all right. Who is that man? I do not think he is a doctor. Is he a doctor come to help you?"

She patted his cheek, then tucked her arm beneath the covers again. "He is a friend who has helped me. Where is Nanny?"

The boy grimaced. "Looking for me."

"You have probably given her a fright."

A pout creased his face. "But she wouldn't bring me down to see you."

"It is still rather rude to cause someone a great scare."

The pout deepened, and Mark almost laughed. This child was going to be trouble.

A flurry of rustling cloth and hasty footsteps sounded outside the still open bedchamber door, and two people appeared in the frame, Epworth and a younger woman in a blue-and-white uniform. She gasped, rushing into the room. "Master William!" Then she spotted Mark, stopping cold. "Oh!" Her hand covered her mouth. "Oh, no!"

At her expression of shock and alarm, Mark could not resist. "What a fine kettle of fish this is."

Judith gave a bark of laughter, then struggled to sit up. Mark slid his arm behind her, bracing her shoulders and helping her scoot up against the headboard as he did the same. They both pulled the covers up to their chests, tucking them in tightly.

Epworth, a wry grin on her face, stepped around Nanny. "My lady, how do you feel?"

Judith sighed. "Better. I think sleep and"—she glanced at William—"the other helped." She slipped her hand into Mark's. "As did the heat." She nodded at Epworth. "You were correct. Thank you."

Epworth stood a little straighter. "Are you ready for a tray?"

Judith nodded. "Real tea. Toast, I think. And"—she gave a quick glance at William—"a bath, I think."

"Of course." Epworth nudged Nanny, which seemed to break the spell. "Girl, get the child. We need to go."

Nanny jerked, looking from Epworth to Judith, with a bare peek at Mark. "My apologies, your ladyship. I only turned my back for a second."

Judith's smile seemed forced, and she winced as she shifted in the bed. "He is a squirmy one." She pushed the covers back and swung her legs over the side of the bed but did not stand. "Let me hug you."

William almost leapt into her arms, giggling. Judith's back tensed, but she wrapped her arms around her son, holding him tightly. Then she eased him away and pointed at the nanny. "Go. I will visit as soon as I am able."

"Good! I miss you!"

"I miss you too. Now be a good boy today. No more scares for Nanny."

"Yes'm."

Mark watched as William skipped back to Nanny, whose face had gone quite pale. The three left the room, and Epworth pulled the door shut. When Mark heard a key turn in the lock, he chuckled again. "They will be talking about this for months."

"A true scandal." She twisted to face him, squeezing his hand.

"Thank you."

He tightened his grasp on her fingers. Signs of pain still pulled at her face, with deep circles under her eyes and lines along her cheeks. "But you are not yet well."

She took a deep breath, as if to steady herself. "Much improved. The pains are less. The sleep will help."

Mark got out of the bed and walked around to her side. "Let's get you nested again." At her nod, he moved her legs back onto the bed, then slid one arm behind her shoulders, the other under her thighs, shifting her higher in the bed. As he released her, he saw blood had stained his sleeve.

So did she. "Damn it. I am sorry."

He kissed her lightly on the lips. "It will give Howe something to fuss about."

Judith cupped his face with her hands, pulling him back for a second kiss. "You should go. There is a key on the edge of the escritoire. I believe my instructions were that you had to leave before dawn."

"If I were good at following instructions, my mother would not have anything to complain about." He stepped back. "Expect an invitation to dinner shortly."

"For Olivia?"

Mark's chest tightened at how quickly she had grasped his intent. "Yes. And we will not be alone."

"Understood." Her smile seemed less strained this time. "Now go. Epworth and Nanny can be trusted. Edmund and Margaret, not quite so much."

Mark kissed her again, then reached for his trousers. He did not care to remind her how skilled he was at fleeing women's bedchambers in the early morning hours, but in this moment, he felt grateful he could dress quickly and walk without his boot heels thudding on the stair treads. In mere moments, he found himself in the bright morning air of a Saturday morning, his long stride stretching his legs, carrying him home before his own servants would be checking on him.

JUDITH WATCHED MARK dress and leave, chewing lightly on her lower lip. Her thoughts swirled in a miasma, nothing settling. She felt oddly unconcerned that Nanny had seen Mark in her bed—even her lack of concern should have bothered her, but it did not. Nanny and Epworth both could, in truth, be trusted not to gossip about his presence to the other servants, but would Nanny eventually tell Mr. Robins?

Or would William? Her youngest son was not a great keeper of secrets. George had been tight-lipped even as a toddler, and Robbie already had proved to be capable of many closely held thoughts. William, however, had become a rather pronounced chatterbox, even carrying on conversations with his toys or other inanimate objects.

Why did she not care if anyone knew? Was it because they had already declared their physical connection in that bloody wager? Or was it because he was willing to marry her?

Judith clutched her hands together on her lap, staring at them. *Only with you.* She had been close to sleep, but she had heard the words, clear as day. She had not responded, pretending to doze, as it seemed he had not intended her to hear them. And then she had fallen deeply asleep, not truly waking again until she heard her son's voice. Even that had seemed a dream.

A low, dull ache gripped her abdomen. Sore, but not the intense pains of the past twenty-four hours. Whether residual relief from the laudanum or the normal passage of time, Judith could not be sure—nor did she care too much about this either. She usually hurt like hell for at least two days, sometimes three, bleeding for five or more. If the rest, heat, and drug had short-ened the pain, all the better. Being able to eat a bit would aid her as well.

What Judith did care about were all the topics Mark had wanted to discuss, topics they had not touched in the short chat before she had disappeared into the laudanum. That he even sought to discuss these things with her filled Judith when an inexplicable pride, something she had seldom felt. Last night, even in the midst of her pain-laced fog, she had relished his attention, his tenderness, his questions, his touch. She had sent him away this morning out of absolute necessity, but she had not wanted him to leave.

Ever.

Judith covered her face with her hands. *Dear God in heaven, what have we done?*

A soft tap on the door preceded Epworth's entry with a tray. Following her came four other housemaids, with all the accouterments of a long hot bath. Judith eased out of bed, letting them help her. It was time to see if she could have anything resembling a normal day.

❦

CHAPTER TWENTY-TWO

Wednesday, 17 August 1814
Lord Mark Rydell's Bloomsbury residence
Half-past six in the evening

MARK STOOD STILL, taking slow shallow breaths and resisting the urge to toss Howe into the Thames. His finicky valet, now also his butler, had retied Mark's cravat twice, with quaking fingers and reddened cheeks, determined to produce a perfectly symmetrical knot. He now circled Mark with a brush, straightening, pulling, and picking imaginary nits from the black-and-white kit, muttering dire comments about dining room measurements, polished silver, and soup courses.

"She can read a recipe, but can she read a ruler? Apparently not. The knives were too far from the plates, and the silver polish is still in the pantry, looking all the world like sauce for the duck. We are not using two of the candelabras because they are still tarnished. We are not equipped for this. We are not staffed for this."

"You do know I can hear you, correct?"

Howe stepped back, stiffening his posture. "Sir?"

"You're muttering, but I can still hear you."

The valet blinked. "I was . . . muttering?"

Mark tightened his lips to avoid smiling. "Howe, whatever you were thinking was coming out of your mouth. Fine for a valet. Not so much a butler."

Now the red crept up the man's forehead. "Um . . . I . . ."

Mark waved off the thought and sat down to put on his slippers. "Try to remain calm. I realize this is your first meal as my butler, but this is not a state dinner. It's my family and Lady Sculthorpe, and they all know about you, even if they have never met you. Lady Sculthorpe's maid will accompany her but will remain in the servants' dining room. Make sure Miss Epworth, their carriage driver, and the footman get something to eat."

"Yes, sir."

"You go on down. They should be arriving soon. I will join you shortly. And, Howe?"

"Yes, sir?"

"Take a few deep breaths. Neither your position nor your reputation depend on this dinner."

"Yes, sir. Thank you, sir. But I still wish to do my best."

"Of course. Which is why I appreciate you."

Mark watched Howe leave, releasing a long sigh of relief. Since Mark had announced the dinner and sent the invitations, Howe had been relentless in his fastidiousness. In just four days, the house had been cleaned top to bottom, the menu devised and revised, supplies purchased, and the dining room prepped with new linens and china. Clara had turned out to be an excellent organizer and leader for the female staff, as well as being able to calm the much older Howe in the midst of his fits of panic.

Mark's own sense of unease about the evening, however, had little to do with the place settings, the recipes, or any cobwebs the maids might have missed. Because he knew none of his guests would be considering his gifts as a host. Instead, they would be focused on the dark curls and blue eyes of a three-year-old girl. His mother, in particular, would be examining the way Olivia walked, the way she smiled.

That smile.

Mark headed up to the nursery, opening the door to find Rose waiting patiently in a dark-green linen gown, the best of her meager frocks, although it now hung loosely about her frame, and he wondered if she had lost weight again, the way she had during her first illness. Mark had offered to have a modiste make her several new dresses after they had moved in, but she had refused, and he did not want to push the matter at this time. They faced far too much adjustment to the new living arrangement. Rose, in complete opposition to her daughter, remained a quiet and private person who doted on her granddaughter.

Said granddaughter looked up at Mark, a smile spreading over her face. She had been sitting at a low table, combing the hair of a doll almost as tall as she was. Mark, who knew nothing about buying clothes or toys for little girls, had thought the doll would be more of a decoration for the room, occupying one of the small chairs. Instead, it had become Olivia's constant playmate, an escaped princess named Elizabeth but dubbed Lizzie.

Tucking Lizzie under one arm, Olivia crossed to him. "Are they here?"

He squatted, stroking her arm. "Not yet. Are you ready?"

She nodded vigorously, her curls bouncing. "Will they be nice?"

His relationship with his mother crossed his mind, but he set it aside. "They will. It's my brother and his wife, my mother, and a good friend of ours, Lady Sculthorpe. They just want to meet you. They may ask a few questions, but it will not take long. Then you can come back up here, change out of this fancy thing, and play." He tugged the skirt of her frock, a high-waisted white muslin dress with a royal-blue cotton slip underneath and a matching ribbon around the waist. Blue ribbons dotted her hair, which had been pulled away from her face in an attempt to tame at least a few of the curls.

Olivia giggled. "I feel like a princess."

"You are a princess."

Her eyes widened. "Does that make you a prince?"

"Oh, no. I am a nobody."

"But you are my papa."

The word still caught Mark off guard, and his breath hitched. "I am."

She gave a single sharp nod. "Then you can be my prince."

He kissed her on the forehead, then stood, addressing Rose. "They will gather in the front parlor before we go into the dining room. I will send Clara up when we are ready. It should not be long. I think I heard the first knocks as I came up."

Rose nodded, her hand pressed hard across her stomach.

His whole household was a bundle of nerves.

Heading downstairs, Mark heard the mantel clock in the front parlor chime the hour, the tone echoing through the foyer and over the soft muttering of voices. Mark listened as he approached the room, immediately hearing the rough rumble of Matthew's words, along with the strident tones of his mother. Sarah, Matthew's new wife, spoke with a soft alto that inexplicably soothed his brother's temper. He heard Judith's dulcet words . . . then another, higher pitched voice that caused Mark to halt outside the door.

That made one too many people. He had only invited Matthew, Sarah, his mother, and Judith. Then who . . .

He pushed open the door, and they all turned to face him, falling silent. Except for one of them.

"He still does not look like a doctor, even though he has on clothes."

JUDITH WATCHED THE color drain from Mark's face as Matthew snorted a laugh, and Sarah gripped her husband's forearm in reprimand. Phyllida sniffed and clutched her hands together in front of her, murmuring, "Seen. Not heard."

For once Judith would agree. She gripped the back of William's neck and whispered. "Remember."

He twisted to look up at her. "Oh. I forgot."

Judith faced Mark, hoping that he would not be too angry by her surprise guest—and that the heat in her cheeks did not mean her face had turned beet red. "I thought perhaps—"

"It was my idea." Phyllida stepped forward. "The children are almost the same age, and no child should be left alone, especially when there is a party in the house."

The gleam returned to Mark's eyes as did the color to his cheeks. "Is that experience speaking, Mother?"

"You should know better than most." Phyllida turned to Judith. "By the time he was five, my second son could not be left unattended. He could shimmy down the lattice on the outside of the house and be under the dining room table causing havoc before anyone noticed him missing from the nursery."

Judith kept her expression solemn. "I take it punishment did not have its desired effect."

Phyllida sniffed. "He has a remarkably short memory of such."

Mark focused on Judith. "Was it truly her notion?"

Judith glanced at her son's face, now wide-eyed at the exchange between the adults. "It was, in truth, although I agreed with her. I have always thought my boys too far apart. So I agree with her wisdom."

"Take care on that score, my lady, as my mother's wisdom often arrives with sharp edges and the occasional thorn." Mark smirked as Phyllida huffed, then he reached for the bell pull. At Howe's appearance he instructed the butler to have Clara bring Olivia and Rose to the room. He then faced them.

"I do appreciate you coming tonight. I was not certain how to integrate Olivia and Rose into the family, but I no longer felt comfortable leaving circumstances as they were. Word is beginning to spread about Stella leaving a child behind and there is growing speculation about who her father might be. The names I heard—dukes, viscounts, even the Prince Regent—put Olivia at even more risk than if I acknowledged her. But this move has not been easy. Her grandmother Rose has never been associated with Society, and she is somewhat overwhelmed and a bit fragile. The maids are helping her, but I felt she needed to meet some of the family with whom she will be associated.

"Not all men would be so honorable or thoughtful." Sarah's

soothing words carried an edge of experience to them.

"Some men"—Matthew cleared his throat—"would have ignored them, left them to their fate, especially given the circumstances of her birth. The city is littered with such children."

"Woe be to us," Judith muttered.

Mark tilted his head as he looked at her. "Indeed. And that attitude is precisely why I invited you as well." He looked down at William. "You were a surprise but are welcome."

"But you are still not a doctor?"

Mark blinked, and Judith suddenly realized neither of them had actually answered his question. She stroked William's hair. "No. He is not a doctor."

"But he helped you."

"He did."

Mark smeared a hand across his lips as the other three Rydells looked puzzled. Further commentary, however, stalled when the door opened to reveal an older woman in a loose and plain green gown and the most beautiful young girl Judith had ever seen. Dark curls had been coiffed into tight ringlets held in place by a plethora of blue ribbons, which matched the slip beneath her white gown, a miniature of a woman's ballgown, revealing an intimation of the beautiful woman she would become. Enormous blue eyes scanned the room as her focus moved from one person to another, finally settling on William. Her face lit as she spotted him, and she took a step forward, only to have the older woman put a hand on the girl's shoulder, holding her back.

Phyllida gasped, one hand covering her mouth. Matthew looked from the girl to his brother several times before his gravelly words echoed what everyone seemed to be thinking.

"It is rather obvious who her father is, is it not?"

Phyllida whispered, "She is Daphne made over."

The girl looked up at Mark. "Who is Daphne?"

"My sister."

"There are more of you?"

"A lot more."

The girl grinned. "Good!"

Mark touched her shoulder but looked at the others. "May I present Mrs. Rose Ashley and Miss Olivia . . . Ashley."

His hesitation before saying the girl's last name told Judith that "Ashley" would not be her surname for much longer. And his face softened as he gazed down at her, his eyes becoming moist.

"Never thought I would see that."

They all turned to Matthew, who shrugged. "That's the way Father used to look at Daphne." He squatted and held out his hand. "I am pleased to meet you, Miss Ashley. I am Matthew Rydell."

Rose released her, and Olivia went to him, her small hand slipping into his. "The same, sir." She looked around at Rose, who nodded, motioning her encouragement with a flick of her hand.

When Matthew lifted her hand to kiss the back of it, the girl's mouth opened in a quiet *O*. She did not move until Sarah bent and introduced herself, as did Phyllida. Olivia then stopped in front of William, who did not say a word.

"Who are you?"

William simply stared.

Judith leaned over. "I am Judith Lovelace, and this is my son, William."

"Are you family too?"

"No," Judith said, nudging William, who resisted.

"Not yet," muttered Matthew, earning another squeezed forearm from Sarah.

"How old are you?"

At William's continued silence, Judith murmured, "He is four."

Olivia nodded, her ringlets bouncing. "Do you have a rocking horse? I have a rocking horse. It is brand new. Would you like to see it?"

William looked up at Judith, who looked at Mark, who looked at Rose, who nodded. Mark turned back to Judith. "Rose and Olivia had planned to eat dinner in the nursery. William may join them, if it is permissible."

"It is."

Olivia bounced up on her toes, and all semblance of polite civility vanished as she grabbed for William's hand, tugging him toward the door. "Come on! I'll race you!"

With one startled look back at Judith, William broke into a run. "I'll win!"

As their thundering footsteps raced up the stairs, an awkward silence settled on the room. With a nod to Mark, Rose followed the children.

Judith watched her go, an odd worrying nagging at the back of her thoughts. She could not quite place it, but something about Rose Ashley felt strangely familiar.

Phyllida sniffed, jerking Judith's attention back to the room. "Well, that was . . . unexpected."

Judith felt her face heat again. "My son has not been around many other children. Just his brother, who is ten and already a bit full of himself."

Phyllida nodded. "As all ten-year-old boys tend to be. Unfortunately, most of them never grow out of it."

Sarah gave a short laugh, and Matthew a growl. "We are right here, Mother."

"If the cap fits . . ."

Sarah caught Judith's eye, and they both laughed, causing the men to look highly affronted. Fortunately, Howe appeared to indicate dinner was ready to be served.

Mark offered Judith his arm, which she gladly accepted, her fingers curling around his elbow. As they walked toward the home's small dining room, he leaned closer. "How are you feeling?"

"Back to normal. It never lasts too long. But I do appreciate all you did. Thank you. Do you need me to return the vial?"

He shook his head. "Not yet. Does this happen every month?"

Judith looked away, her cheeks warming again.

"My apologies. My mother will tell you I have never been very good at knowing what is and is not appropriate topics of conversation."

"Then I suspect you have seen many a young lady grow red in the face."

He chuckled. "More than you can imagine." After a pause, he whispered. "Are you wearing it?"

She tightened her fingers on his arm.

"I will take that as a yes." His voice dropped even lower. "No matter what you hear tonight, keep one thing in mind."

She peered up at him. "Which is?"

"First choice."

CHAPTER TWENTY-THREE

Wednesday, 17 August 1814
Lord Mark Rydell's Bloomsbury residence
Half-past ten in the evening

MARK CARRIED A sleeping William to the Sculthorpe carriage, laying him across one seat and covering him with a soft coverlet borrowed from the nursery. Both children had played hard, falling asleep on Olivia's bed well before the adults finished their dinner and retreated back to the parlor with port.

Except for William's presence, the evening had progressed much as Mark had expected, with a delicious meal and what felt like hundreds of probing, detailed questions about his plans for Olivia and Rose, as well as details from Judith on how the tactics for the Blackwell ball progressed. He had dodged as many questions as he could, Judith peering at him with expressions of curiosity as she stepped into several gaps, often turning the conversation back to the ball. The three ladies she coached seemed taken with the scheme, and Sarah—whose first husband had been an arrogant, abusive man, much like Atkinson—offered suggestions on how to lure him deeper into the charade.

Only when they were settled with the port did his connection with Judith enter the conversation, with his mother pointing out they had already traipsed into the territory of scandal, with the wager and his acknowledgment of Olivia. If the plot against Atkinson failed, Italy might be a good option for exile. Or perhaps Greece, where their aunt lived and Daphne currently visited.

Matthew, who had plans to rejoin Wellington as soon as they

had settled Sarah in place to run the duchy, objected strenuously to that possibility, as he wanted Mark to remain in England to help Sarah. Judith had remained silent in the heated discussion that followed, observing all of them instead of participating. Mark had also said little, as he had long since stopped caring about his own reputation and did not wish to discuss any of his intentions at the moment. Too many of them were still not fully formed. He did worry about how all this would affect Judith and her family, especially if they were not able to rectify Edmund's financial difficulties.

The main point of the evening, however, had been to introduce his family—and Judith—to Olivia and that had gone as well as could be. And Mark reluctantly realized that his mother's suggestion for Judith to bring William had been a good one, despite the initial awkwardness.

Mark tucked the coverlet beneath William's feet, then eased backward out of the carriage, trying not to rock it much. He moved away as the footman helped Epworth and Judith into the vehicle, then peered in through the door as they settled.

"I appreciate you coming, Lady Sculthorpe. I believe your presence made the evening progress much smoother."

Her eyebrows arched. "You consider that a 'smooth' evening?"

He smirked. "Where my family is concerned, remarkably peaceful."

"Hm." She leaned back against the squabs. "Something to keep in mind."

Mark chuckled and stepped away as the footman latched the door, mounted his post, and thumped on the roof. The driver clicked the reins, and the carriage moved forward, down the street and out of sight. He waited as the Embleton ducal carriage pulled into its place. His brother escorted their mother and the lovely Sarah down the steps from the foyer, where they had been waiting. As the footman opened the door, Phyllida stopped, studying Mark.

"What is it, Mother?"

Her next words were a pronouncement. "You need to marry that woman."

Matthew and Sarah looked as startled as he felt. "I beg your pardon. I thought you said she was a—how did you put it?—a 'damnable hussy.'"

"As she is. But so are you."

Matthew laughed.

"I'm sorry, what—"

"But I have never seen you with a woman so well suited to your outrageous personality. And she looks at you with affection instead of lust, as so many other women do."

"Mother—"

"Do you think I am blind? Or that I sit in ballrooms and not observe how people look at you? I have tried to steer you toward the ones less obvious in their lascivious gazes at you, not that it has had any effect."

Mark's patience evaporated. "Then stop trying. I think it is time you put off your mourning clothes and got up and danced instead of nosing into everyone else's affairs."

"Mark!" Matthew moved forward as if to step between them. Phyllida threw up a hand, stopping him as Mark went on.

"Father once told me that you were the finest dancer he had ever squired onto a floor. You had no equal. And it has been almost a year since he died." He gestured to his brother. "Matthew is the duke now. The head of household. Let him *be* it. You are a beautiful woman, and you do not need to spend the rest of your life doing nothing but overseeing and prowling through the lives of your children!"

The air went still. No one moved or spoke. Then his mother snapped toward their stoic-faced footman and held out one hand. The man leapt to her aid, and Phyllida disappeared into the carriage. After a moment, Sarah joined her with a bare glance at Mark.

Matthew shook his head as he reached toward the carriage

door. "There will be repercussions."

Mark let out a long breath. "Of course, there will be. There always are."

Matthew clapped him on the shoulder, then joined the ladies. The footman secured the door, and Mark stepped backward as it lumbered away from the pavement.

He and his mother had fought often, starting early in his life. Spats, mostly. His father had explained that Mark and his mother shared a similar temperament, something he could not see then— or now. He had been ten when the first major row had occurred, but for the life of him Mark could not remember what it had been about. Something to do with Matthew going off to school probably. He did remember spending the night in a tree in their back garden. His mother had forbidden anyone to help him or bring him food or drink. He had even pissed from his high perch, much to the amusement of his younger brothers. He had not eaten for two days, until he had apologized.

The first of many rows . . . and many punishments. "But I am not in a tree anymore," he muttered as he entered the house.

"My lord?"

Mark jerked, startled by Howe's presence in the parlor door-way.

"Pardon me, my lord."

Mark motioned for Howe to close the front door. "Let us bring this evening to close, shall we? Tell the maids they can reset the parlor tomorrow. I will not be using it." He turned toward the stairs.

"Uh, my lord? May I pose a question?"

Mark paused two steps up. "What is it?"

"Lady Sculthorpe's maid."

"What about her?"

"You did call her '*Miss* Epworth,' did you not?"

Mark kept his face still. "I did. Why?"

"I-I-er—I merely wanted to make certain."

Mark grinned. "You finish down here then get to bed. I'll

undress myself, and you can tidy up in the morning."

"Yes, sir. That will work out nicely." Howe gave a slight bow, then turned toward the kitchen.

Mark decided to check on Olivia before retiring, and he opened the door to the nursery slowly, taking only one step inside. Mark had offered Rose her choice of a separate room or to have a bed brought into the nursery. She had chosen the room, which most likely allowed her to rest more soundly, even though it was adjacent to the nursery, and if Olivia roused during the night, her grandmother would hear her.

Mark watched his sleeping child. Her face appeared more peaceful and sweet in her slumber, her breathing even and her muscles relaxed. One arm draped loosely over Lizzie. Moonlight streamed in through the high windows, casting long strips of silver light across the room. The toys, silent now, waited patiently for the next engagement.

During their time in the parlor, Judith had continually glanced at the door or the ceiling, as if she had been listening for the children, as if she were ready to bolt the room to get to them. She had seemed distracted, almost withdrawn from the conversation, answering questions briefly. Had something occurred during dinner to put her off their scheme? A scheme she had devised?

Or had something happened to put her off him?

Mark eased the door closed but lingered in the hallway a few moments, his mind going over the evening once again. Nothing extraordinary stood out. Rolling his shoulders against exhaustion, he headed down the stairs to his own bedchamber. Whatever had distracted her would come out eventually, he knew that for certain. In the meantime, they all had to prepare for one of the most important events of all their lives: the Blackwell ball.

JUDITH STARED AT the canopy over her bed, her thoughts

whirling. Sleep would be hard to achieve this night, despite her exhaustion. The evening had not been unpleasant, but a great deal of information and number of details had crossed over her tonight, and Judith had trouble lining them up and making sense out of everything she had heard and witnessed.

And Rose Ashley's appearance still nagged at her. Even though Mark had warned them that Rose was reserved and fragile, Judith had been surprised by the look of her as well as her reticence. Rose had said nothing, nor had her expression changed much, nothing that would indicate whether she were hale and hardy or needed a doctor. She had hung back from everyone, watching Olivia but little else, wincing any time voices were a little loud.

Which, given the nature of the Rydell family, was most of the time. Judith had honestly never met any family like them, with the relentless bantering and insults tossed at each other as if they were Christmas trinkets. Sarah, new to the family, spoke rarely, watching Matthew with pure adoration in her eyes. What had seemed casual sparring at first had grown increasingly snappish, as if some underlying anger lurked, waiting for an opening.

Judith's emotions had further warred within her as she thought about how Mark had responded to the children. She had honestly expected to spend much of the evening with Olivia, getting to know the young girl. Instead, Olivia and William had whisked themselves off to the nursery while the adults strolled into dinner. Neither had been seen again until Mark had brought her sleeping son downstairs. The children had spent the evening only in the company of the frail Rose, with her gaunt face and purple circles around her eyes. The woman could not be much older than Phyllida, yet she looked like—

Edmund.

Judith sat up in bed.

Rose looked like Edmund. Like Edmund in the last stages of his disease, when the once hale earl had withered, weakened, and finally retreated to his bedchamber, unable to even tend to the most personal of needs.

Rose Ashley was dying.

Did Mark know? Is that why he was so determined to move them into his house so soon after taking it over. Is that why he was acknowledging Olivia now, after three years of remaining at a distance?

If that were the case, what other secrets might be skulking behind those blue eyes and sharp wit? Is that why his bantering became crisper, more defensive as his mother had probed and prodded, not just about the Blackwell ball but his plans for the future?

Judith crossed her arms. "I do not know him. Sweet God in heaven, I do not know the man at all." Tears gathered in the corner of her eyes, but she brushed them away. "No. I will not do this."

This was a distraction. Only one thing mattered: saving her family. Making sure Atkinson paid for his arrogance, his manipulations. Rectifying all that had happened to Edmund and Margaret and ensuring their future and that of her three boys.

Nothing else should occupy her mind at this time. Including Mark Rydell.

CHAPTER TWENTY-FOUR

Friday, 19 August 1814
Residence of Lord and Lady Blackwell, Grosvenor Square
Quarter to eleven in the evening

V INCENT ATKINSON LOOKED nothing like Judith had expected. With what she had heard about his ambition and successful businesses, she had searched the crowd at the ball for a handsome young blade kitted out like Beau Brummel. When Edmund finally pointed him out to her, she had stared, trying to take in that this man held her son's marionette strings.

The Blackwell ball had launched with a rousing success, a glittering evening crowded with the *ton's* most elite members. People Judith had not seen in years were attendance, and the women's finest gowns gleamed under the golden light of the room. The Blackwells' ball had always been supreme, and this one carried a theme of ancient Greece, complete with a chalk painting of the Acropolis on the dance floor. Columns and statues dotted various areas of their ballroom, which was expansive enough to hold more than three hundred people. Beverage tables lined the walls, and footmen wondered about with trays, collecting empty glasses and cups from every available flat surface. Anchored at each end with tall doric columns, each beverage station held cups of lemonade, goblets of ratafia, and flutes of an inexpensive rosé wine. Judith always chose the lemonade, pleased to know that—as with everything else at this ball—it was perfection. The orchestra, almost forty pieces strong, sat in a semicircle before the glass doors leading to the terrace, their instruments filling the air with tunes meant to keep feet moving and marriage-minded mothers happier than usual.

Although Judith had danced a few times, she had mostly found a chair among a gathering of the dragons of the Beau Monde, observing, waiting for the arrival of the Embleton clan, and studying her nemesis, whose very presence annoyed her, even though she had arranged for it to happen.

Vincent Atkinson's clothes, constructed of the finest materials and made with precision, declared his wealth. But the style more reflected Italian trends with colors better left to barnyard roosters. Obviously a man who told his tailors what to do instead of taking their advice. And while he had brought his current paramour, a gaunt woman whose gown matched the gaudiness of his kit, he often abandoned her to hobnob with the male nobles in the room, inserting himself into clusters of conversation where he found a polite but wary welcome. Judith soon realized the woman spoke no English and wandered aimlessly from one beverage table to the other, avoiding others and waving off invitations to dance.

This made her despise Atkinson even more than she already did. And apparently, she was not alone. More than one aristocrat extracted himself from one of those conversations to head in a straight line to their host, Lord Anthony Blackwell. While Lord Anthony remained calm, often his guests walked away less than pleased, some muttering under their breath.

So much for the stoic English demeanor.

Judith tried to remain aware of Atkinson's presence without staring at him constantly, reminding herself that she had come to this ball for a number of reasons, including her affection for Lord and Lady Blackwell, to remind those around her that the Sculthorpe family had not yet stepped over the brink of bankruptcy, and to enjoy a number of enthusiastic trips around the floor.

Judith, wearing one of her finest gowns, had accepted only a few dance invitations throughout the evening. The men flirted with her in mild and chatty ways, often hinting at the wager in White's book without addressing it directly. Amused that men adored gossip as much as women, she teased them with her own hints but not too many details. One did ask her why she had not danced with Lord Mark Rydell that evening, and she pointed out that none of the Embleton clan had yet to make an appearance.

For which Judith was grateful. She remained irritated with him, which made her question her own heart, her growing affection for him. Gratitude for all he had done, all the help he had offered warred with questions about his intentions and the obvious plethora of secrets he kept. Tonight he would be a distraction.

A distraction who had not arrived. She looked again around the room, and this time her search sent an odd tension through her gut. The Embletons were not the only ones now missing from the room. Several other high-ranking members of the elite had disappeared.

Including the host and his wife.

Judith rose slowly from her chair, studying each cluster of nobles who remained. *Where had everyone gone?*

"Lady Sculthorpe?"

Judith turned to face a young footman. "Yes?"

"Lord Anthony requests your presence."

Ah. "Very well. Where is he?"

The footman gestured toward the room's entrance. "This way, please."

Puzzled, Judith nodded. "Lead on."

She followed as he led her from the ballroom, down a long hallway past the retiring room for the ladies, and down a second, short hallway, pausing at a closed door long enough to knock and wait for the command inside to enter. He announced her and stood aside as she stepped inside.

And stopped, her eyes widening and her breath catching in her throat. Judith stared, barely hearing the door close. Before her stood Lord and Lady Blackwell, four dukes of the realm with their duchesses—including Matthew and Sarah Rydell—five earls, two counts, a viscount, and an assortment of lesser male and female nobles and attendants. In the midst of this array of aristocrats sat a short, round man with a headful of riotous brown and gray curls and a waistcoat that threatened to pop every button within seconds. His ruddy cheeks and bulbous nose spoke of a great deal of alcohol consumption, both tonight and in months passed. His overstuffed chair sat atop sturdy legs the size of small trees that had been ornately and intricately carved with lions' heads. A throne fit for royal. A very short, very round royal.

George, His Royal Highness, the Prince Regent.

Judith dropped into her deepest curtsy, hoping not to lose her balance. "Your Royal Highness."

The prince motioned for her to come closer. "Lady Sculthorpe, I understand you are the reason I am in attendance tonight."

She straightened and took a step forward. "Sir, I—"

"I do enjoy the entertainments of my dear friend, Lord Anthony, but he tells me this was your idea. That you are trying to entrap some odious criminal."

Judith's stomach clenched. "I—um—yes, sir. Lord Anthony is correct."

"How do you think I can help? I do not even know this man."

Judith took a deep breath, and her words tumbled out, spelling out Atkinson's ambitions, his noted offenses, and his attempts of coercion against reputable members of Society. She ended with, "We wanted to ensure his presence here tonight, and we—I—believed your attendance would make it impossible for him to resist or even be suspicious. He will most likely fawn all over you or those closest to you. Anyone who he thinks can help achieve his goals."

The prince gave her a wry smile. "Most people do fawn over me, Lady Sculthorpe. An advantage as well as a disadvantage of being the prince."

"Yes, sir."

"Far too many people want to join the aristocracy, do they not? But they generally want the privileges without the responsibilities. And I understand you do this devious thing for the sake of your family?"

"I do, sir." Judith glanced around. Edmund and Margaret were not in the room. "My son—he has strayed from those responsibilities and has paid dearly. But much of it is my fault. My responsibility. I failed to give him guidance after his father's death or even to bring on someone who could do so."

"You seek restitution."

"I do, sir. And reconciliation between my son and his peers."

The prince studied her a moment, then gestured for Lord Anthony to bend closer. After a hushed conversation, Lord Anthony straightened, and the prince continued. "In a few moments I will enter the ballroom with my attendants and make a circuit, greeting old friends. Lord Anthony will introduce me to your"—he waved a hand—"intended culprit. It will be a short visit. I cannot stay for the supper as I have another engagement. But I will make sure your aims are met." He paused, his gaze raking over her again. "Lady Sculthorpe, I do not appreciate being lured into other people's dramas. I assure you I create enough of my own. But I will not argue with a beautiful and clever woman determined to risk so much for her son, her family. It is not a sentiment I share or have experience with, but it is one I can envy from afar. It is, my dear, a gift."

Judith curtsied again. "Thank you, sir."

He waved her back. "Let us get on with this charade. I am sure we all have much to attend to this evening."

Judith straightened and backed away as fast as she dared, not wanting to trip on the hem of her gown. A footman opened the door behind her, allowing her to move into the hallway. It closed again, and Judith stared at it a few moments, gasping as she realized she had been holding her breath.

"Pudgy little devil, is he not?"

Judith whirled, her hand on her throat, her head swimming.

Mark's eyebrows arched above his smirk. "I did not mean to startle you."

"Did you"—Judith swallowed and pointed at the door—"did you know that was going to happen?"

His eyes narrowed in confusion. "You knew Prinny would be here. It was your suggestion."

Her hand dropped. "But I did not expect to be dragged in for a private audience!"

"You did not think he would want to meet the woman behind this mad scheme?"

"I just thought Lord Anthony would *invite* him. Not *involve* him. Did you know he had informed the prince of the reasons behind the invitation?"

Mark shook his head. "Not until we arrived and a cadre of footmen commandeered us, escorting us into rooms on this hall. A few moments ago, one came to claim Matthew and Sarah, releasing me to go into the ball."

"But you waited here?"

"I saw them escort you in. I wanted to make sure you were all right. Meeting with the prince can be . . . unexpected. Even those close to him never know how he will react. He can be entirely civil or a complete beast."

Judith studied him, chewing her lower lip. Worry gripped every muscle as she envisioned the evening going wrong in the worst ways. "He was civil but annoyed about being involved. He knew about the scheme to lure Atkinson in, just not who he was. Now someone is sure to warn Atkinson about the plot. The supper will never go as planned."

Mark glanced at the door. "Not if they think it will upset the prince to have this go awry. Risking his wrath was never a good idea, even before he became regent. To do so now is to court ruin. Or worse."

"Where is your mother?"

"For some reason, she decided her presence would not be warranted this evening." A growing rustling behind the door warned of people on the move, and Mark offered her his arm. "Shall we dance?"

With a brief hesitation and a glance at the door—the noise grew ever louder—Judith took his arm.

MARK TRIED TO keep his gaze forward, but Judith continued to worry her lower lip until it reddened and began to swell. Her habit whenever worry consumed her—or fear—and he realized how much she relied on this evening to go as she had planned. For Atkinson to be found out and Edmund to be freed of the man's machinations. But other resolutions could be worked out. Other options almost always existed for any difficulty.

"Judith, if this evening does not go as you intend—"

Her words almost hissed as her grip on his arm strengthened. "Do not say that! Do not even think it! It has to."

"Other options—"

"Margaret is with child. There is no time for alternatives."

Mark let this statement ferment in his mind as he escorted Judith through clusters of people in the ballroom. "I am not . . . why would that—"

"If he can prove Edmund prefers men . . ."

Ah. A new possibility for blackmail would linger on the horizon. "Understood." He guided her toward a spot near the orchestra and against the wall. As they stopped and turned to face the room, Judith peered up at him, her face abnormally pale.

"I thought we were going to dance."

"Just watch," he whispered.

At the entrance to the ballroom, a footman appeared, rushing toward the orchestra. Although a dance had been in progress, the footman whispered into the conductor's ear, and the man brought the music to an abrupt halt, then signaled for the musicians to stand. This action turned irate looks from the dancers to those of astonishment as everyone turned toward the door as the herald announced the arrival of the prince regent.

The boisterous room fell silent as the prince entered, his round figure and waddling stroll reminding Mark far more of an overweight peacock than a monarch. The man whom painters often portrayed as statuesque and handsome in truth stood almost as wide as he was tall, without the height of his father or the posture of his mother. His thick hair billowed around his head in brown and gray waves, and his double chins sat atop a tight cravat like so much whipped cream on a pudding. He moved slowly through the room, nodding to this or that noble, as the crowd parted before him like the Red Sea at Moses's beckoning.

A movement near one of the beverage tables caught Mark's eye, and he realized Atkinson slowly wormed his way toward the prince regent, a hungry light in his eyes. Mark watched as the two paths crossed, Lord Anthony stepping forward to make the introductions. Atkinson bowed before the prince regent, and the few pleasantries exchanged left Atkinson looking smug and satisfied.

Until His Royal Highness stopped a few feet away to greet the Earl and Countess of Sculthorpe. At Mark's side, Judith began a series of low whispers, her hand on his arm quivering. "No . . . no . . . no . . . do not do this. Please do not do this . . . no . . ."

To no avail. The prince hailed her son with a hearty call of "Sculthorpe!" and held his hand out to Margaret, kissing the back of hers with a warm—and somewhat lecherous—smile. Edmund and his wife stood frozen, eyes wide as the prince they had never met brushed Margaret's shoulder, his fingers lingering on the bare skin over her collar bone as his eyes examined Edmund, head to toe. Even from where Mark and Judith stood, they heard the prince regent's pronouncement. "Your father was always one of my favorites, as are you and your lovely wife. Woe befall anyone who brings ill to your door!"

"Bloody hell!" Judith's hand tightened on Mark's arm to the point of pain.

He looked down at her, then followed her focus, which was not—like everyone else in the room—on the prince regent. Instead it fell on Atkinson, who looked as if he had been punched, his face as red as a rose, brows so furrowed his eyes almost disappeared beneath. With a rough shove, he pushed his way through the trailing mass of aristocrats, almost barreling over two footmen as he strode out the door.

Judith made an odd gasping sound, and her weight fell against Mark. He looked down just as her knees gave way. Pulling her backwards, Mark scooped her up, pushing out pass the orchestra and through the terrace doors behind them.

CHAPTER TWENTY-FIVE

Saturday, 20 August 1814
The garden of the residence of Lord and Lady Blackwell, Grosvenor Square
Half-past midnight

"I DO NOT swoon."

"Trust me. You swooned."

Judith's head ached, a deep throbbing that started at the base of her neck and outweighed any sense of mortification that Mark held her in his lap. "My stays must be too tight."

"Do you wish me to loosen them?"

She glared at Mark, eyes narrow, hoping he could see in them her desire to strangle him as she pushed away from him, sliding off his legs to sit next to him.

"I take that as a no."

"How long did I . . . did I swoon?"

"Long enough for Prinny to leave and everyone else to go into supper."

Judith looked away, trying to decipher what had happened in the ballroom. "Atkinson left."

"He did. As if someone had dropped fireworks in his britches."

"He ruined it. The prince. I should never have suggested he come. Or insisted Lord Anthony not tell him."

"Prinny is the most unpredictable man on the planet. With the possible exception of his father."

"Who is mad."

"Well, there is that. I'm sure he asked, and Lord Anthony would never have lied or misled him"

Judith took a deep breath, relishing the fresh air tinged with the light scents of the summer flowers that stretched along the manicured pathways of the garden. They sat on a stone bench near the edge of one path, the sounds of the ball wafting over them, blending with echoes from the street and the dozens of carriages waiting for the festivities to end. Mark remained silent as she listened, a sense of pure despair settling over her. "It's all for naught." Her voice grated. "We are lost."

He cupped her hand in his, the warmth of his palms oddly soothing to her entire being. "Possibly not." His words seemed equally calming. "Prinny's words were a sound caution—"

"Which will infuriate Atkinson. Make him more evil and determined."

"If there is proof of the blackmail . . ."

"There is not. A man approached Edmund outside that . . . establishment in the Strand. A lad from the Rookeries picks up the payments, but he is merely a runner. He has no information. Believe me. I tried."

Mark straightened. "That is correct. No actual proof of the vase's theft exists either. Or Edmund's visits."

"If the men there talk—"

"They will not. That has been handled."

She peered at him, fighting a sense of relief. "You took care of it?"

He grinned and stood tugging her to her feet. "Of course I did. The men who visit, who work there, all make their way to At Wheel's End. Offering unlimited credit to the ones who saw him closes many a mouth." He looked around, then leaned over to kiss her forehead. "Come with me. I have an idea about where Atkinson went."

"But how—why—"

"Enraged men often make horrific mistakes out of their anger. If he wants to wreak vengeance on Edmund for what he thinks is a royal slight, he will probably up the ante."

"By doing what?"

"Think about it. If you think someone who you've been extorting is suddenly protected from that extortion, what is your next move?"

She blinked. "I do not—"

"You would want to prove them guilty." Gripping her hand tightly, Mark headed toward a gate at the back of the garden.

"Where are we going?"

He pushed through the gate, then began weaving them through the carriages lined up on Davies Street. "Your home. I think Prinny had in mind. He does not like people who wish to worm their way into the aristocracy. He is all about the birthright. He probably believes he can prompt Atkinson into revealing himself."

Judith, still a bit confused and lightheaded, trotted along behind him, trying to regain her bearings. Although only a few blocks lay between the two houses, she could feel her silk slippers begin to tatter against the rough pavement by the time they reached the front of Sculthorpe Manor where they came to a dead stop, staring at the commotion. A cluster of men mingled before the house and the front door had swung wide open. Inside, backlit by the chandelier in the entrance hall, their butler and Epworth stood, each holding what looked like a fireplace implement. In front of them was the Bow Street Runner, Jeremy Smith, who scribbled on a piece of foolscap with his short but ubiquitous pencil.

Mark took Judith's arm, urging her forward, as one of the sidewalk men approached them. "Sorry, folks—"

Awareness surged through Judith, and she broke free from Mark, shoving the man back. "This is my house. Get the hell out of my way." She picked up her skirts and raced up the steps, confronting Smith. "What happened?"

The three stared at her, silent for a moment, then Smith acknowledged her with a nod. "Lady Sculthorpe."

"Why are you here?"

Smith glanced over her shoulder at Mark, who had followed her up the steps. "As we discussed, we had men waiting outside the Blackwells', expecting Atkinson to make a move after the supper. But one of Lord Blackwell's footmen came out with the suggestion that the move might take place sooner rather than later. Which it did. They sent an alert to me, then followed him to a warehouse, where he picked up a package and came here. He broke in through the servants' quarters but met with some resistance before we could stop him." He nodded at Epworth and the butler.

Epworth's chin went up. "We were waiting the family's return. The villain apparently thought we would be asleep with the family out. But he was not as quiet as he tried to be."

Mark looked down at the poker in her hand. "Is that blood?"

Judith followed his gaze, her hand coming to her mouth.

Epworth sniffed. "Yes, my lord."

Mark snorted, looking at Smith. "No one messes with Epworth."

A grin flashed across Smith's face before he turned somber again. "Indeed." He checked his notes on the foolscap. "Atkinson had apparently planned to stash the vase in his lordship's bedchamber. He put up a significant struggle when thwarted, threatening everyone until"—he glanced at Epworth—"suddenly silenced." Smith cleared his throat. "The package containing the vase has been taken to the magistrate. It will probably be returned to Devonshire by tomorrow afternoon. Atkinson will be tended to by the doctor at Newgate."

"That will be a change of scenery," Mark muttered.

Judith tried to scowl at Mark, but her pride in Epworth and their butler pushed out any other emotion. She gave a sigh of relief. "Thank you both."

Smith folded the foolscap and tucked it into a pocket, along with his stub of a pencil. "I will make a full report to the magistrate in the morning. If we have any more questions, we will let you know."

Smith trotted down the steps, shooing the other men in front of him, as Mark closed the door. Judith turned to Epworth and the butler, unable to contain her joy any longer. "I thought everything was lost. You saved us!"

They both seemed to glow, and Epworth even raised up on her toes. "It was an unexpected pleasure, my lady."

The butler nodded. "The blackguard had it coming."

"You are gems, worth your weight in gold. I will make sure his lordship knows what happened tonight."

They both smiled, then before her very eyes, they resumed their roles as servants, straightening their backs and forcing their expressions to become staid. Epworth gave her a slight curtsy. "I will meet you upstairs, my lady. I know the evening must have been exhausting for you as well."

"I will return to my pantry and await the family, my lady. Do you think they will be very late?"

Judith, who suddenly realized she had no idea what stage the ball had reached when they left, looked at Mark.

"They had served the supper and champagne, so they probably will not be much longer."

She nodded. "I will also wait in the receiving room."

"Very good, my lady."

As they turned to leave, Judith touched Mark's hand. "You do not have to stay."

He peered down at her, one eyebrow arched. "You have had a private audience with the Prince Regent. You have swooned in the midst of a ball—"

"I do not swoon."

"And your home has been broken into, a notorious criminal assaulted by your staff, and he has been hauled away by a Bow Street Runner. Do you even dream that I would leave you alone?"

Judith looked down at her hands a moment, her thoughts and heart a jumbled mess. Pride and gratitude blended uneasily with worry and a touch of fear. The affair with Atkinson seemed resolved but so much else felt topsy-turvy and unsettled. Her heart had driven her steadily toward this man who had stood beside her, while her mind sent out too many questions. She straightened her shoulders, then turned toward the receiving room as Mark followed her, determined to speak her mind and either find peace with their relationship—or step away.

"I have been—uncertain—the last few days, about what has passed between us." She pushed open the door and entered.

He left the door open a bare crack. "Why have you been uncertain?"

Judith looked up at him, her stomach roiling. "I have"—she pressed a hand to her abdomen—"your family, in a group, can be a bit . . . overwhelming."

He smiled. "And that was only a few of us."

"Precisely. And you seemed to be holding Olivia at bay."

He hesitated, looking away toward one of the windows.

"Mark, I know Rose is dying."

He snapped back toward her, his expression sharp. "How do you—"

"Her appearance. I thought she seemed oddly familiar that evening, and I finally realized . . . she looks like Edmund did—my Edmund—in the last weeks of his life. She has cancer, does she not?"

The harshness in his face eased, his shoulders sagging. "She does. And I did not want to take Olivia away—take her affection—away from Rose in these last few months. Doctor Oakley has told us both it will not be much longer. Olivia needs this time with her."

"Does Olivia know?"

"She knows her grandmother is ill. She seems to understand that Rose will not improve, but I do not know if she grasps what that means."

"That's a hard concept for a child her age. My Robbie was eight, and it still took him a bit to fully understand. William still does not truly understand that his father is dead. He just knows he is not around." She touched his arm. "You must be tender with them both."

"I am trying." He moved toward her, his gaze soft as he took her hands. "I do not have a great deal of experience being tender. Yet."

"This does not surprise me, growing up as you did in a household of so many boys." She paused. "Yet?"

He nodded. "I believe you could change that. Would you like to join that household?"

Judith stilled, as did Mark. He blinked first, his cheeks reddening. "Um . . . I had not meant to say it quite like that."

She chewed her lower lip a moment. *Was he truly asking . . .* "How had you planned to say it?"

The red deepened. "Something incredibly romantic, foolish perhaps. Appropriate to a rake who has discovered he has lost his heart to a child and a woman at the same time."

"Maybe in the nursery then, among the toys."

"You are the one who has proclaimed all children precious."

Tears blurred the corner of her eyes. *He could not be . . .* "So I will come in second place to a child?"

Mark reached for her hands, folding both of them into his and kissing her fingers. "No, my dear. Olivia may have won my heart, but you will always and forever be my first choice—for my life. For my world." He kissed her, a soft brush against her swollen lips. "For my wife."

EPILOGUE

Two Years Later

Saturday, 25 May 1816
Blackthorn Park, country estate of the Earl of Sculthorpe
Half-past ten in the morning

"COME ON, WILLIAM! Stop dawdling!"

Judith watched from her bench in the garden as Olivia twisted in her saddle, urging William to drive his Highland Pony a little harder toward the back of the property. Olivia's pony—a sturdy, plodding mount—also moved with a constant steadiness, ignoring her urging for more speed as well. But she had gotten a head start on William, who had been helping the groom saddle his pony, his eyes squinting as he approached the task with a determined precision.

Over the past two years, as William had become more judicious and studious—like his brothers—Olivia's contagious energy had urged him into ever more adventurous play. William had ridden far longer than Olivia and had the better seat, but she maintained more control. Her cleverness seemed to spark livelier every day, especially since they had asked Mr. Thompson to take her on as a student as well. The two had become remarkable, devoted, and mutually beneficial friends.

Mark, observing the children from a more agile and restless steed, called out instruction to both, correcting their posture and handling of the horses, as they rode away.

Judith's heart swelled as she watched her family, bundled up in their woolens even in May, their faces red, eyes bright. In the strange, unrelenting cold of the year the breaths of children and ponies fogged around their heads like clouds.

As the sounds of children and horses—and her husband's voice—faded, Judith tugged her shawl tighter around her shoulders and turned her attention back to the letter she had been composing for the past three days, following the receipt of one from Mark's sister, Daphne, who had returned from Greece the past Christmas with a surprise in tow. Now the Rydell family experienced an unfamiliar turmoil and division. Their stubbornness and pride fueled a rift that could not stand. Judith felt it in her bones; family was far too important to let this go unanswered. But any resolution would require tact and diplomacy.

Judith read both letters again—she had to make this reply absolutely perfect.

Dear Daphne,

I truly enjoyed meeting you and Sophia this past Christmas. I had not realized that Mark had not told you about me—or Olivia—or I would have contacted you sooner. No one should come home to find so many brothers unexpectedly married, some with children already running about. As I love all my family beyond reason, I hope that you and Matthew especially can make amends in the future. I realize that as head of the family, he takes his responsibilities seriously, but I also know he loves all his siblings without reserve.

Until then, please feel free to write me at any time with questions, and I will return the favor by offering as much information as possible. I have already broached with Mark the idea of us visiting you and Sophia once you have settled at her estate in Yorkshire.

I am not sure, however, how many details I can offer. Since Mark, William, Olivia, and I have retired to Blackthorn, we do not see London much nor the rest of the family. You know that Sarah and Matthew had their Robbie (named for your father) last year. Sarah is with child again, with the arrival to come later this summer. Mark is forever grateful to have shed his designation as Matthew's heir and seems rather content these days with the horses and the business of the Blackthorn estate. Like you, his disdain for London Society grows ever stronger the longer he is away. And this seems to be a family trait. Timothy, of all people, has traipsed off to America, and Paul has retreated to your family's country property. My Robbie and George have done well this term and will spend this coming summer here.

Mark runs Blackthorn on his own, as Edmund has made him its manager. My oldest seems relieved not to have the responsibility on his mind. He still has fences to mend in London as well as things to prove to those around him.

Judith paused, looking again toward the direction her children and husband had taken, and tried to decide how much to tell Daphne. Blackthorn, for all its size as an aristocratic country home, had a relatively small back garden that overlooked the rolling fields of the main grounds. In the distance grew the scrubby blackthorn trees that gave the estate its name, and beyond them the first of the tenancies that helped the property earn an income.

In just two years, Mark had been instrumental in turning the Sculthorpe finances around. He had sold At Wheel's End, using the proceeds to invest in the Sculthorpe estate. He had established close relationships with the tenants, and last year's income from the farms had been double of the year before. Which, given the current weather, looked to be beneficial. If this year's crops failed, they still had some in store and a reserve to keep the tenants solvent.

Judith doubted Daphne would want to hear all that, nor would she care about Atkinson, who had been convicted of his attempts at coercion as well as the murder of Stella Ashley. His wealth and connections had eased the blow somewhat; he wound up being given the option of transportation instead of hanging. He had obviously chosen to live, and he now existed somewhere in Australia. Most likely running a gaming saloon and bilking the locals.

"Judith?"

Judith folded both letters before turning around.

Phyllida strolled the one narrow gravel path of the garden, the skirt of her thick green woolen riding kit brushing her ankles. "I wish to join the children. Will you not ride with me?"

Judith shook her head. "Not today."

"Still not feeling well?"

"Just a bit queasy. I do not think riding a horse would be a good idea."

Phyllida peered at her. "And probably not a good idea for a while."

Judith smiled but said nothing.

"Is that letter from my daughter?"

"It is."

"And you are responding?"

"I am."

Phyllida sniffed, then turned on her heel and headed to the barn at the far end of the garden.

Judith sighed. By showing up with a woman at Christmas, Daphne had sparked a rift in the family that would most likely take years to heal. She could have simply declared her companion to be a close friend, but that type of discretion did not seem to be a part of Daphne's constitution—she was far too like her brothers and her mother for that. The result had been volcanic, after which the two women departed, with only Judith and some of the children seeing them off. Sophia had an estate in Yorkshire, and Daphne had gone there to live. The rest of the family now tried to behave as if their sister no longer existed.

Judith was not having any of that. Family was family. Mark and Phyllida knew that she wrote to Daphne, but they did not want to hear about it. But Judith knew people could change; she would not give up on this.

After all, Phyllida herself had made a major change in her own life after the Blackwell ball. After disappearing that night, she had emerged a week later with the first of several day gowns in every color of the rainbow. She had thrown off her clothes of mourning and emerged as one of the most vibrant dragons of the ton. The widowers of the city flocked after her but left unsatisfied. Then, after two London seasons, she had started spending more time at her own country estate as well as Blackthorn.

Judith suspected this had more to do with Matthew's growing family and Sarah's astute running of the Embleton household than Phyllida's need for fresh air. No one liked to feel as if they were in the way.

As Phyllida on her thoroughbred cantered across the fields, Judith pulled the letters out again, deciding to save the rest of the information for a future missive, closing quickly.

Your mother is also staying the summer. London also seems to bore her these days, something I never thought I would see.

Please know that I wish you and Sophia well, and I hope we may visit someday soon. Please write whenever you feel the need.

Your loving sister-in-law,
Judith

Judith folded the letter, tucking it away again. She would seal and mail it later. For now, the chill of the morning air had eased her upset stomach. She wanted tea and toast, a bath, and a fresh gown. Epworth, whose knowledge of Judith had already alerted her to what lay in store for the next few months, would pamper her appropriately. Judith wanted to be at her best for her husband tonight, for the moment had come for her to explain to him exactly what could happen when he claimed her as his first choice. His only and forever choice.

The End

To My Readers

Thank you for reading *The Heart of a Rake*, the first book in my Silver Vixens series. I dearly hope you enjoyed it.

When I begin to create a series, one element I always consider is if I can link the story to others I've written. I love finding ways to "cross pollinate" the tales. In the case of *The Heart of a Rake*, there are connections with several other books, including the next two in the series: *The Mind of a Widow* (which features Luke Rydell) and *The Soul of a Lord* (which features Paul Rydell).

Several members of the Rydell family also show up in stories I've written for Dragonblade's shared world series, the Lyon's Den. The romance between Matthew and Sarah Rydell was featured in my first book for the series. *Into the Lyon of Fire* shows how the infamous Black Widow of Whitehall, Mrs. Bessie Dove-Lyon, brought them together. Another Lyon's Den novella tie-in, *To Uncage a Lyon*, featured the youngest brother, Timothy. Their cousin, Gordon Rydell, is the hero of "To Tilt at a Lyon," included in the *Night of Lyons* anthology, and Mark and Phyllida are featured characters.

Readers can get a glimpse of Daphne and Sophia's story in the fourth book of my Ashton Park series, *The Duke I Came For*, in which they are prominent secondary characters. To bring the tie-ins full circle, characters from that novel carry over into another Lyon's Den tale, *A Lyon in Waiting*.

I hope you enjoy my work and that you will consider reading these books. I would love to hear from you. You can sign up for

my newsletter at my website for more news (abigailbridges
author.com) or follow me on Facebook or Instagram.

Happy Reading!
Abigail

About the Author

Abigail Bridges wrote her first historical romance, titled *The Belle of the Ball*, when she was thirteen. It was, of course, horrid. But it firmly established her love of all things Regency, a mild obsession with Georgette Heyer, and a determination to become a writer. After a master's degree in English and years of being paid to write and edit other types of material, she has returned to her first love. She is busily binge-reading all her favorite authors, resuming her study of the history and culture of the Regency era, and plotting like a madwoman. She does all this in a small cottage near Birmingham, Alabama.

X: @AbbyBridgesAuth
Instagram: @abigailbridgesauthor

www.ingramcontent.com/pod-product-compliance
Lightning Source LLC
Chambersburg PA
CBHW051236070726
47594CB00013B/262